The Elf Queen

By

Lyndi Alexander

Fantasy Novel

Published by
Dragonfly Publishing, Inc.

The Elf Queen
Fantasy Novel

First Paperback Edition
EAN 978-1-936381-03-6
ISBN 1-936381-03-6

Story Text ©2010 Barbara Mountjoy
Cover Art ©2010 Dragonfly Publishing, Inc.
Dragonfly Logo ©2001 Terri L. Branson

The term "Denny's" has been used with permission.

Published in the United States of America by
Dragonfly Publishing, Inc.
Website: www.dragonflypubs.com

For my husband Eric, who has been through the ages my beloved partner and best inspiration.

CHAPTER 1

"YOU'VE got to be kidding me!"

Jelani Marsh bit her tongue as she nearly tripped, running for the uniformed Missoula police officer beckoning a tow truck toward her seven-year-old sedan.

"No, wait!" She lunged for the car door, the taste of blood in her mouth. "I've got to get to work! Hey!"

The tall officer grabbed her wrist and pulled her back.

"Miss Marsh, I'm sorry. Laws are meant to be enforced."

She peered up through long dark bangs. "Richard?"

He at least had the decency to look sheepish. "You've got half a dozen unpaid tickets. I'm within my rights."

"This doesn't have anything to do with tickets, you jerk! This is because I quit going out with you. Bite me!" Embarrassed as her neighbors slowed to stare at the patrol car and flashing lights, she leveled a kick at him which he barely avoided.

He waved the tow truck on its way. Her silver sedan with its faded multi-colored bumper sticker reading "Mother Earth: the original uppity woman" disappeared down Rattlesnake Drive.

She could not give him the satisfaction of hearing what she really thought.

Swallowing the rest of the bad language that came to her tongue, she started walking, feeling his disappointed gaze burn into the back of her head. Fabulous. It would take her twenty-five minutes to get to the coffee shop now. She'd be late. And late for the fundraiser for the Wildlife House after that.

As she reached Broadway, a worn blue bicycle pulled up next to her, horn screeching over its rider's distinctive squeal. "Where is your car, woman?"

Jelani eyed her best friend, Iris Pallaton, whose blonde hair swirled above the bright cloud of a magenta blouse. "Richard had it towed."

"Rat bastard!"

"Tell me about it. I'm late." Jelani headed off again.

Iris pedaled along the curb beside her. "You should call his supervisor and complain."

"And what? Humiliate myself because he's a jerk? Screw him!"

"Maybe you should." Iris laughed. "Then he'd be too awed to bother you again."

Jelani glared as they crossed the street. "Funny."

On the far side, she caught the glint of glass in the middle of the sidewalk. "What idiot would drop a bottle when there's a trash can right there?" she grumbled. "I'll get it. First karma points of the day."

Iris climbed off the bike and put down the kickstand. "What *is* that?" She bent down near the object. "Oh, sweet Gaia! It's a glass slipper!"

No kidding. It really appeared to be a shoe made out of glass. A large one.

"Who would have left this here?" Jelani picked it up, looking around for a prankster camera team. Something kept her from tossing the shoe.

"Try it on," Iris whispered. "It would get Richard Snyder off your mind."

"Richard is not on my mind. He's on my shit list."

"Oooh. Sorry." Iris ran her finger over the shoe. "You're chicken anyway."

"Don't even go there."

"Chicken. *Bawk-bawk.*" Iris giggled.

"Fine! If it means I can get to work." Reaching down with her right hand, she unzipped her boot and kicked it off. "Ready? You want a picture?"

Iris dug for her cellphone and raised it, ready to take a shot. "Just in case your prince shows up right then."

"I don't need a prince," Jelani complained. "I don't need a man. I need a new life."

Setting the shoe on the ground, Jelani slipped her foot in it and gently stepped down, not sure to what expect.

The slipper shattered, slicing into the sole of her foot.

Nauseous, Jelani screamed and could only watch in disbelief as tiny men sprang from the blood trickling under the broken shoe. She lost track of how many.

With the biggest maybe two inches high, the men scattered into the shadows around the nearest building and disappeared.

She lifted her foot, shaking off the blood, and examined her sole to see if glass remained buried in her skin.

"Did you see that?" Iris gasped, nearly breathless. She grabbed at the wall, eyes closed for a moment.

Jelani felt faint, too, suddenly washed out. "I don't know."

There were no glass fragments in her foot or anywhere. The shoe had vanished. The only trace of the whole incident was dark blood, slowly drying in the sun on the sidewalk. As she watched, the cuts in her foot healed.

Iris knelt down to peer at Jelani's foot. "There were little people. Naked little people. They ran away. I swear they did."

"Did you get pictures?"

"I almost forgot!" Iris got up and activated the screen on her cellphone, pressed the arrow. Jelani leaned close to watch the whole thing replay in living color. "Oh. Bless. My. God," Iris said, in her shock reverting to the male deity.

Jelani nodded. "And the horse He rode in on."

* * *

CHAPTER 2

THE Butterfly Herb Company was one of the many coffee shops on the north side of the Clark Fork, the river that divided Missoula. When Jelani arrived even later than she'd anticipated, her harried employer, Mrs. Sutton, simply waved her behind the busy counter before retreating up the wooden steps to the loft office.

Jelani was grateful to escape an expected reprimand, but her mind remained in a whirl. However she considered what had happened, no explanation presented itself.

"You look puzzled, missy."

The familiar voice penetrated Jelani's thoughts, as she measured espresso in the small brew basket for her next order, and then flipped on the brew cycle.

One of Jelani's favorite customers, Dee, rated a sincere smile. The older woman was perhaps of Native American descent, her long straight and black hair dramatically streaked with gray at her temples.

"Not puzzled. Annoyed. How are you, Dee?"

"I saw a pair of hawks this morning."

"A good sign." Jelani poured the deep-toned chocolate hazelnut coffee over ice and handed it to her waiting customer, wishing she had time for one herself since it was her personal favorite. She was about to ask Dee for her order, when she saw the woman had a steaming cup in hand. "You've got coffee already."

"We couldn't wait," Dee apologized. "Astan has errands."

She gestured over her shoulder to a dark-eyed young man in a black pea coat and slacks who stood nearby, perusing a rack of greeting cards. He reacted to his name with a curious but brief glance.

"You remember my grandson?" Dee asked.

Jelani smiled at the young man of the brooding good looks. She'd noticed him on other days with Dee, but he had yet to speak to her. "Hello, Astan," she called to him, before she took the next customer's order.

He mumbled a response and withdrew with his own steaming cup to the candle display closer to the front of the narrow shop.

Figures. The ones I like have no need for me.

"He's shy," Dee said. "Around girls."

"I don't bite." Jelani laughed and took the next customer's request. Even if he stole her car, she wouldn't bite him. Kick him a little, maybe. "What message do you think the hawks bring?"

"I'm not sure yet. A change is in the wind, though. Of that I'm sure." Dee's smile was mysterious. She studied Jelani's face a moment. "I see something is on your mind. Do you seek a message of your own?"

"It's nothing," Jelani replied, realizing after she'd spoken that she'd mixed a double espresso instead of a single. Better not overdose someone on caffeine without consent. She set it aside and began again with a dark laugh.

"I've discovered one myth from my childhood is just a myth. There is no such thing as Prince Charming."

"I brought you something," Dee replied with a cryptic smile. She pulled a narrow wrapped package from her large hand-woven shoulder bag. "Hang this over your bed."

Jelani paused as Mrs. Sutton passed by, heading for the front counter to help another regular visitor with a bulk coffee purchase. Since Butterfly Herbs competed with a dozen other local shops including several little drive-throughs, every regular was treasured.

While Jelani waited on the coffee to brew, she took a quick peek in the bag. Inside was a beautifully woven dreamcatcher, made from thick gold and umber threads, embellished with tiny pinecones and blue jay feathers.

"It's beautiful."

"The blue jay symbolizes clarity and courage," Dee said. "He brings voice to what remains unspoken."

"Oh." After the brew finished, Jelani set the dreamcatcher aside a moment to foam the latte milk with practiced hands, before passing it to her impatient customer. "Thank you, Dee. Even if I don't know what's 'not spoken', you know I don't have a hard time telling people off."

"One cannot say what one has not realized." Dee's smile remained mysterious.

Well, no kidding. Jelani turned to the next customers in line, students, by the look of them, and tried to keep their orders straight while her mind wandered. The next time Jelani looked up, Dee and her grandson were gone.

Odd. But then, the whole day had been odd.

After Dee's visit, she couldn't get on track again. In the next hour, she botched several orders in a row, so she pled a headache and asked to go home. Mrs. Sutton frowned, but let her go.

Her small one-bedroom apartment was not where she intended to brood, alone. Instead, she detoured to the small second floor apartment of the people most likely to set her straight.

* * *

CHAPTER 3

JELANI climbed the narrow wooden stairs of the old storefront off Orange Street, frowning as the bare light bulb overhead flashed and threatened to go out. The air held faint traces of the smell of a cooked dish that teased her mind, not clear enough to identify.

Or maybe she was just too distracted by the scene from the sidewalk that morning. Impossible to believe, even when she'd watched it again on Iris' cellphone as she'd walked.

When did fairy tales come to life? Where did those people go? Why did her foot heal? What the hell had happened?

Maybe now she'd get some answers.

The light flickered, intermittently illuminating cobwebs along the ceiling, thick with dust. She knocked once. Paused. Knocked two times. Paused again. Then knocked once more. Though she heard the bass line thump of heavy metal music inside, she knew no one would answer without the Code. When no one answered anyway, she leaned close to the unmarked wooden door with the paint tiredly starting to peel.

"Come on, you guys, it's Jelani! Open up!"

The door opened a crack. A narrow slice of pale face appeared between the door and frame. Thick dark bangs nearly covered the nervous eye that studied her.

"About time, Crispy." Jelani waited with annoyance as the chain slid back. Then she stepped inside when the door creaked open. The door was shut closed behind her.

"You can never be too careful." The skinny little man shuffled past her up the hallway. One foot dragged as he walked. Jelani had never heard why. They just all knew that Ron "Crispy" Mendell had done too many drugs in his difficult and misguided youth.

Jelani followed him through the hall's dim light toward the music. Peering around the corner into the living room, she eyed the Cave.

Built from computer towers, monitors, data storage bins, file cabinets and dozens of empty Creamy Cupcake cartons, the Cave was the place from which Crispy's roommate Delano Donatelli viewed the world. The man most called Lane currently had four computer screens active, rotating on his wheeled desk chair to access their slaved keyboards in random order.

Crispy retreated into the kitchen, mumbling. Jelani leaned closer to hear him. "Watch out for the camera," he repeated.

"What camera?"

"He got a webcam. The government can hear us now."

"The government can't hear us just because I have a webcam," Lane scolded from the other room. His tone made it clear it was not the first time he had said it, and that it wouldn't be the last.

Crispy shook his head, as he took the whistling teakettle off the stove. "We're doomed." His half of the beige-walled room was spotless, the half not responsible for the detritus of the Cave. The sparse furnishings were a step in class down from hers, early rummage sale instead of late Salvation Army.

She idly plucked dead leaves from a scraggly schefflera. *This is too far from the light*, she thought, her affinity for growing things kicking in. "Come on little friend. We'll get you to a healthier place. But you must do your part to flourish." She picked up the eight-inch terra cotta pot and placed it by the window. "How's it going, Lane?"

"Just fine and dandy." Lane gifted her with his wide, crooked grin. He proudly showed off his ample black T-shirt emblazoned in magenta: *For the Horde!* "Had a great flame session with some total noobs. PWN'ed 'em, clearly."

Jelani raised an eyebrow, not well versed in computer lore. "Is that good?"

"You computer virgins are so cute." He cackled at her confusion. "What brings you here?"

"Yes," Crispy said, coming up behind her. "You haven't

come for a week." He set a tray with a steaming teapot and three glass mugs on the table. The spicy scent told her he'd brewed chai. Several powdered sugar cookies graced a blue plate, as well. "Iris comes more often."

With a chuckle, Lane rolled his chair over to the small table with its green felt placemats, pulling out a chair for Jelani before his fat fingers grabbed a cookie. "Iris has the earth-shaking task of prying you from our humble abode into the great outdoors, Crisp. Five years into that continuing voyage of agoraphobia where no man has gone before. When Jelly Bean comes, it's just to see us."

Crispy frowned a little and took the other chair. "Iris is my friend, too."

"I know she is, Crisp. No worries there." Lane turned an amused gaze on Jelani. "Heard Richard had your car towed. Asshat."

"Did Iris call you?"

"Nah. Got a permanent hack into the police broadcast frequencies." He shrugged back toward the Cave. "He was going to file obstruction of justice on you, too. You kicked him?"

"He moved."

"Ah. Smart man." Lane leaned over to examine her boots. "Steel toed?"

"No." She tried not to smirk and poured some tea.

"Too bad."

"You should never date a government agent," Crispy said in a dark tone.

"It wasn't a date. He had tickets to the Jazz Festival at the university and I was broke and it was my birthday and I really wanted to go." Jelani sighed. Now that was karma. Use a man just to see a concert and he has your car towed.

"Come on, girlfriend. You know you went out with him five times." Lane smirked and took a second cookie.

Jelani glanced over at the Cave, a little unnerved. "Are you spying on me?"

Crispy nodded. "Webcam. We're doomed." He stirred his tea, clanking the spoon on the inside of his cup at exactly the nine and three o'clock positions, and then twitched as he set down the spoon.

"I'm not. Really." Lane laughed, leaned back in his well-worn chair. "That, Iris told me about. She was worried you were in over your head. Especially after Arik."

"Great. Just great." Annoyed, Jelani picked at imagined lint on her chinos. Iris was the kind of girl men loved to date, pretty and blonde and witty. She hardly had a weekend that wasn't scheduled with something light and fun. *Me, I just seem to choose all the losers.*

Lane let her off the hook with a wink. "Come on, Jelly Bean, you know we love you."

She did know that. Over the several years she'd known these men, Jelani had come to appreciate their awkwardness, the way they didn't seem to fit the world any better than she did. Affectionately dubbed "the Boys" by most who knew them, the two were a real Mutt and Jeff. She and Iris dropped in frequently, since Crispy never left the apartment.

"Now, let's turn that frown upside down. Cough it up. What's bugging you?"

Jelani pulled Iris' cellphone from her pocket. "You have to see this." She held out the phone, activated the playback, and then watched their warm smiles change to dead shock.

"Where's that from? You pull it off the net?" Lane took the cellphone from her, played it again.

"No! That's on Broadway just before Higgins Street. That's Iris' phone. That's my foot."

Lane stopped and looked at the phone. "Oh. So it is."

Crispy gasped. "Aliens!"

"What?" Jelani stared at the now shaking man.

"Aliens! You must have been taken aboard the mothership! Maybe that other summer, remember, when you disappeared for a week."

She tried to grab his hand, but he was too agitated. "Crispy. Crispy, listen! I didn't disappear for a week. I told you that. I went to Mount St. Helens with the University's ecology club."

Lane rolled his chair into the Cave to start tapping on a

couple of the keyboards. "Yeah, buddy, remember? She even brought you some ugly chunk of lava from the last blow."

Crispy's forehead furrowed, trying to recall such an event. "Yeah. Yeah, I guess." His smile was only tentative. "Maybe they got you some other time."

"Aliens?" Jelani bit her lip. She couldn't rule it out. The little men did have an E.T. kind of feel to them. But, no. No way. That would be crazy.

Lane was still moving from screen to screen, clearly searching for something.

Jelani couldn't decide whether or not she found it comforting that he had an actual answer in mind. That made the whole crazy mess seem way too real.

"Not aliens," Lane finally said, after an uncomfortable silence that seemed to stretch on forever.

"Great! What then?" She walked over, watching where she stepped once she crossed the threshold of the Cave, wary of thick wires and unrecognizable bits of discarded food on the floor. He had plugged Iris' phone into a wire that led somewhere deep in the tangle of cables behind the nearest computer tower. The enlarged video blurred and broke up into small squares when anything moved, but there were the little naked men, fuzzy, and revealed in more detail than she'd been able to see on the tiny cellphone screen. They had faces, fingers, and small….

She blinked, as she realized they were anatomically correct.

Crispy inched closer, obviously unwilling to come within range of the webcam. "Not aliens?"

Lane shifted his bulk in the chair, rolled to a second keyboard where he brought up several pictures of other little men who resembled those running in a continuous loop on the first screen. "Homunculi. Just like the ones in *Fullmetal Alchemist*," he said in admiration.

"Full Metal what? Isn't that a Vietnam movie?" Jelani was puzzled. "They're Asian?"

"*Manga*," Crispy interjected softly.

"Oh, comic books."

"No!" Lane growled. "Manga are not 'comic books.' They're

an art form." He rolled back to the first screen, studied it. "In *Fullmetal Alchemist* the homunculi were artificial humans, named for the seven deadly sins, with a piece of the Philosopher's Stone instead of a heart. Magic enemies."

"Magic?" *Was he nuts?*

"Deadly sins. I don't like the sound of that." Crispy twitched back over to the table and cleared the dishes, taking them to the kitchen. A few moments later, a lighter snapped, followed by the unmistakable sweet odor of a clove cigarette.

"Ugh. That's a nasty habit, Crisp."

"He won't listen. I've printed out studies showing clove cigs have more nicotine and all that bad crap than regulars. Doesn't help. Guess if he can stand to live with my idiosyncrasies, I can tolerate his paranoia, OCD and cloves, huh?" Lane smiled at her.

"I don't see how you guys live together at all."

Lane and Crispy had been foster brothers for a number of years, both sets of parents found unfit by the court system. Neither had worthwhile family connections they wanted to renew, so after they each turned eighteen, they had moved in together. They were very close. Some thought perhaps they shared more than the apartment. Jelani had never asked.

None of my business. Long as they're happy.

Both men preferred to stay in 24-7. Crispy's agoraphobia had progressed, after five years of working with Iris, to a point that he could go out under the porch canopy into the fenced back yard to tend a few plants, but that was the extent of it. He received disability checks from the government, but Iris was convinced someday Crispy would be back in the workforce.

Lane, on the other hand, had no physical disability. He just preferred electronics to people. Lane freelanced various consulting jobs on a variety of topics over the Internet. While he was responsible for the errands, he preferred to make arrangements over the computer. Their bills were paid online, and all groceries and medications delivered by cyber-order. The pair had a beat-up red pickup truck some fifteen years old, but Jelani hadn't seen it driven more than a dozen times.

Lane eyed the video. "What did Iris say about this?"

"Not much. We were both late for work, thanks to Richard. I told her I was going to come here and she gave me her phone." The small apartment quickly started to reek of smoke and she crossed to crank open a window.

"Smog day." Crispy scolded from the kitchen, peeking around the door frame.

"I'll take my chances." Missoula's beautiful valley location unfortunately lent itself to occasional bouts of inversion, where smoke and other pollutants would be trapped by the surrounding blue-gray mountains. "Besides, it's May now, not winter. You should be fine. At least long enough to keep the rest of us from dying of lung cancer."

Crispy's dark eyes studied her with pity. "Everything gives you cancer."

"Thanks, Crisp. I'll make that my cheery motto of the day." Jelani took the cellphone from Lane. "So, what am I going to do about this? Do we report the…ah, magic little men to the authorities?"

Lane burst out laughing. "Awww. That's so sweet. You'd do anything to call Richard, wouldn't you?"

"What? No!"

"Calm down, honey. It's all good. You let Brother Lane do some research, okay? Let me see what we can find about similar occurrences, whatever. I'll hit Snopes, Urban Legends. I know a couple of guys." He boosted himself from his chair to hug her awkwardly. "I can call you when I've got something."

She sighed and hugged him back, grateful they hadn't just laughed at her. "All right. You guys need anything?"

"Nope. Got Tipu's bringing over curry and naan for dinner. Was that masala or tharka dahl, Crisp?"

"Masala. It's organic. No commercial poisons."

Jelani thought of the thick spicy soup and her mouth watered. "Mmmm. I'm jealous. I've got a skinny girl's frozen meal. Chicken and something green." She shrugged.

"Yummy." Lane wheeled back into the Cave and activated two new screens and computer keyboards, started tapping in commands, already lost in the hunt.

"Bye," Crispy said, peeking from his safe haven behind the kitchen door.

"Catch you guys later, then." Jelani checked to make sure she had the cellphone and let herself out, hearing quick footsteps follow and then the scrape of the chain lock behind her.

She walked down the street to catch the bus, the realization her car was still held hostage by a petulant patrolman burning in her memory.

The sky had clouded up again, but the bus came before it started raining. The other passengers were lost in their own thoughts, so Jelani replayed the tiny video capture, wondering as she watched if she might not just be going crazy after all.

* * *

CHAPTER 4

ASTAN left his grandmother Djana, also known as Dee, in the kitchen to plant yet another pot of aromatic herbs for her windowsill, and retreated into his attic room.

Something was coming.

Djana and her customary circle of old wise women had met in the morning and again in the afternoon, twisting dried herbs into the wreaths that graced every window in the house and drinking steeped wood tea that left a lingering odor. When he was a boy, he used to sit just at the top of the steps and listen for hours to the old women chatter. He didn't quite understand their talk of exile, royal politics, and old forest conspiracies, but it was fascinating. Almost like a fairy tale.

He thought maybe it was in reference to the Native American histories of the Kootenai and other tribes, which had settled in western Montana before the coming of the white man. When he had attended the town schools, he'd been teased for his odd dark eyes whose corners tilted more than those of his classmates.

As his olive skin tone made it clear he was not of Asian descent, they finally decided to dub him Yahoo the Indian, and the quiet boy was harassed to the point of violence. In Astan's second year of school, Djana took him home one day and he never returned.

"Am I an Indian, Nana?" he'd asked, feeling the tears on his face as they walked along the sidewalk to her small house.

"You are not an Indian, Astan. Nor is any child of the soil who has lived on this land since the early days. Indians come from India. Those little monsters at school mean Native Americans, those who were here before the humans." She stopped a moment with a small frown. "Before the Europeans."

Although he'd heard the self-correction, he had been much

more interested in the scraped knee received at the playground when one of the other boys had shoved him. "Are we children of the soil, Nana?"

"We are," she replied in a warm tone. "We are indeed."

From that day, she'd taught Astan at home, along with many of the other children and young people who lived with Djana's women friends. They provided him with resources, both written and oral, each of the women generous with the knowledge they held in one subject or another. He read everything she could get him, even texts from the Mansfield library at the university.

He was consumed by the history of the land of the Bitterroot, where glaciers once covered the Mission Mountains in silent mounds of ice. As he left childhood and entered his second decade of life, Djana and the other women taught him the healing herbs of the forests, the flora and fauna of the region, and above all respect for nature. He and the other boys and girls banded together as a cohesive group, excluded from the lives of the townies, but open to possibilities that the townies would never experience.

Astan stared out his bedroom window at the fading snow atop the mountains. For nearly a year now, some mysterious excitement had consumed the circle. In the past two weeks, their activity had ramped up considerably.

Djana had made repeated stops to Butterfly Herbs, often dragging a reluctant Astan along with her. She'd bought him coffee, though she knew he liked it even less than she did, and she brought presents for the young woman who worked behind the counter. Magic presents, gifts steeped in tradition and folklore.

Astan would have preferred to be out in the woods, where he'd spent most of his youth. The woman didn't interest him. Her jewelry, sleek haircut, and trendy dark clothes gave him the same vibe as those students at the school of long ago. The townies were self-important and unaware of much beyond the need for consumption.

Better to stick to one's own kind.

But something in his grandmother's obsession with this

person over the last few days signaled her importance. Whatever was about to happen, Astan was sure she was at the center of it. He'd discovered over the years that Djana and the women didn't gather without good cause.

Why does Nana push me toward this girl?

One of his grandmother's favorite sayings came to mind: *The best weapon against ignorance is the search for knowledge.*

Astan set his mind and his heart on that search, and went back downstairs. He pulled a chair away from the table, turned it so he could straddle it, and studied his grandmother intently.

"So," Djana said, offering a smile in his direction, "you finally want to know who she is. It's about time."

* * *

CHAPTER 5

JELANI'S bulky key ring jingled when she let herself into her small apartment, many of its colored baubles and attachments gifts from Iris, who felt Jelani disguised herself in a wardrobe that included mostly shades of black.

She dropped her mail and Dee's dreamcatcher next to her fat black cat stretched languidly on the counter.

"Hello, Azrael," she said, giving the cat a kiss before kicking off her boots.

Iris found it amusing that the cat was named after the archangel of death. While Jelani would agree the cat had a mischievous streak, he was no devil. She'd named him after a cat from an old cartoon she had loved in her childhood.

She put on the kettle for tea and absently scratched Azrael's neck. He stretched in ecstasy, nearly falling off the counter.

"Whoa!" Jelani blurted, catching him before he tumbled onto the floor and bruising her elbow on the counter in the process.

Azrael jumped down and walked away into the bedroom, tail stiff with disdain.

"Fine. Be that way." Jelani pouted and followed him, climbing onto her bed to hang the dreamcatcher in just the right place, the blue jay feathers dangling above her pillow. Perhaps it was silly and a waste of time to suspend the pretty webbed circle to catch bad dreams.

It's the thought that counts, she reminded herself. And she needed all the help she could get.

Taking the pitcher of rainwater that had collected on the front steps during the day, she moved through the two rooms, giving her multitude of plants a fresh drink. Iris complained she lived in a rain forest, but Jelani needed green things around her. They thrived under her touch, and she kept them well tended.

She spoke to them and it seemed that they followed her commands, though she knew that was silly. Her ability extended to the plants outdoors, too, and the other volunteer staff at the wildlife rehabilitation center often asked her help with their troubled trees and vines.

When she'd emptied the pitcher, she returned to the kitchen to sort through the mail, the majority of it tossed directly into the trash bin. She stashed a couple of utility bills on the small shelf where she kept such things with her checkbook and credit cards, and came to the last letter. Staring at the return address, a chill crept into her midsection.

Kokomo, Indiana.

Her stepmother's measured, flowing handwriting.

A thousand memories.

She dropped the letter on the counter, as if it had burned her. For several minutes, she fussed with her yellow-flowered mug and jasmine tea, delaying the decision whether to open the white envelope or trash it with the other stuff she no longer needed in her life.

After some soul-searching, she relented. It had been eight years. A long time to hold a grudge. "Might as well see what she wants."

She picked up the letter and carried it, with her tea, into the tiny living room to her beige-cushioned papasan chair, her single brand-new purchase. She held the envelope in her hands, while memories trickled around her.

Her father Vincent Marsh had married Carolyn when Jelani had been very small. He had died in a Montana forestry accident when Jelani was fifteen. Carolyn had invited the bereaved girl to stay with the only family she'd known.

Jelani didn't remember her mother, who had died at Jelani's birth. In fact, she couldn't even recall seeing a picture of her. All she knew was her name, Linnea. She must have been dark-haired because Jelani was a brunette, while Vincent's family members were all blond. Though they visited occasionally with Vincent's extended family, no one ever turned up on her mother's side.

Vincent simply described her mother as a loner, and special.

"You don't need to know," was his universal response.

Despite Carolyn's generosity, neither she nor Carolyn claimed any great love for the other. During the years they lived together, Carolyn's girls, both older than Jelani, had been horrid. Jelani hated them so fiercely that even now her eyes burned with tears, recalling those first lonely six months without her father.

Carolyn had sold the old house on Converse Road, leaving its wooded acreage to move into Kokomo proper. She'd never shared her husband's affinity for the study of nature and escaped from that life as soon as possible. That had been the last straw for Vincent's daughter, who was drawn to the woods, wild meadows, and the depth of trees. Jelani left when she'd just turned seventeen, migrating to the care of an obscure aunt. She hadn't seen Carolyn since.

When college came, Jelani sought out a school in the Pacific Northwest, where her father had spent so much time, the place where they'd lost him. The hope of reconnecting with him, if only by proximity to the land he'd loved, had brought her to the University of Montana at Missoula, and she'd been granted a half-scholarship on the strength of her pedigree alone.

Jelani took a deep breath. "Well, I've stalled long enough. Let's see what she wants." She opened the envelope, drew out two sheets of blue paper, written only on the front sides.

Dear Jelani: I hope this letter finds you well. It has been some time since we heard from you, so I trust you've completed your degree by now and you're working somewhere. Your father would be so proud to know you followed in his footsteps.

Annoyed, Jelani reached for her tea. What a crock. How could Carolyn ever understand how close Vincent and Jelani had been?

Her father had been a renowned forestry expert, evidenced by a multitude of carefully framed certificates and diplomas on his home office wall. When Jelani was young, the phone rang often, representatives from some institution or other looking for a specialist consultant to serve their needs.

The house had photographs and paintings of the forests and mountains of Idaho and Montana in every room, nearly wall-to-wall in her father's study. As time went on, he pored over old photo albums for hours, particularly interested in large trees in the area south of Glacier National Park. It became an obsession. The consulting calls came in less frequently, and he spent more and more time locked in his dark-paneled office, leaving Jelani to the mercies of Carolyn's daughters.

He'd never failed to show his pride in Jelani, though, always attending choral concerts and science fairs. Even in the uncomfortable near-hermit years when he went nowhere else, Vincent would drag himself to school to socialize with the other parents and mingle with the science teachers, who all treated him as though he was extraordinary.

Cognizant of Vincent's national reputation, the teachers would persuade him to give talks to the class, and Jelani would sit in the back with her head down, like any other teenager embarrassed by a parent. But secretly she was thrilled.

She and her father roamed the Indiana woods together, more so when she was younger. She'd learned to identify trees and other flora, knowing their leaves' shapes and all sorts of uses for the bark and sap. While Vincent had showed her how to care for them, he didn't teach her much she didn't know in her gut. What was important to her was that Vincent didn't take Carolyn's girls on these trips. Only her. And he told her he was more proud of what she did there in the woods than anything she learned in school. Those were good times.

She continued with the letter.

Since the other girls are out of the house now, I've been thinking I should move into a condo, and so I've sold this house. When I was packing, however, I ran across some of your father's things, papers and books about trees and things. I thought maybe since you're living out there in the woods, it might be useful to you. Come stay a few days and look through the boxes, if you'd like. The sale on the house closes June 30, so it would have to be before then.

It was already halfway through May. Could she buy tickets at some price she could afford? How would she get the papers and materials she wanted to keep back here? She looked around her little rooms, dismayed. Where would she put them if she did?

In the face of all those questions was a sudden overpowering desire to be close to her father again, to touch his life in some way, even only through papers and photographs he'd made. She'd find a way to go, somehow.

Let me know your plans, and we'll look forward to seeing you. Both my daughters have families of their own now. Those little girls will be delighted to know they have an aunt who's all grown up!

I bet, Jelani thought. Those little girls' mothers would just as soon run her over with a gas-sucking Hummer. She put aside the letter. She had some money saved. Maybe she'd feel less like she was going crazy if she got away for a few days.

"Oh, no! My car!"

The longer she left the car in the police impound, the more it would cost to ransom it.

A few phone calls located the vehicle and an attendant gave her directions how to retrieve it, with a warning she would have to pay her fines.

She slammed down the phone, frustrated. "Damn you, Richard. Now I'll have to work Saturdays for a month."

Three hours later and $126 poorer, she parked the car back where it had been that morning and retreated to do some reading before another exhausted sleep.

* * *

SHE awoke in a sweat, a violent dream fading from her mind.

As the smoky remains eluded her mental grasp, all she could remember was the smell of deep forest and traveling with a regiment of black-clothed men.

Two particular men followed close, just out of sight. They seemed very familiar. But their features evaporated with the remnants of the pine scent and the mist.

In the pitch dark, her heart pounded until the pale light from the digital numbers on her alarm clock let her see she was alone. No trees, vines, or other forest flora around her.

Azrael leapt on the bed, startling her, but his presence was soothing. He complained a bit, and then curled up beside her, his purr an engine's roar in her ear.

That customary sound lulled her back to sleep. She didn't encounter the forest or see the men the rest of the night.

* * *

CHAPTER 6

LANE drove Jelani to the airport.

She had really expected him to return from his investigation with his trademark smarmy look and snappy comeback about how it was a real cute trick and *ha-ha-ha, you got us.*

But that hadn't happened.

"Sent your video to a couple friends of mine," he said, after the engine on the ancient truck had finally rolled over, followed by a roar from the rusting tailpipe. "They verified it wasn't faked. It's legit."

Wishing the seatbelt still worked, she eyed him from the passenger seat as they lurched forward. "Well, gee. Thanks."

He grinned. "I had to test it out, Jelly Bean. Not that I don't believe you, but— "

"But?"

"But that's one helluva story. Your foot healed up right then and there, and the shoe— "

"Disappeared before I put my boot back on."

Lane stared forward, waiting for a traffic light to change. "You know some of the Magick-type games hold that wizards use an injured creature's own healing power to mend injuries. By focusing their energy on the pattern of a healthy body inside the injured one, they can speed the process of natural healing, even drawing from their surroundings and other living creatures nearby to jump start the process." He glanced over at her, an odd look darkening his face. "But as much respect as I have for Iris, she's no wizard."

"My life is no D&D game, either." Irritated, Jelani hunched back into the seat. "What about the little men?"

"Yeah, well." Lane accelerated onto Broadway, heading west to the airport. "Those are a little more difficult."

"No, no, Lane, listen. This is where you're supposed to tell me there's no such thing as little men, blue, green, or otherwise. And I should put it out of my mind as a piece of undigested potato or something. You know, like Scrooge and those damned ghosts."

"Blue?" He looked over at her curiously.

"Never mind." She fidgeted with her purse for a moment. Then split her attention between passing cars and the river running alongside the highway.

"My research showed a lot of references to the homunculus, or little man, in all kinds of scientific circles, both biologic and alchemist. Back in the Middle Ages, they had mondo theories how you would make little men, just like you described. Did you ever hear of a mandrake?"

"The magician guy?"

Lane cackled. "I thought you didn't know about comics. No, not that kind. This is a kind of plant whose root grows to look like a human form. Legend held that mandrakes would grow from the sperm hitting the ground when a hanged man convulsed and ejaculated."

"Ugh! That's disgusting."

"Do you want to hear this or not?" Lane gave a dramatic sigh. "You had to have a black dog retrieve the root for you. You'd feed it milk and honey until it became alive. Then it would do your bidding."

Jelani snickered. "Better than a real man, apparently."

"Not really. The homunculus would run away from its creator after a while."

"Oh, just like a real man." She looked out the window, her own left-at-the-altar experience still raw after nearly three years.

Lane was silent, and she could see she'd hurt his feelings. Like Crispy, he often took serious offense to what she considered gentle teasing.

"Is that the only way?" she asked to draw him out again.

He sulked for a few minutes. "Sometimes, alchemists would take a bag and put in bones, pieces of skin, and human sperm. Then they buried it in dung for an entire lunar cycle, during which the embryo formed. Then presto! One home-grown homunculus!"

Lane pulled into the turn lane, waiting for the cross-traffic to pass. Then turned onto the wildflower-lined airport drive, and continued along the route to the Departure gates.

Surely, Lane didn't believe all that crap. "But that's all myth, right?" Jelani asked. "I mean, alchemists aren't really scientists. Not like, you know, doctors? Right? They're quacks."

"Well, true. There aren't a whole lot of them around today. The most common uses I found of the term 'homunculus' in modern times are a bio-psychological theory of a small man inside a brain, kind of overseeing the body. And, second, some women finding dermoid abdominal cysts with hair and teeth in them. But they've got to be surgically removed. They don't just appear out of your blood on a sunny sidewalk."

There were a fair number of people waiting to check their bags, as they pulled up at the departure curb. Already nervous, she hoped they wouldn't all be on her flight. "You think those little men came from my blood?"

"Where do you think they came from?"

"I thought they must have come from the shoe. I mean, I cut myself at work all the time. If little guys were going to escape through my blood every time I needed a bandage, I'd have repopulated the city with them by now." She climbed out of the truck and retrieved her overnight bag and her purse, planning to carry everything with her to avoid delays. She'd steadfastly emptied all her liquids and chosen thin-soled sandals she could just slip off at the security gate.

Lane set the hazard flashers. Then climbed out and walked around the truck. He studied her for a moment, concern etched on his face. "I'll keep researching while you're gone. You sure you're going to be all right with the wicked stepmother?"

She smiled. "It's been years. I'm sure she doesn't remember all the bad crap I said to her. It was the stepsisters who were the real pain in my ass. As long as those girls keep away from me, I should be just fine."

Jelani hugged him as if she'd be gone for several months

instead of just a weekend.

"Look," she said, "I appreciate what you've found. Whatever it means. I'll think about it. If you find anything I need to know, Iris has Carolyn's number. Or you can email me. There's got to be a computer somewhere in Corn and Soybean-land."

She walked into the terminal, taking just a moment to look back to see Lane waiting alone like a lost child.

* * *

CHAPTER 7

ASTAN sat across the table from his grandmother, disconcerted by the serious look on her face, the kind of look adults often used when they were getting ready to share bad news.

"We had to keep it from you," Djana said. "We couldn't risk a chance slip, in case any of Bartolomey's men were about."

"Tell me again about this Bartolomey."

Chewing on a greenstick, Djana paused for a moment. "He is by default the leader of those of our clan who remain in the woodlands. The son of the king." Her expression betrayed more anger than sorrow.

"So if he's our leader, why aren't we out there with him?" Astan asked. "I know I'd rather be out there among the trees than here in these cold concrete boxes."

"This is why I made sure Grigor and the older boys took you under their wings as you came up, my boy. So you would learn the ways of our clan, as was proper. But also so you would stay far from the notice of Bartolomey and those who cleave to him."

"Do Grigor and the others know the truth? Were they trusted, even if I was not?"

"Some do," Djana admitted. "The older ones, who are responsible for your training. The others will be told when the time is right."

"Huh." He made sure the single syllable was fraught with contempt.

"Astan." Her warm smile cut through his pain. "I know how hard this is. Consider how difficult it has been for us all these years, protecting you until you were ready to know, until our lives were ready to change. And all the while worrying that Bartolomey would discover you. There's no telling what revenge he might take."

"You think he doesn't know you're here?"

Djana gestured at the window, where she'd hung a wreath of holly and calendula. "We have gone to great lengths to disguise our whereabouts. These herbs guard us from his sight."

"So we're down here in the city. And he's up there with how many? A hundred or more? Can't we just go take our territory back? You make it sound like he's not entitled to it."

"He isn't." Djana's lips smacked around the greenstick. "A dozen old women and a handful of young ones could not challenge him, Astan. Not if we hoped to survive. But the wise elders of the clan took steps those many years ago to ensure our future. These years, while Daven and his men slumbered in nothingness, you and your friends have been taught by other exiles, masters of the Elven art of defense, preparing for a future we were never sure would arrive. We had begun to lose hope for this generation, but a miracle has happened. Now there is a chance to restore the proper order of things."

"So you've told her?"

"No, it is not yet time." Djana's brow furrowed with concern. "She is even less prepared for the truth than you are. So long we were without hope. We had nearly given up. Our long consultations, plans, and prayers have given us one chance. And for that chance we had to wait until she had passed her twenty-fourth year. The protections that had been laid for her since birth have now begun to fade. If she is frightened away, if she is exposed before her feet meet the destined path, it will all come to nothing."

Cautious as always, his grandmother kept her counsel very close. "Astan, I'm sure I have told you enough today that it will take you a week to digest it. Consider what I've said. Be patient, and know plans are in motion that will come to a head very soon. You are a grown man now. I will expect you to take your place in the fight. Your training masters have found you to be a very apt student and a fine elf as well. There is a true leader inside you."

* * *

DAYS after his grandmother shared the revelations about the

dark-haired girl from the coffee shop, Astan found it almost ridiculous.

Elves? Conspiracies? Humans? That was what he had spent his life training for? A rescue of mythic proportions?

He considered the implications, while walking a trail in Pattee Canyon. He'd had to get away into the forest and let the scent of the ponderosa pines clear his head of the smog produced by the humans in the city below. The plaintive peep of the Lewis' woodpecker and the occasional twitter of a flycatcher were like a chorus of bright lights on the deserted trail. These were things he understood. The animals. The plants. His world.

Not the fact that everything he'd been taught was a cover up for a much bigger picture, a more dangerous threat.

He had realized from a young age that his family was not like the other families on the street. He had a grandmother. Not a mother. Not a father. But that was all right, because Djana loved him as much as a whole family could have. Questions he had asked about his parents had been diverted or answered in half-truths, he realized. He had been happy with the lies. He hadn't known better. Until now.

The long conversations his grandmother and her women friends used to have about their royal upbringing echoed in his mind. He had always thought they were fantasizing, comforting themselves for something missing in their lives, the way suburban housewives sometimes latched onto soap opera queens or babushkas told tales of the old country that became more grandiose and fictitious with each telling. But no, her revelations to him the prior afternoon confirmed they were real. His grandmother was of royal blood, at least as far as his people were concerned.

His people? They weren't even people. Not human, anyway.

Frustrated, Astan leaned down to pick up a small granite chip, which he then tossed far into the distance. His fine tuned ears heard it ricochet off one of the tall pines. Ah, yes, another 'gift' from his heritage. Excellent hearing. Keener eyesight. More acute sense of smell. All of them superior, because of his blood. The blood of wood elves.

He climbed up on a large gray rock shot through with quartz crystal, sitting there as he looked back down the trail. As he sat still, his eye caught the movement of small animals, a couple of rabbits, a deer, and the ever-present overhead whisper of wings as birds flitted from branch to branch, catching insects midair. He'd always felt that he could blend into the forest scene, his breath one with the breeze, his skin part of the fabric of the woods. Now he knew why.

Astan looked out into the distance at a pair of hawks gliding on the updraft. Djana had been skimpy on the details in the brief conversation, but somehow that girl figured into her plans. She was the miracle.

"Your father will be so proud of you," Djana had said. She had kissed him on top of the head and walked out into the back yard to tend her herbs, before the implications of her statement had sunk into his brain.

My father? I have a father? He's alive?

* * *

CHAPTER 8

THE plane bumped around as it came down through the upper clouds.

Jelani clung to the seat's hard plastic arms, holding her breath. She liked flying, as a rule. It was the not flying that bothered her. It was the lumps, the bumps, the air pockets. And the landings. Especially the landings.

The college student in the next seat smiled, and she saw he was holding on for dear life, too.

She had to laugh. "Where are you heading?" she asked, to help distract them both from the possibilities.

"Going to see the 500," the young man said from under a Colorado Rockies cap, azure eyes standing out from a tanned face.

Not being a race fan, it took her a minute. "Oh, the Indy? Sure." The realization also explained the difficulty she'd had booking a seat. Memorial Day weekend meant the Indianapolis 500. Most of her high school classmates had obsessed yearly over every detail of the events while they decked out their own cars for hot-rodding at the Bunker Hill drag strip. In Indiana, Indy car racing was nearly as big as basketball.

"I've been three times, but my guy Mike is finally in the top ten," the guy began, and he just kept rolling, spilling statistics and data faster than she could absorb after a night of very little sleep. He must have noticed her interest drifting, because he trailed off with a self-mocking laugh. "Sorry. I'm really passionate about this one. You going to the race?"

The plane leveled off, and she felt safe to release her death grip on the seat. "No. I have family obligations."

Her smile faded as she considered the upcoming two days with the family she cared nothing about, and her companion took the hint to leave her alone.

Carolyn had agreed to meet the plane, to save Jelani the expense of a rental car. She could always get one later, if she needed to escape the house. Even on the phone, her stepmother had seemed kind and generous. Jelani tried not to believe there was a hidden agenda in the invitation.

When Vincent died, Jelani had felt completely alone. She had few friends, though those she accepted became close. She particularly distrusted men.

The exceptions, of course, were Lane and Crispy. But they were more like, well, brothers than men.

The pilot announced they were coming into Indianapolis. The temperature was a balmy 75-degrees, he assured them and suggested it was time to fasten that seatbelt once again. She shared a smile with the young man on the way to the races and spent the rest of the time praying the pilot's sexy voice was enough to win them an actual secure landing on the tarmac.

The doors from the airplane to the terminal opened with a noticeable change in air pressure. After a few claustrophobic moments in the aisle, her overnight bag over her left shoulder and purse strap over her right, she walked up the gangway to the terminal.

Posters and memorabilia commemorating the upcoming Indy 500 decorated the walls, and tourists crowded the walkways. A scan of the crowd beyond the security barriers revealed no one who even looked familiar.

Had Carolyn forgotten?

Debating whether to walk further ahead to seek her stepmother, Jelani stepped aside to let other anxious vacationers pass while she fumbled for her cellphone.

"I almost didn't recognize you," a woman's voice sounded close to her ear.

Startled, Jelani twitched and turned to look behind her.

The woman in the pink sundress wasn't nearly as tall as she remembered, and the hair that used to be dark blonde was now platinum, cut in a chic style over dangling gold earrings.

"Carolyn?"

Her stepmother's blue eyes twinkled, new crows' feet appearing at their corners. "It's so good to see you." She reached across to hug Jelani over the security cables.

Burdened by her bags, Jelani could only press her cheek awkwardly to Carolyn's, catching a whiff of the perfume she'd always worn.

"Come on." Carolyn let go and slipped back into the crowd, reappearing at the open exit.

Jelani bumped her way through, letting Carolyn take her by the arm to escape the worst of the race-happy throng.

Out in the sunlight, Carolyn offered to take Jelani's bag.

"It's not heavy," Jelani said, caught off guard by this new soft-spoken, girly stepmother. She could almost like this woman. Almost.

Carolyn led her to a deep green Subaru SUV, unlocking the door with the push of a button on her keychain. "Just stash your bags in the back, then." She continued to the driver's door, the heels of her taupe platform sandals high enough to accentuate the slimness of her calves.

Feeling awkward and young, Jelani climbed into the front passenger seat. "It was really kind of you to ask me here. You didn't have to do that."

Carolyn smiled. "Those months after your father died overwhelmed me. So many things to take care of, papers to deal with, you know. Many questions that were never answered." Her smile faded. "When you left so suddenly, we never got a chance to talk about what really happened to your father. I hope we can now."

Surprised beyond speech, Jelani watched out the window as Carolyn negotiated the traffic with ease and pulled onto the interstate.

It had been a month of bombshells. Jelani couldn't tell at this point which had provided the most shock or even whether the revelations were over yet.

* * *

CHAPTER 9

JELANI had never been in the home where Carolyn lived, but she'd seen pictures in the carbon-copied obligatory Christmas newsletter she'd received faithfully every year. Jelani had not replied, because she knew they would never be a real family.

Carolyn pulled into the driveway of a condominium. All along the street there were fine-trimmed lawns and a complete lack of trees from one matching property line to the other.

Jelani considered, with a pang of loss, that her father would have been thoroughly unhappy here.

Inside, the house was fluffy and bereft of the world of nature, like Carolyn herself. The only plants were silk flowers, which Jelani found hideous, arranged in mauve and lilac splendor in nearly every room. She tried not to react when she caught a whiff of some air freshener, one of those that sprayed every so often.

"I've put you in the guest room," Carolyn said. She tapped the answering machine with one pink-polished fingernail to play messages, mostly social communiqués from tearoom afternoon lunch ladies. "It's the last one on the left down that hall."

Jelani carried her bag to her room. Off-white walls matched the French country bedroom suite, while ubiquitous silk plants added a mauve and lilac garnish. She ducked around the corner to the small frilly bathroom. Even the pale pink soap had curlicues carved in it. She washed her face and returned to find Carolyn fussing in the kitchen.

"I'm so sorry. I've got to run out for an hour to help one of my bridge club members take care of a crisis. Will you be all right? I feel so bad. You've only just arrived."

More relieved than annoyed, Jelani's smile was genuine. "I'll be fine."

"You're an angel. At least I can show you your father's books and things if you'd like to get a head start. We can talk later. Come on." Carolyn crossed to a door on the far side of the kitchen and disappeared.

Jelani hesitated a moment, and then followed.

The door led to a finished basement, the steps clear of any clutter. Even the shiny washer and dryer in the far corner were unblemished by piles of clothing, clean or otherwise. The floor was off-white tile. Carolyn crossed to a space behind the stairs, where a card table awaited, clearly intended as workspace. Several small cardboard boxes and a couple of large ones were piled discreetly to the left of the table.

Carolyn switched on an overhead fluorescent lamp.

"Here you are. I haven't really looked at these things since we packed up the old house. I don't even know if they'll be useful to anyone at all. There might be some clues." Carolyn shook her head and then checked her watch. "Be back soon as I can. We'll talk. I promise." With a faint smile, she scurried up the stairs.

What was Carolyn trying to say with all these mysterious references? That Vincent hadn't died? That the truth remained to be shared?

Jelani opened a folding chair next to the pile of boxes, glad to be left alone to explore her father's belongings. The door upstairs thumped closed. She took a deep breath and tugged open the flaps of the largest box.

She slid out the framed photographs, one at a time, becoming reacquainted with old friends. The largest was a twenty-four by thirty-inch photograph of a huge Douglas fir, one that looked to be about 150 years old. The tree was photographed in loving detail, shadows from the surrounding trees creating shades of color along the gray-brown bark. Close-up, a photo would have revealed deep red tones inside the canyons of the craggy bark. Jelani had seen many of them when she spent time hiking in the Missions and northward. They were one of her favorites.

This picture had hung over her father's desk as long as she could remember. Staring into it, she could almost believe herself in his study at the old house, the cherry scent of his pipe smoke sweet in the air while he told her stories of his days in the Idaho and Montana woods. He had seemed to light up when he spoke of the firs and the mountains, the clear, cold lakes and bright-colored fields of midsummer.

She'd asked him several times why they didn't live in those forests if he was so fond of them. His face would cloud over then, and he'd retreat into silence or send her off to do chores. Eventually, she quit asking.

As she laid out the pictures on the floor, she realized for the first time that most of the pictures were of the same tree from different angles. The fir seemed huge by the usual standards, so it might be remarkable for that reason alone. But based on the scale given by men in the picture, it wasn't larger than many she'd seen. The flora around it was not unusual in any way. There didn't seem to be natural flaws that distinguished it.

Why was this tree so important?

While Carolyn tended to her business, Jelani lost track of time, buried in the memories that surfaced while she went through the photos. Others she recognized, but hadn't known their origin. She could now read the words in her father's scrawl on the back of each, a sentence or two identifying people and places depicted.

Many were of the Bitterroot Valley, the dull points of its snow-covered mountains dominating the background while yellow and pink vistas of summer flowers brought color to the landscape. There were a few pictures of the chill beauty of Glacier Lake and Flathead Lake, and even a couple of old photos of the downtown area of Kalispell, circa 1930. But most of them were of trees, Ponderosa pines and other firs.

But that one Douglas fir's location was never identified.

* * *

CHAPTER 10

CAROLYN appeared at dusk with a couple of takeout salads, something delicious with crunchy bacon and sweet dried cranberries.

The two of them sat on the porch after they ate, watching the sunset, clearly unobstructed by trees, an awkward silence stretching between them. Some older children in the next yard played badminton, and Jelani silently cheered the underdog.

Carolyn swirled the ice in her glass of tea and stirred in artificial sweetener and released a deep sigh. "You look good, Jelani," she said, crossing her legs, leaning back in the woven rattan chair with its cushions of mauve and lilac. "Are you happy, at least?"

Jelani shifted in her chair, not sure how to answer. They'd been through her failed college life already, and her job as a barista. She'd even opened up enough to talk about the non-wedding.

Well, wedding was too strong a word. She and Arik, a senior accounting major, had decided to get married on a lark, both seeking romance. Over time, teasing had become a vague commitment, and they had chosen a date almost to call the other's bluff. Though Iris had agreed to be maid of honor, she had nattered on that something wasn't right. The morning they were to meet at the university chapel, Arik had sent her a text: *Sry babe I can't. See U round.*

"A text?" Carolyn hissed. "He didn't even tell you to your face?"

Jelani shook her head. "Just said he couldn't go through with it and wished me all the happiness in the world. As if."

"You're better off without him," Carolyn muttered, and then realization washed across her face. "That's why you dropped out.

Isn't it?"

"It helped." Jelani pried an ice cube from her glass and crunched it to avoid further answer.

"I'm so sorry you had to go through that alone. You should have called." Carolyn gave a warm and sympathetic smile. "I understand why you wouldn't. It was hard when you lost your father, especially when there was no one else."

Unspoken criticism for the absent mother drifted between them like misty regret.

"Thanks." Jelani observed the kids next door, tears threatening. She'd really cared for Arik, though she'd never known how much until he had gone. She'd convinced herself after that she was just fine without a man. Certainly Richard had never been a real prospect, and his recent antics didn't improve his chances.

The sun edged toward the horizon, and they listened to mothers and fathers call in their children for the night.

"Did you find anything you wanted to keep?" Carolyn asked.

"I did. I think I'll probably take most of it. Some of the papers, I'll wait to sort through until I get them home."

"Good. I'm glad you found them useful."

"I'd forgotten some of those old tree photographs. So many from around Flathead and outside Glacier."

Pain crossed Carolyn's face. "Where he died," she said.

"There?" Jelani studied her stepmother's expression. "That tree's in the park somewhere?"

Carolyn stared down into her glass. "He'd never say. From the time we met, I knew he'd left his heart in those woods. Something he never finished. I thought it was a woman, but as hard as I looked, I never found any trace if it was. No pictures, no phone calls. Nothing."

Jelani was loath to interrupt the train of thought, the trail of ugly feelings slithering from the depths of Carolyn's past. Another woman? Jelani couldn't believe it. She tried to remember discord between Carolyn and her father, but nothing came to mind except Carolyn's tight-lipped disappointment when Vincent retreated to his office again and again without explanation.

"Did Vince ever tell you how we met?" Carolyn glanced at Jelani, eyes shining in the reflected light from indoors. "We lived down the street from each other in junior high. You know, one of those middle-school romances, where it's 'oh so dramatic' and all your friends swoon?" She laughed, staring off in the distance. "One of my friends got mad at him and we broke up. But I always loved him."

Carolyn took a sip of her melted ice. "All of a sudden, he reappeared in my life. I was a single mom, working as a secretary, barely making ends meet. And there he was, a famous scientist left with a newborn, making a nice living. And Vince still looked great." She smiled. "He took me out a couple of times, brought you over to the house to meet my girls. They fell in love with you, a little living doll they could play with and dress."

Was Caroline kidding? Whose childhood was she talking about? Certainly not Jelani's.

Jelani bit her tongue, instinct telling her something more was coming.

"So Vince asked me to marry him. He promised to take care of us, and I said I'd take care of you. But it didn't take long to see his attention was engaged elsewhere. He must have thought I was blind, that I wouldn't notice. Nothing I did ever attracted him as much as his forest. *That forest.* But I loved him the best I could. And you, too."

Jelani felt tears come into her eyes and saw that Carolyn had tears, too. "I'm sorry if— "

Carolyn held up a hand. "No. Let me get through this now. I'll tell you, and then I never have to think about it again." She wiped her eyes and took a deep breath. "Your father didn't die in an accident. He was murdered."

Why hadn't anyone told her? Who could have done it?

A chill started in Jelani's stomach and slid out to her extremities. "What?"

"Vince made plans to go to Montana a dozen times over those last years, and cancelled them every time. I'd find him in his study late at night crying. He was nearly irrational. I wanted him to see a doctor, but he wouldn't."

Jelani's wits raced. Murdered? She couldn't wrap her mind around that word. Not her father. Not Vincent Marsh.

"One night he got a call. Some guy named Mad Dog. I don't know exactly what he told your father, but then there was nothing that would stop him. He had to get on a plane the next day. He left some notes." Carolyn's voice broke. "I found them on his desk the next day. They said something about an elf, an emergency in Flathead County, life or death situation."

She took a tissue from the box on the patio table next to her, blew her nose. Both of them were crying now. She sniffed and looked at Jelani. "I did some research. Found out that this Mad Dog was active with a group out there that called themselves ELF. Terrorists are what they are. They blow up things. Kill loggers. Vicious people. I tried to explain all this to the police, but they said your father wasn't killed in an eco-terrorist attack. He was killed by someone who wanted him to feel pain. Jelani, he was tortured!"

Jelani stared at her weeping stepmother. It was too much to absorb. Tears rolled down her cheeks. She felt hot and cold and trembling and ready to go out and kick down someone's door just for answers. "How? Why didn't you tell me? I deserved to know!"

"Maybe you did. But I had to do what I thought was best at the time. They never found who did it. And I couldn't bear for you to see what I'd seen. His body."

Carolyn shuddered and wiped her face again. "So I told everyone he'd been killed in an accident and we had him cremated." She gestured to Jelani. "You remember. You scattered his ashes in the woods."

She nodded numbly. "Because he'd want it."

"Exactly. Exactly." Carolyn seemed to pull herself together. "Now you have his things. And you know the truth." Her voice grew firmer. "I've done all I can for you. If you want to pursue it further since you're out there, that's up to you. But the police never had answers for me." She stood up. "I'm exhausted, Jelani. This has—it's real hard for me."

Jelani stood, not hesitating to embrace her stepmother. "I'm so sorry for being a brat. I didn't know." She tasted salty tears again, and the two clung to each other for several minutes, in mutual comfort.

"Go on to bed now," Carolyn finally whispered. "I've got to put this behind me. In the morning, let's not talk about it any more. All right? Please?"

Jelani, despite all her questions, couldn't bear the pain in Carolyn's voice. "All right. Thank you for being honest."

"You deserve it. You're so like him." Carolyn held Jelani at arms' length for just a moment, studying her in the artificial light, and then walked into the house.

Jelani sat on the porch in the dark, thinking.

* * *

AS she'd promised, in the morning neither broached the subject of Vincent's death.

Carolyn helped her pack up his things, and Jelani wondered whether her answers were hidden within those sealed boxes. She'd have Carolyn mail most of them. Several folders, though, she intended to carry with her.

Then she helped prepare a luncheon for the threatened gathering of the family. Despite her fears, there was no bloodshed. The two wicked stepsisters had grown into fashion-conscious, self-absorbed soccer moms who doted on their frilly little daughters, as did their grandmother. The little girls, preschool darlings, were appealing enough, but all the same, Jelani was glad she didn't have any. She could hardly take care of herself. She'd never be able to be responsible for a houseful of other people.

The potent late May sun felt heavy there on the back porch with mothers cooing over the antics of their tots.

Carolyn tried to include Jelani in the conversation, but they both knew other topics crowded the young woman's mind. "Perhaps you want to finish packing," she suggested softly. "What time does your flight leave?"

"Five." Jelani escaped to duck into the shower for a long cool refresh, returning to the porch in her traveling clothes to keep up the kiss-kiss charade for another hour. The others said nothing of particular interest to her. She tried to return the favor. Finally, one of the wickeds said she had to run home to make dinner, and the other quickly joined her. No one insisted they must do this again soon.

Three hours later, Jelani clutched the arms of her seat when the plane took off to wing her back to her Rocky Mountain nest.

* * *

CHAPTER 11

ON the trip home, Jelani resolved not to tell anyone about what she'd learned. Not yet.

Carolyn had said the police wouldn't tell her everything and much mystery still remained. Jelani hadn't decided yet whether to forgive Carolyn for not telling her the truth in the first place. Sure, she'd been young, but this was important.

One thing was certain. Jelani was closer to the truth because of where she now lived. She could dig around with Lane's help, and maybe discover what had really happened. Records like that didn't just disappear. Those responsible could be confronted and forced to face punishment.

We won't take no for an answer, Dad. We'll find out.

Thoughts like that comforted her through the seemingly endless ten days until the boxes arrived by parcel post. Iris stopped by Jelani's apartment to help her unpack everything. The sheer volume of boxes in Jelani's small space seemed to overwhelm her.

"What are you going to do with all these pictures, Jel? I mean, trees? Don't get me wrong, I'm as much a nature lover as any other hippie born in the wrong decade, but look out the window. See a dozen of them." She propped them in single file against the wall. "Hey, isn't that the same one?"

"Tree? Yeah. This one, and that one. And that. And that." Jelani went on down the row pointing out the rest of the photos, all framed, some in color, others more stark and shadowed in black and white.

"What's that about?" The blonde poured them both some iced green tea, the only kind she'd drink.

"Beats me." Stacking the boxes in the corner for now, Jelani laid her thick files of papers on the small table that served as desk, eating space, and ironing board. "But I'm putting some of them up."

Iris shrugged. "They're yours. Might as well. But there are so many."

"Maybe I'll see if the Boys want some."

"Yeah, maybe." Iris flounced onto the papasan chair, propping up her feet. "Maybe take some up to the Red Poppy in Ronan. You know, if you'd mat these and frame them, they'd make a real nice display."

Creating a one-woman show was really not high on Jelani's list of priorities. "Lane hasn't come up with anything else on those little men, has he?"

"Nope. He's worked round the clock, from what I've seen when I'm there. I think he feels like one of the Scooby gang. But he doesn't know anything." She gave a grin laced with mischief. "We actually went back to the scene of the crime to see if we could track down any of the little buggers."

Eyes wide with surprise, Jelani straightened from her work. "You what? Did you find anything?"

"Sorry, hon. Not a trace." Iris sighed. "If we didn't have that video, I'd think you and I just had a mental break."

Jelani blew out a deep breath. "Well, I can't define my life around a mental break. I've still got work and bills." She studied her mostly bare walls. "You gonna help me put these up?"

"Sure." Iris grabbed a hammer off the counter. "You sure the landlord will let you put nails in?"

"I didn't ask him." Jelani shrugged and grabbed a folding chair, pulling it over to the wall.

Iris made a scolding noise. "It's in your lease, dummy. But you never stop to look at the rules."

"Ha! You're one to talk. After you got ditched in the middle of that date on Saturday. Lane said the guy walked out to take a leak and never came back. And you had to pay the bill."

"I know, I know. Never date a guy who spends so much time with his bicycle. And doesn't read." With a rueful smile, Iris handed Jelani several slim nails and a couple of the framed photographs she'd set along the wall on the floor.

"Seriously. You've got to have some bottom line of equal intelligence. Literacy is a good start." Jelani drove the nails in, hanging one picture lower and to the right of the other, pleased with the artistic effect.

"Still think it would have been cool if the glass slipper had really led to Prince Charming," Iris groused. "There were lots of those little guys. Maybe we could have each picked one."

"Exactly what would you do with a guy two inches tall?"

"Oh. Um. I don't know. Maybe they got bigger." She covered her blush by handing over more photographs.

"Right," Jelani said with a sarcastic tone. "They all grew up and found Internet Love and bought purebred Afghans and ate arugula and lived happily every after in the 'burbs with a white picket fence. Why not?"

"Well, they could," Iris pondered.

"You see a good man around every corner. I've yet to find one." Jelani looked at the big tree picture, waiting in the far corner of the living area. "Except maybe my dad. Guess no one will ever measure up to him, huh?"

"That's what the headshrinkers say." Iris grinned. "It's nice that you can have a little bit of him here with you."

"Yeah. Yeah, it is." Jelani smiled and continued hanging pictures, feeling that tenuous connection grow just a bit stronger.

* * *

CHAPTER 12

THE week after Jelani's trip to Indiana, Dee's grandson Astan became a daily visitor to the coffee shop.

He always dressed in neutral colors, as if trying to fade into the woodwork, and was accompanied by a tall clean-cut man with broad shoulders and dark brown hair framing wide-set hazel eyes. During their frequent visits, the two would let someone other than Jelani wait on them, and then take a seat at a table by the wood-framed back door. From there, they would watch her surreptitiously and talk in quiet tones. They were good-looking and never offensive, even jumping up to hold the door for older customers. Everyone noticed.

Wednesday evening, the manager Mrs. Sutton, apparently tired of the surveillance, pulled Jelani through the swinging door into the storage room. "Do you know them?" she asked.

Jelani glanced through the glass window into the café, studying the two men. The stranger was calm and self-assured, while Astan fidgeted, always in motion as if he didn't want to be there. "The one is Dee's grandson. You know, the Native American lady who always buys the chai mix? He's harmless enough, I'm sure. But the other one, I have no idea. I've seen them together here a couple of times. Is there a problem?"

"I don't know how they know your schedule, but Bailey says they only come when you're here. Have they said anything to you? Harassed you? Bothered you?"

"Never. I don't think I've even served them." With a faint smile, Jelani turned back to the manager, ducking as one of the other girls passed by with a tray of clean cups. "I think I'd remember. They're real good-looking."

"It's not funny, Jelani." Mrs. Sutton crossed her arms. "I'm ready to call the police."

"No, don't," Jelani pleaded. "It's not a problem. I swear. They haven't said a thing to me."

"All right, then. I won't take any action at this time. But you be careful when you're behind the counter. And in the parking lot. If you need any help, you ask, hear?"

"Sure, thanks." Taking another peek through the window, Jelani thought Mrs. Sutton was overreacting a bit. But when it came to men, who knew? She returned to serve the next person in line, her attention now caught by the two men who continued to study her. Trying not to blush, she carried on with her duties, even restocking the coffees and teabags to delay her departure time.

Finally, the two men exited the shop, and then Jelani felt safe to leave.

It was sinister. Yes, sinister, she insisted in her head, liking the sound of the word. The two traveling always together like Siamese twins just reinforced her perception of their creepiness. At the same time, though, she was a little bit aggravated they only watched and didn't actually speak to her. Especially the tall handsome one. Something in his smile really appealed to her.

When she got to the Boys' house for dinner, she made the mistake of mentioning the odd pair from the coffee shop.

Lane actually stopped typing for thirty seconds to stare at her, while Crispy twitched his way into the kitchen, muttering.

"That's not normal," Lane scolded. "You should report them for stalking."

"They haven't said a word to me."

"Stalking doesn't involve speaking." Lane spun back to the Cave and tapped out a query. "Section 45-5-220. Stalking. Number 1. A person commits the offense of stalking if the person purposely or knowingly causes another person substantial emotional distress or reasonable apprehension of bodily injury or death by repeatedly: (a) Following the stalked person; or (b) harassing, threatening, or intimidating the stalked person, in person or by mail, electronic communication, as defined in Section 45-8-213, or any other action, device, or method."

Jelani raised an eyebrow. "That implies they actually have to do something to bother me. All they've done is walk in and buy coffee in a place that is in business to sell coffee." She shrugged.

It was his turn to mutter. "You want me to come down and set them straight?"

"No!" She laughed. "They don't look harmful, Lane, not in the least."

"This what's been on your mind, babe?" Lane's broad face wore lines of concern. "You haven't been yourself since you came back."

Before she could reply, Crispy carried over a crock-pot full of chicken and dumplings, and she smiled, glad for the rescue. "Oh, wow. You've outdone yourself, Crisp. Thanks for asking me to dinner." She smiled, hoping it would encourage him.

"Might as well get a good meal," he muttered, "before they find you lying dead in an alley."

She sighed. "All right! I'll do something." Just as Lane started to speak, she cut him off with a raised hand. "But I'm not calling Richard."

* * *

AS it turned out, Richard had noticed the men all on his own.

He came to the coffee shop in full uniform on the following Friday night, strolling in, taking time to examine each and every patron with his classic stone face and beady eyes before he approached the counter.

Jelani finished waiting on her double shot soy latte with a hint of nutmeg, trying to ignore him.

"Jelani."

She shook her head and turned away to restock the coffee beans in the box next to the grinder.

"Jelani." More forceful. His 'your license and registration' voice.

Rolling her eyes, she picked up the tub of dirty dishes and walked into the back. Why couldn't he just drop dead?

A loud police whistle sounded in the café. "Miss Marsh, I'm afraid I'm going to have to ask you to come with me," he called, knowing she could hear him through the door.

She caught sympathetic looks from her co-workers, but when the boss came down out of her office, Jelani knew she had to handle the disturbance before it hurt business. "I'm going, I'm going," she muttered.

Marching out front, she saw the two men come in the door. Astan's face showed some alarm, as he noticed the uniformed officer. They turned away with a sudden interest in the glass jars of loose tea on the wall, but she could see they were still observing her.

She gave Richard her best Evil Eye. "What the hell do you think you're doing?"

Richard's gaze darkened, when he saw the two men. "Jelani, I'm looking out for your own good, even if you won't. The other girls told me you're being stalked. I'm hurt you wouldn't come to me yourself."

"I don't need your help. I don't want your help." She sloshed a porous cloth through the bucket of treated water behind the counter and then scoured the counter with it, wishing she could make him disappear as easily as the crumbs.

"Are these your new friends, then?" Richard peered over at the men with suspicion.

"Yeah, I thought we'd have an orgy later," she said in a tone dry enough to crack skin. "You're not invited."

"Come on, Jelani. The girls are real worried." His pitch approached a whine, something she just couldn't stand.

She took a Styrofoam cup, filled it with black coffee and held it out to him. "Here you are, Officer Snyder. Thank you. Please come again." She stared at him hard, daring him to take the cup.

"I don't know why you have to be so stubborn. I just want to help." Red-faced, he pushed his way through to the front door and left the shop, the bells jangling as he stepped out to North Higgins.

No less embarrassed than the lovelorn officer, Jelani tossed the coffee in the sink and went into the back, heart pounding. Feeling deprived of oxygen, she told Bailey she needed some air and went out the back door.

She leaned against the rough surface of the brick building,

closed her eyes, and tried to calm herself with a few deep breaths. When that didn't work, she started shredding the heads off scraggly tall weeds that had forced themselves up through cracks in the alley's concrete.

She had just turned twenty-five. By most accounts, that made her a grown-up. Why was everyone trying to tell her what to do? They were just imagining a dangerous situation that didn't exist.

"Excuse me."

The strong male voice startled her. She hadn't even heard a footstep. She glanced up to find the warm hazel eyes of the tall stranger studying her.

* * *

CHAPTER 13

JELANI'S first reaction was shock mingled with a bit of fear. She took a step back and felt her shoe scrape the brick wall. What did these guys want?

"Can I h-h-help you?" she choked out.

The hazel-eyed man's face broke into a devastating smile. "It seems we have caused you trouble. I assure you that was never my intention."

She didn't smile back, thinking how much taller he seemed standing close to her. "You know what they say about intentions."

"I don't, actually." His blank face seemed to indicate genuine puzzlement.

Jelani shook her head. Either he wasn't too bright or he was playing dumb on purpose. She looked past him to Astan, who fidgeted behind him. "So what was your intention?"

"We needed to make contact. Events are moving faster than we expected."

A raised eyebrow was her only initial reaction. Then she straightened and wiped the weed pollen from her hands. She looked around, satisfied that the lights from the parking lot next door made her visible to any passersby. Besides, the two men maintained a respectful distance.

"I see. Events. Now it's James Bond time. Look, my friend, I don't even know you." She eyed Astan. "Did your grandmother send you?"

Astan shook his head.

"Exactly," the other one replied. "It is time we met."

Jelani felt lost in the gaze he fixed on her as he spoke. His feet never moved, but she could feel him closer. Her instinct was to retreat inside the coffee shop, but something about him kept her rooted where she was. "Who are you?"

"You don't know?" He reached to take her hand, never releasing her gaze.

Absorbed by his intense regard, she didn't pull away from him. Somehow she knew his name was Daven Talvi and that his companion was Astan Hawk. She could hear his voice inside her head. It was all at once familiar and strange, thrilling and frightening.

Our people have been in hiding for many years. The dangers averted by the quick action of those who saved the queen have not vanished. Your father was wise to conceal you. He let go, and the voice was gone.

She stepped away, a bit overwhelmed. Did he just talk to her through telepathy? What the hell kind of man was he?

"Our people?" she asked. "What are you talking about? And what danger?"

The warmth of his mental tone made it sound like he knew Vincent Marsh. Could he have been involved in her father's death? That seemed unlikely, because he did not look much older than she was.

Astan Hawk, alert and looking over his shoulder, whispered in Daven's ear.

Daven nodded and turned back to Jelani. "It would be best to speak of these things in a less vulnerable place."

"You're talking crazy and you think I'm going somewhere with you?" she blurted. "Ha! Best get over that, chief."

She felt her attention come back to the real world, anchored even more strongly when one of the other girls leaned out the back door looking for her.

"I'll be back in a minute," Jelani promised.

The girl smirked when she saw who Jelani was talking with. "Sutton will have a cow."

"No, it's okay," Jelani said, at the same time wondering why she was so certain. But there was more to Daven than the words. Something in his mental voice conveyed safety and support.

The other girl cast narrowed eyes on the two men and then disappeared inside.

Daven gestured to the door. "She will call the uniformed

man."

Jelani scowled. "She better not." More attention from Richard was the last thing she needed.

Astan Hawk whispered again, looking down the alley.

"Is there a place?" Daven persisted. "We have much to speak about. Warnings for you. Trouble for us all."

There was just something about him. As odd as the scene was, she thought she could trust him. But not at her apartment. Even losing her mind, she was still smarter than that.

"How about Denny's on Brooks Street in about an hour?" she suggested. "That's when my shift's done. After the game lets out, no one will care what you say unless you strip naked and table dance."

"Very well. Shall we wait for you, to guarantee your safety as you travel?"

"No," she said, a little annoyed. "I think I can handle that. If Richard doesn't have my car towed again."

"We will see you there." Daven brushed her hand once more. Then he and his taciturn companion walked away without another word.

Jelani toyed with the thought of calling Lane, but her stubborn streak wouldn't allow it.

I can do this. I can.

She returned inside and took the worst parts of the closing routine to make up to the others for the drama she had caused, filling sugars, restocking, and washing the floor. Then she closed up and headed to Denny's.

* * *

THE restaurant was well populated in the hour before midnight, the post-barhopping crowd from the University mingling with high school kids and truck drivers drinking endless cups of coffee.

Jelani stepped inside and paused by the register a moment to ruffle her hair with her fingers, a nervous gesture to delay the meeting.

"Just one tonight?" asked the fresh-faced hostess.

"No, I'm meeting some friends." Jelani flashed a smile she hoped would mask her hesitation.

The hostess helpfully surveyed the large room. "I see. Are they here?"

Jelani didn't see them in the main room. "Can I check out the back?"

"Um, sure, I guess." The hostess's smile lost about half the wattage of its original incandescence, and Jelani could guess she was wondering if this was some kind of dodge to snag a table in front of others who were waiting.

"Thanks, babe," she replied and hurried off to scout out the larger room in the back. A glance over her shoulder showed the girl had moved on to the next people in line, so she relaxed while studying the occupants of each booth as she walked.

Rounding the corner, she spotted Daven and Astan in heavy conversation in an isolated booth in the far back corner of the restaurant. She took a deep breath and marched over to the table.

Neither man stood up, so she opted to slide in on Daven Talvi's side, sitting on the vinyl seat as far from him as she could. She eyed them both, as if they were something distasteful on the bottom of a bench at the city bus station.

"Thank you for coming," Daven said.

"It's not like you gave me a lot of choice, right? If I hadn't, you'd have reappeared at the shop, which means Richard would have started again. Not exactly my happy holiday picture," she snapped. "So I'm here. What do you want?"

The waitress walked up to the table and her charm flipped on as she went into tip-earning mode. "How are you all this evening? Can I get you some coffee?"

"Ugh, no," Jelani said. "Water, with a slice of lemon?"

"Sure, hon. For you gents?"

Astan asked for herbal tea for both he and Daven and ordered an appetizer plate. The waitress scribbled the order and hurried away.

Uncomfortable, Jelani wondered why she had agreed to come. A loose piece of skin along one nail became the target of her jangled nerves, and she picked at it idly till she drew blood.

The silence grew and she finally looked up, annoyed. "Well? What do you want?"

Daven looked at his hands on the table. "We need your help."

"My help? What for? You seem perfectly capable of getting coffee on your own." She frowned. "Even if you want herbal."

Astan studied her without smiling. His dark eyes had no flecks of color to brighten them. His jacket was made of denim, but didn't look like a designer brand. Seemed practical, Jelani thought.

"Herbs are a natural brew," he said. "More healthful."

"Great. See, this is why it makes no sense that you come to the cafe night after night and drink coffee." She eyed him, doubt eating at her again. Having devastated the small piece of skin, she moved on to shredding the napkin the waitress had set in front of her. "You seemed to think I should know you. Why is that?"

Daven and Astan exchanged glances.

Here it comes, Jelani thought. The pitch. The plea. Give money to a charity. Be someone's surrogate baby-mamma. Let a foreign banker make you a fortune by handing over your bank account number and password.

Without a verbal response, Daven laid his hand over hers on the table. In an instant, her mind's eye was transported back to that sidewalk in the shadow of the building when she'd tried on the glass slipper. Now she saw the event from the viewpoint of one of the little men. She and Iris appeared huge, distorted from that angle. Yet there was no fear, merely the shock of the sudden birth into the world. Then the need to hide somewhere safe.

She looked into his eyes, confused.

Yes, that was me. Your life force has reanimated our people at a time of great need. We beg your help, daughter of Linnea. The sincerity of his mental voice never faltered.

What was happening? She felt lost in a wave of unreality, still shocked at the words in her head. Jelani's ears buzzed with a rush of blood.

Then she passed out.

* * *

CHAPTER 14

JELANI awoke in a rush of noise and action.

The concerned waitress dabbed at Jelani's face with a damp cloth and Daven held her head in a gentle embrace.

Astan scowled at the attention they were receiving. "My Lord," he warned, jerking his head at Daven.

Dizzy, Jelani sat up and pulled out of Daven's grasp. To her relief, none of the curious faces in the red vinyl booths that turned in their direction were familiar to her, as most of the University students during her tenure had moved on by now. She took a sip of her water, letting the ice cubes rest cool and attention-grabbing against her lips, and waited to catch her breath.

Daven dismissed the waitress. He watched Jelani closely, but didn't touch her again. "Are you all right?"

"Sure, I'm just great." She looked from one to the other. "No. Not great. You're making my head hurt."

Astan removed a leather packet from his pocket and took out a couple of dried leaves, which he then crumbled into her water. "Drink it."

She frowned, eyeing the particles in her glass. "I don't think so. How do I know what that is? Wacky tobacky?"

"It will heal you." Astan's dark eyes glittered like jet beads. He pulled his jacket close around him again and surveyed the noisy restaurant crowd with disdain. "My grandmother says it has taken years to find you. She and her Circle have put much effort into what you have just experienced. Believe me, the last thing we would ever do is harm you."

Before she could reply, the waitress ventured back with the food Astan had ordered and set it gingerly on the tabletop. "Sure you're okay, hon?"

"I'm fine," Jelani said with an edge.

Daven waited until the waitress had left the table to slide a little closer to Jelani and then lay a hand on her arm. His action and his warm smile seemed to relieve the curiosity around them. "I apologize for the suddenness of our approach," he said in a soft voice. "Of course, it is difficult for you to accept the truth when you are presented with it in such a shocking manner. Come, let us share food and talk like friends."

For we will be friends, Jelani.

She looked at his hand, realized his ability to communicate with her through telepathy was activated by touch.

Yes. I must be in contact in order for you to hear me. At least for now. That may change if…. His thought trailed off, even though he did not release her arm.

"If what?" she said aloud.

We shall see. He let go and wrapped his hand instead around his hot china cup.

Jelani glanced at Astan, but he was fixated on the plate, eating breaded zucchini strips dripping with white sauce as if he hadn't eaten in weeks. They had a strange dynamic, these two. Daven Talvi was definitely the face, the spokesman. Astan conducted himself as he did with his grandmother, as someone on the periphery. But it was different, too, she realized. This Astan was more like a watchman, almost like a military aide, always advising but not controlling.

Frustrated, she eyed the leaves in her glass and then sniffed the water. Minty. The two men didn't seem so dangerous, even if Daven was a little homunculi man. And how had that happened? Did she even want to know? How did he get so big in a matter of weeks? Surely that wasn't possible.

Daven nodded to her. "The water is safe." He reached for some of the vegetables, eating them more thoughtfully than his companion.

She took a scant sip of herb-laced water. It wasn't so bad. After a few moments she did feel more alert, but was that real or an imagined effect? Who knew?

"What do you mean, my life force did that?" she asked.

"Made all those little men?"

Daven smiled. "When your blood came in contact with the shoe, it mingled with our essences. We were able to regenerate."

Essences. Right. "So you put the shoe there? Hoping someone would find it?"

Daven hesitated.

"The shoe was left for you," Astan declared, "and you only."

"How could you know?" She could have been on a hundred different sidewalks that morning. She should have been in her car. That meant someone had been watching her, studying her habits. She eyed Astan. "Your grandmother's involved with all this?"

He nodded, but offered no explanation.

Jelani thought of Dee and all the gifts she'd brought over the last several months. Had she been set up somehow? The little herbal wreaths and the dreamcatcher, what did they mean? All this time, she'd just believed Dee was thoughtful, a concerned grandmother reaching out to a young woman living on her own in the city. A feeling of betrayal came, and went. In her Montana months, she'd studied Native American culture, and her eco-work had certainly taught her the value of natural plants. None of the items she had received were dangerous. None of this had hurt her. Yet.

"So Dee's been stalking me. And you're still not talking."

"It's not my plan."

When Astan looked away, she sighed and turned to Daven. "What about you? You said you'd been searching for me. What do you want me for?"

"There's no easy explanation for that." Daven leaned back in the booth with a sigh.

"Should be easier than the one about how a bunch of little men came out of a glass slipper when I stepped in it." She eyed him, water in hand. "When it was apparently left just for me to find. Somehow."

"Both questions are troubling." He managed a smile. "Your father told you nothing of this?"

"You said something about him before. That he was wise to

hide me. No. He never said anything about this. Or you."

She watched the headlights of passing cars through the windows, envying people who had only normal occurrences in their lives and knew nothing of homunculi and stalking cops and mellowed stepmothers. And murdered fathers.

Daven offered her the fried vegetables left on the plate, but she shook her head. He finished the last bits cheerfully and wiped his fingers with his paper napkin. "We should prepare to meet with the Vincent then. He will be able to advise us of the best way to proceed."

"Well, there you're out of luck, pal. He's dead." Jelani leaned back against the bright vinyl with a sigh.

Both men froze, staring at her.

Daven looked horrified. "It cannot be true."

"Well, that puts a crimp in those lofty plans," Astan said with an edge. "How are you going to save her if the Vincent is no more?"

"Djana did not know. We'd thought he was simply in hiding, as this girl had been." He fidgeted a moment, twisting his fork in his hands. "Perhaps there is another way." He turned to Jelani. "When? When did he pass from this plane of existence?"

Really mystified now, Jelani took a moment to study them. They seemed genuinely distressed. What was that 'the Vincent' stuff? Who needed saving?

"Ten years ago," she said after a moment.

"Ten years!" Astan just stared.

Weird upon weird. She was not telling them anything else. "You knew my father?"

Daven nodded, his face somber. "Yes. He helped us save your mother, Linnea, in the last cycle. We expected that he would be able to tell us how to resuscitate her."

Jelani raised an eyebrow. "Linnea? She's dead, too. She's been dead since I was a small child."

"No, Jelani, she is not." Daven shook his head. "She is very much alive, preserved in a safe place until we are able to bring her forth without danger. But danger now threatens her, and all of us, once again."

"But my father said...but he married Carolyn! But...."
Things started to get fuzzy again and she took a deep drink of
water. "I don't understand."

"Perhaps it is too much for her to absorb in a single sitting,"
Astan commented with a hint of annoyance. "She does have
human blood, after all."

"And what does that make you?" she shot back without
thinking. "Freaks of nature?"

"Actually," Daven said, "we're elves."

* * *

CHAPTER 15

THE next afternoon, Iris, Lane, and Crispy stared wide-eyed, as Jelani told them the story.

The four had gathered in Lane and Crispy's small living room to sort through the remaining boxes Carolyn had mailed.

"Elves?" Crispy was aghast. "You mean little cookie-making tree-dwellers?"

Lane rolled his eyes. "Yeah, Crisp, just like those."

He turned back to Jelani. "So. Elves. Assuming for the sake of argument that they really are, and I believe what you say about the mind-reading and telepathy, hon. I mean seeing the glass slipper thing from that end must have blown your mind. But how did they know your father?"

"That, I'm not sure of exactly. Something to do with my mother."

She frowned and rubbed her eyes, the revelations of the night before having left her with troubling dreams and not much sleep. "After that, Astan freaked out about some woman who wouldn't stop staring at them, and they split."

Iris studied her friend with concern. "So that's it? 'Hello, we stole your life force and grew into big giant men who aren't really men, but elves, and hey, it's so sad your dad is dead. And oh, by the way, your mother isn't?' That's it?"

Lane cracked up. "Iris, dear, you do have the gift." He opened the box at his feet. "So our mission, should we choose to accept it, is to find out who these guys are, and how your father knew them."

"And the mother," Crispy interjected nervously.

"Right. And why your mother who's been dead some twenty-five years isn't dead."

Jelani went for some lemonade. "That's about it. Think we

can handle it?"

"We've got enough coffee and cupcakes," Lane said, patting the box of confections next to him. "What else do we need?"

Iris snagged the smallest of the photographed-stuffed boxes and set it on the rickety coffee table between them. "Let's divide things into stacks and then attack each stack. Um, letters over here. Photos in the middle. What else is there?" she asked, as she started lifting things from the box. "What's this?" She eyed a thick bound manuscript and opened it to the first page. *"Ecosystems of Old-Growth Forests in the Pacific Northwest.* Vincent Marsh, 1996."

"Hmm. Yeah, he was kind of an expert on that stuff," Jelani said, reading over Iris' shoulder as she leafed through the pages. Several sheets were marked with yellow highlighter and one such marking caught her eye. She read it aloud to the group.

"Old-growth forest contains a biodiversity unlike any on the North American continent, with as many as 1,475 different species living among the trees. It is possible that native plants in the old coniferous forests could be used to heal human ailments and diseases, similar to some of those in the rain forests of the Southern continent."

The statement reminded her of Astan and his dried leaves. He seemed to be prepared with exactly the right thing she needed. Could it all be true?

"You said he was a scientist, but I didn't know it was like this." Iris closed the book. "Talk about esoteric. No wonder you're— "

"I'm what?" Jelani demanded.

"You know, kinda hard to figure out sometimes." Iris shrugged a little, a smile on her face.

"Well, what kind of a scientist did you think I meant?"

"Ladies," Lane scolded gently as he rolled his chair over to the Cave. "What I don't understand is what science has to do with elves." He slid a keyboard into his lap and tapped in a query.

"I'm not sure," Jelani said.

Lane scrolled through several screens. "Elves were part of Scandinavian and Norse mythologies. Section on German elves.

Then the myths cross over into England and Scotland. Mostly noteworthy in high fantasy like Tolkien's *Lord of the Rings*. And then there's Elf Princess Rane, but that's clearly only for the anime *otaku*. That means it sucks." He read on, brow furrowed. "Now if we were playing WOW, elves could be a hell of a cool ally. I mean, they really kick ass."

"The most important part of all that is they're not real," Jelani said dryly. "Like most of your world, Lane."

"Maybe they're spies." Crispy's eyes narrowed.

Iris laughed. "Right. Because spies claim to be elves all the time."

"Did you ever meet a spy who told the truth? Haven't you seen any spy movies at all?" Crispy grabbed a pile of letters and started skimming them, his foot tapping.

"Crisp," Jelani said more gently, "there are plenty of things a spy could claim to be, like a garbage man or a teacher. Or, you know, lots of things. Why would he choose an elf? I mean that's clearly fantasy."

Lane rolled backward out of the Cave for just a moment. "Why would a spy be after you, Jelly Bean? Maybe your dad ran into some top-secret shit out there. You think maybe your pal is a spook?"

Jelani considered Daven and Astan. The first was smooth and personable with telepathy. Could she have read deceptive intent in his thoughts when he'd touched her, if he meant her harm? Astan, on the other hand, seemed a little paranoid, sharp and easily provoked. Neither fit her notion of a spy.

Lane retreated into his hole again, while the others looked through the stacks that had come out of the first box.

The whole thing was bizarre. Elves? In downtown Missoula? She knew she should just discard the whole concept as a crazy flight of imagination. But after the glass slipper it was all anti-climactic. The controversy also distracted her from what an ass Richard had been.

She plopped onto the sofa with a stack of letters dated in the early 1990s, many of them from her father to the Forestry Service, U.S. Department of the Interior, and the Montana

Logging Association, regarding the intended logging of an area near Flathead Lake. He clearly advised against it, and from the replies he'd apparently received his word had counted for something. The logging had never taken place.

As she came to the bottom of the pile, she found two letters that were scrawled in heavy black ink, left-slanted writing, signed "Mad Dog."

The man who lured her father west for the last time.

Her face must have showed her surprise, because Crispy immediately alerted to her distress. "Jelani? What's the matter? What is that?"

Jelani couldn't make her lips move. The letter's cryptic words seemed to burn themselves into her mind. The others hurried over to stand behind her, reading as she did.

Vince: Still Patrolling quadrant C. Several unsavory types snooping big-time. Troops keeping an eye on things. Thought you'd like to know. ~ Mad Dog

"Mad Dog? Who's that? Some badass biker or something?" Lane grabbed the paper from her hand. "Where's quadrant C?"

"He's a murderer."

She stared at the next one. It was dated two weeks before her father had left Indiana for Montana.

"Murderer? Honey, who did he kill?" Iris slipped in beside her on the couch, put an arm around her shoulders. "You don't think he killed your father?"

Jelani didn't answer, absorbed in the next letter.

Vince: Spotted Stinky for the first time. Must think they're getting close. Lot of movement in those woods, old friend. We've staked out some trees to keep watch. Let's say, condition yellow, heading for red. Stay in touch. ~ Mad Dog

"You think that guy murdered your father?" Crispy asked, his voice nearly a whisper. The terror in his eyes seemed as great as what gripped her heart.

"Jelly Bean?" Lane prompted.

The story Carolyn had told her didn't seem any less disturbing, when she shared it with her awestruck friends. She finished to the empty silence of shocked disbelief.

Finally Lane leaned back in his chair with a deep sigh. "You said this guy was with ELF? That's some bad mojo."

"Twenty years ago, right, Lane?" Crispy appeared nervous, as though he expected someone to burst through the door. "He's probably fallen out of a tree by now, right?"

Iris made a little gesture, and Lane nodded. "I'm sure he's long gone, Crisp. Those guys lead pretty volatile lives. Explosives, blades, you know. I'm sure we're fine." His tone definitely held a question though.

"Let's keep looking at the other stuff, shall we?" Iris asked cheerfully. "Here are more pictures of that tree."

"That's the one you have the big photos of?" Lane asked. "Is it like the biggest tree in the forest, or something?"

"I don't think so." Jelani leaned forward to examine the photos carefully encased in sheets of thin plastic.

Crispy's thin finger tapped one of the small rectangles. "Is that your father?"

"Where?" Jelani took the picture in question and examined it. "Yeah, that's him."

He looked about forty then, a tall, medium-build man wearing knee-high rubber boots and a lumberjack jacket in red and black plaid. His hair wasn't as gray as Jelani remembered, and he actually wore the better part of a smile.

"That's the Tree," Iris said.

"It is?" Jelani held the color picture up to the light. "Oh, yeah, I think it is."

"Anything about your dad that might clue us to what's going on? What's his history?" Lane asked.

"His mother was a housewife, his father was an accountant, back in Oregon somewhere. Medford, maybe. He grew up an only child, went to college, majored in biology with a specialty in botany. Then went to work in the woods." Jelani put the picture down and sipped her lemonade, still feeling a bit of a tremble in her hand. "He built up quite a bit of fame and worked as a consultant for many years." She even told them about how he lost interest in everything but his old pictures, still wondering if he hadn't gone a little mad. "I swear he never said a damn thing about ELF. Or elves."

"He sure loved trees," Crispy said, handing Jelani a photograph.

She looked at the picture and frowned. It was her father, taken on a different day, as he had no boots and wore a short-sleeved shirt, but his arms were around the trunk of the tree, and his cheek pressed close against the bark.

She didn't need Iris to remind her which tree it was.

* * *

CHAPTER 16

NO matter how many hours Jelani put in at the wildlife rehab center, she never tired of the work.

Instead, her time with the animals seemed to rejuvenate her. Shirley Wright, the veterinarian, said she had a gentle touch, one that soothed the troubled patients into a positive response.

It was late in a June evening, and Jelani had cleaned most of the animal area. This was the kind of work that most of the volunteers did, making sure animals had food and water and clean hay in their cages.

After two years at the center and some paraprofessional training, she had been invited to help treat the animals, as well. At first she only assisted Shirley. Now she was trusted to perform nursing tasks on her own, such as wound management, medicine checks, and so on.

She had almost finished tending to their clientele of the week, checking a handful of rabbits, a pair of young raccoons, and a half-grown fawn. Shirley had nearly turned away the deer, concerned about the epidemic of Chronic Wasting Disease prevalent in neighboring areas, but the young age of the deer was enough to sway her opinion. It stayed. In a matter of a few days, it would have recovered from the effects of some sort of trap that had badly scraped its foreleg, and be ready to return to the woods.

Jelani had fed the black bear in the back, but she knew enough to leave it otherwise undisturbed in its strong silver cage. Even when it seemed friendly, it became aggressive in an unwary instant. One of the other volunteers had discovered that when he'd nearly lost a finger trying to help the furry black animal scratch an itch against the chain link fence.

These animals are wild through and through, and always will be,

Shirley had said. *No matter how attached they might seem, they aren't pets.*

Although Frank, the night caretaker, had already scolded her for dawdling, she insisted on taking the last few minutes of her scheduled shift. She'd left the best for last, a male golden eagle, a young adult with a wingspan of about seventy-inches. Affectionately dubbed Romeo by the center staff, he'd been there ten days, healing from a break in the light bone between his wing tip and outer joint. Shirley planned to remove the splint in the next few days, giving Romeo a chance to try out his wing and strengthen it before releasing him back into the wild.

Most of the large birds that came into the center stayed an average of four to six weeks depending on the extent of their injuries. Those that had serious injuries were usually transferred to the Montana Raptor Conservation Center about 200 miles to the southeast. Jelani was one of the few volunteers who could work with the big birds. When she first approached them, of course, they went all a-flutter and tried to escape. But once she touched one, it would get quiet and let her perform what attention was needed.

Like when Daven touched her.

Her head said that theory was ridiculous, but something inside her insisted it was not. She knew when she heard his thoughts that he was telling her the truth. It was almost as if she were reading words written on his heart.

Astan, though, seemed restrained, controlled by those around him, like one of these animals in its cage waiting to be free once it was whole again. What might have happened to him to keep him so guarded, so trapped?

Jelani found she wanted to know.

She checked the eagle's broken wing, removing the splint just long enough to rinse the healing wound in hydrogen peroxide. She then replaced the worn gauze with a fresh one wearing a dollop of antibiotic ointment.

Shh. Hush there, my pretty. You are healing so well. Soon you'll be back in the sky.

Jelani replaced the splint, and then heard another bird's

strident cry outside the low building. When she bent to peek out the window, she caught a glimpse of another eagle, swooping past in a flutter of multi-shaded brown feathers. Then it was gone.

The bird in her hands responded, trying to fly despite its bandaged wings. She could feel the power of it, its small heart beating so fast she thought it might burst. Romeo seemed to be straining toward the window.

"Is that someone you know, little one?" She smiled. Romeo had a Juliet, then. She'd not thought this one old enough for a pairing yet, but it was possible. She wondered if this pair had chicks in a cliff-edge nest somewhere that were waiting for parents to hunt together. Even nature seemed predisposed to couples. Well, that still didn't mean it was for her.

She calmed the bird enough to return it to its cage area and frowned as it made aborted efforts to take off, falling from its perch to the ground a couple of times before it gave up, frustrated.

In time, my friend.

"You about done down there, sweet thing?" Frank's gruff voice held more than a hint of irritation.

"I've just got to clean up," she said. "Five minutes, okay?"

His grumbled response brought a smile to her lips. She hurried to wash her hands and put the medical supplies back where she'd found them. A quick sweep of the area with the push-broom finished her work. She checked the back door to make sure it was locked, turned off all but the security lights, and wished her patients a restful night.

"All right, Frank, I'm done," she called, locking up the animal barn. "I'll see you Saturday!"

"About time. Got me a hot date down at the Silver Dollar." The pudgy, flannel-shirted man grinned when he met her at the front door. "Gal name of Rosalinda. She's a redhead." He waggled his eyebrows suggestively.

"Far be it from me to thwart the path of true love," she said with a laugh. As they walked out to the parking lot, she took off the long-sleeved hooded sweatshirt she'd worn to protect her skin against nervous claws and beaks. The evening air felt warm against tank-topped shoulders.

"Dunno about love," he said, "but definitely some red-hot lust." He winked at her, then waited for her to get into her car before he revved up his fifteen-year-old Chevy and headed into town.

Jelani chuckled as she started her car and started to pull out of the lot, but stopped when she thought she saw movement in the trees. Not just a couple of chipmunks or squirrels, either. Something large. She stared into the shadows under the pines, expecting a deer or maybe an elk to emerge, but it was a man. There shouldn't be anyone up there that time of night. Maybe it was some of those people who protested zoos, thinking animals shouldn't be caged.

She parked the car and stepped out, cellphone in hand. "Who's there?"

To her surprise, the man stepped into the circle of light under the security pole, she recognized Astan Hawk.

"What are you doing here? Following me?" Jelani put her hands on her hips.

The dark haired man came closer. "Would that be so bad? It could be dangerous out here at this time of night." He looked over his shoulder, taking a long survey of the trees around them.

"I'd be on my way home, if you hadn't distracted me." Her gaze followed his, seeking his constant companion. "Where's Daven?"

"He was called away to deal with other matters." Astan brushed dust from his light jacket.

Though he was several inches shorter than Daven, he was still taller than Jelani. His dark eyes burned with unspoken words. She wanted to be annoyed with him. Somehow, she couldn't be.

"Okay." Jelani crossed her arms and eyed him. "What do you want then?"

"I wanted a chance to talk with you." He looked around the parking lot. "In private."

"I hate to point out the obvious, but we are in the middle of nowhere."

"Exactly. Difficult to tell who may be listening. Perhaps we should go back to your apartment."

"Is that a line? 'The woods are dangerous, let's hit the hay?' What?"

Astan frowned and whipped around, pulling her behind his back as he gaze swept the darkened forest. "We must go. Now." He shoved her toward her car.

"What?" Her heart-rate jumped at his urgency.

Astan opened the car door. "Inside."

"Excuse me?"

"No time to argue. Either you drive or I will."

She had no intention of letting the guy into her apartment. The fact he'd followed her here alone made it worth calling the cops. All the same, she chose bravado.

"This is about my father and the forest. And that tree," she said. "Right?"

Startled, Astan stiffened. He grabbed her arm and shoved her into the driver's seat. As she started to jump out again, he held a hand out in her direction, fingers spread. She found she could not move. Hurrying around the car, he climbed in and locked the doors.

Furious, she launched into a string of hostile words, which he promptly ignored. His hand still held toward her, palm out, she felt herself reach for the key and start the car.

"Please, Jelani. I trust you to drive more than myself." Astan studied the darkness behind them, as a coyote howled very close by. "There isn't time to argue. Please."

"Oh all right." She figured if worse came to worse, she could just drive in circles. How would he know where she lived?

She headed back toward the city, planning to turn off as soon as she could, watching the roadside for deer or even moose that might run into her path, as they tended to do this time of night.

"Daven and Djana believe the best approach is to come to you slowly with this. They were not raised among humans, as I was. I know humans can handle much more than their thin skin might suggest." Though there was a harsh edge to his voice, she didn't think that his annoyance was aimed at her. "They also don't recognize how hard it is to deal with an understanding that your whole life has been one giant conspiracy."

Jelani glanced over at him, wondering what was making him so emotional. Emotion in a man meant unstable in her book. Unstable was not a good thing. She reached for her cellphone, which had dropped between the seats when he put her in the car.

"It won't do you any good." Astan was a silhouette in the dark, lit only by the headlights of the occasional passing car.

"What? You'll whammy the cell waves too?"

"Whammy?" He laughed softly. "No. But I expect they won't believe you. At least not about the whammy part."

She mumbled and turned onto Highway-93, heading south. "You know you and your friend sure have turned things upside down since you showed up."

Astan laughed, but he didn't sound amused. "I could say the same about you."

* * *

CHAPTER 17

AS soon as Jelani and Astan entered her apartment, Azrael bounded across from the bedroom and jumped into Astan's arms. Purrs of contentment filled the air, as Astan scratched behind the cat's ears.

Jelani frowned. Maybe Astan was not so bad, if Az approved of him.

The gut-twisting reminder of Carolyn's revelations and of Mad Dog's writing filtered into Jelani's mind like smoke. And what was so important that Astan decided to follow her halfway to Ronan?

"You said my life's a conspiracy," Jelani began. "What makes you think that's true?"

"Because they did the same to me."

"They introduced you to a pack of elves? No wait. You are an elf!" She eyed him suspiciously. "So how is your life a lie?"

She read indecision on his face.

"I thought my grandmother was the only relative I had until six weeks ago," he said with a shrug.

"Six weeks? You mean until the glass slipper?" She paused, staring at him. "Those men were your family? Daven?"

"My father." He nodded. "The rest are uncles, cousins, kinsmen. All elves. I had never known my own history until then."

"So we both grew up screwed up. It happens. And Daven, why has he waited till now to make his big comeback?"

"Nothing had changed until you turned twenty-five."

That stunned her. She had just attained that age, the concert she and Richard had gone to for her birthday. "What happens after that?"

"I can't believe you know nothing of this. The Vincent must

have wanted to wait until you were of age, but passed before he could tell you. Was it a sudden thing?"

"My stepmother thinks he was murdered."

That seemed to phase the elf-man. His rich complexion paled. "Bartolomey."

"Who? No, some guy named Mad Dog, I think."

He turned away from her and urged the cat out of his arms. Azrael ran across the room and leapt with his usual plodding grace onto the counter where he observed the two of them with some disapproving cat expression.

"Stranger and stranger. That doesn't make sense." He seemed to gather his thoughts as he came to face her. "Jelani, there's no time for Daven's slow method or for the usual courtesies he might use to woo you. The danger may come to a head very soon, and you are the bridge between our two peoples. We must have you with us. Do you understand?"

"I don't understand any of it!" she cried. "What the hell is going on?"

"I think it's time you learned."

A little startled that someone had finally agreed to speak straightforwardly, she relented. "I think I need a drink. Want one?"

"It might make the hearing easier, if not the telling."

She picked up her purse and keys and put them on the cluttered counter before she ducked behind it to score two pale ales from the refrigerator. Handing him one, she gestured to the worn brown chairs in the corner of the apartment that served as the living room.

Astan walked over to the large picture of the tree and stared at it, almost as if hypnotized.

Curious, she watched him. That was as good a place as any to start. Finally someone seemed to know what was happening, and why, and was willing to share. She juggled a hundred questions in her mind. Then realized she was more likely to get answers, if she asked them in manageable bits. Start with the picture.

"You've seen that tree before?"

"Many times." His voice was almost reverent.

"Where is it?"

"North of here in the old forest."

"Why would my father have so many pictures of this tree?"

"Your mother's spirit lives within it."

The words hit her like a brick. "What?" Staring at the picture, his words seemed to echo in her head. Her ears buzzed and she felt dizzy.

Astan quickly guided her to a seat in the papasan chair, rotating the half circle backward on the frame until her feet were elevated.

"Take deep breaths," he said. He laid a hand on her forehead, and she soon began to feel less disoriented. "I'm sorry. There is no easy way to share such news."

"You're serious."

"Very serious. The people had hoped that she would be released to govern once again before now." He hunkered down next to the chair.

She watched him, taking the deep breaths as he'd suggested. "My mother is…in that tree." She thought of the photograph of her father holding the tree as if for dear life, and Carolyn's words came back to her: *Your father left his heart in those woods.* "Carolyn never said, even when she told me about what happened. She must not have ever known."

"Carolyn?"

"My father's wife. She raised me most of my life, until my father died."

She wondered idly whether Vincent had ever told Carolyn the truth. She doubted it. Not that she would have believed it. All the same, it felt like a betrayal, one she wouldn't have expected from the father she loved. How could he have married Carolyn, knowing he was in love with another woman? A woman in a tree. Unreal.

Jelani couldn't decide if she should laugh, or cry, so she drank her ale, all of it, while she was considering her next words. Astan spoke to fill the silence, a compassionate warmth in his dark eyes.

"So you see I understand exactly how you feel, having to pick up a new life with little preparation." Astan sipped at his ale and then looked at the bottle. "Nothing like elven ale. You'll have to try ours."

"I'll get right on that," she said dryly. "So now I'm twenty-five. What does that mean? I'm an old maid? I get the quarter-century of service watch? What?"

"We had hoped the Vincent had started training you to use your powers."

"Why do you call him 'the' Vincent?"

Astan grinned. "His existence has grown into almost a legend, considering the glory of his undertaking. As a human, and as one who has gained the respect of our people, they have called him that."

By then she had digested the rest of his sentence. "Now, wait, wait, wait. Powers? You mean like that hocus pocus stuff you just did? And Daven with his telepathy? You think I have powers?" She struggled with the idea, and then decided against it. "No. I don't think so."

Could the day get any stranger?

He frowned, stood up, took a long drink of his ale. "I thought you understood. Linnea is one of us."

* * *

CHAPTER 18

"MY mother is one of…." Jelani stopped to gulp more air. "She's an elf?"

With a solemn nod, Astan stood straighter and looked at the picture again. "She was born to be the next matriarch of the People. Her mother was our queen, to use the human word. When she passed to the next world, Linnea was the chosen successor. Our people govern through matriarchal lines, the heart of each queen guided by Fate to find the king we need to lead during that generation."

"But that means— "

"Yes. You're half-elf, half-human."

"So, what does that mean? My father was the king?"

"He may well have been if Linnea's life had progressed without interference. As much as the Elders tried to discourage Linnea, she believed your father was the one, despite the fact that he was human. She would hear nothing against him."

"What did you think? Did you like him?"

"I did not know him, Jelani. I was a babe when Linnea and the Vincent met and became lovers."

Surprised, she sat up straighter, wiggling the chair upright again. "But Daven said he knew my father."

Astan nodded, stretched as he stood up. "It is true. Daven Talvi knew the Vincent. Twenty-five years ago, when the clan became divided over Linnea's choice, Daven wanted to allow the union, as did many others. But there was also a faction in fierce disagreement with what they called the 'tainting of the Blood,' led by Linnea's own brother Bartolomey. He claimed she forfeited her right to govern by choosing the Vincent, a human instead of an elf. But in fact our tradition does not speak to any hard and fast rule on this point."

"So who was in charge? Didn't they come up with some kind of decision? I mean the king or queen or whoever? You said the traditions weren't binding." She held the chilled bottle to her forehead, her dizziness finally fading.

"Yes." Astan shifted a little, glanced back at the picture. "Djana says that Linnea's father Lorenz decreed the union should proceed. Many, including my grandmother, admired the Vincent, of course, for he was a fine human. It is just there have been so very few relationships of mixed heritage in the histories of the People. No one knew what the result might be."

Jelani rubbed her forehead and tried to absorb the information. "I wish Lane was here. He'd have some context." She could imagine her friend typing furiously, as he pulled all sorts of facts from the ethers. Feeling more like herself, she squiggled around to rebalance the chair in an upright position so she could drink the chilled ale. "So how did my mother, how did Linnea get in the tree?"

Leaning against the kitchen counter, Astan drained his bottle of ale. "Bartolomey was not satisfied. When the Elders would not accept his claim to rule, he and his followers arranged a strike against Linnea and the Vincent. Someone loyal alerted her, but not in time to save her body."

"So she is dead." Some part of her concluded this was a strange conversation. Maybe there was something in the ale. A bad batch. A hallucinogen of some kind that made people believe all kinds of weird crap.

"Her body was injured beyond repair. But one of our healers was able to save her consciousness, and place it within another living thing. One we prayed would be safe through the years to come."

"You can do that?" Jelani asked, amazed.

"Each of us has a gift we can use when it is needed by the People."

"A gift. Like a power. That's why you said that." She understood the point he was trying to make, no matter how absurd it seemed. It still didn't mean Jelani had a power. "What happened then? Did you have a war?"

"War?" Astan's expression clouded with sorrow. "War is a human invention. We have other ways." His voice held a distinct disapproval of the human race this time, and she was pretty sure it included her.

"So did they punish this Bart guy at least?"

"No. Our clan, formerly harmonious, split into three communities. The first, the one in which my grandmother stood, left the forests and moved into the human world. She took me with her, to protect me and to allow my training. We are now scattered, aging as do the humans, awaiting the time the clan will reunite.

"The second, of which Daven is a part, opted to—what do you humans call it?" He snapped his fingers. "Hibernate. Nearly fifty of those trained to use their special gifts were frozen in time by a spell woven by one of the Elders, their beings and spirit reduced to a simple essence."

"So when I stepped in the glass slipper— "

"Your blood mingled with their dried essence. And your life force, blood of the direct royal line, re-animated them. Made them whole once again. They have returned to the forests, but have avoided the others."

"The others? Oh, that third group. Who's in that?" As she spoke, the answer came to her. "Bart and his folk, right?"

"Yes. Bartolomey wanted to be King, and so he is of a hundred men, perhaps. Only a few women remained with his group, most of the others alienated by his refusal to follow tradition." He tossed his empty bottle at a precise angle some twelve feet into the recycling bin, and gave a little smile as it landed squarely in the plastic box.

"I don't know how many his band totals now. But I do know, as Daven and his men have scouted them out, that they have aged as we have. Even living among the natural things in our former world. Their numbers are not sufficient in magic to maintain the protections of our kind."

"What kind of protections?" She struggled to swing the chair down and he reached out a hand to pull her to her feet.

"As a people we are healthy, long-lived. We use our talents

for the betterment of the clan. We were strong once. We will be strong again."

There was a long silence, and Jelani disposed of her own empty bottle. "So the slipper was like a test. If my blood could activate these cells and make dried people reconstitute into real grown up people, then I must have powers?"

He grinned at her description. "Exactly."

"Okay. So let me see if I've got this straight. Half-elf. Powers. Of some kind. And my mother is in a tree in the forest."

"Yes."

"Is someone protecting her? Why hasn't old Black Bart gone after her?"

"As far as we know, he does not realize which tree she inhabits. The Elders have gone to great length to disguise it from his eyes."

"But if he discovers which one it is, if they cut the tree down, she won't survive, right?"

"Right. That is why we hope to release Linnea from the tree to return to her rightful place."

"No one's tried that before?"

"I have been told all my life that we must steadfastly avoid the area where I now know Linnea awaits. Once attention is drawn by any of us to that tree, surely Bartolomey will try to destroy her again. But it is not likely that he will randomly discover her. That particular section is old forest. It hasn't been logged by humans. Many of our sacred spaces lie within its confines."

"You get herbs there?" Jelani recalled the page of her father's work that they'd read at the Boys' place.

He knew what she meant. "Yes. Our medicinal herbs grow there in profusion."

Something else nagged at her. "So the plan is to get her out of this tree, at which point the clan will magically heal itself and all will be well in Elf Country." She flashed a grin to show she was being a little bit facetious. "But what if you don't pull this off? If she doesn't survive, who will rule? Bart wins? I thought you said that his part of the clan wasn't thriving. Will they just die off?"

Astan looked at her for a long moment. "The clan could reunite under the next surviving female of Linnea's line."

She gasped as the implication set in. "You've got to be kidding me."

"There is no need to consider such a future at this juncture. We must try to set the situation to rights. Then those who have returned and those in the human world can return to our world."

He seemed to be more pleased with her now that he had shared what he had to say. "I am sorry if I hurt you or frightened you at the shelter. Real dangers exist all around us. Some you cannot see. Those who rose from the glass slipper guard you, but we suspect there are others of Bartolomey's faction who are always watching."

"Do they know about me? I mean, being Linnea's daughter?"

"From what I have now been told, only a few of the Elders realized that Linnea was with child. Djana said that they caused you to be born in the Elven way, and the Vincent took you away with him to hide you until the time was right. My grandmother and her Circle discovered you had been called back to this area two years ago."

"Called back? No. I just came here to go to school, that's all."

"Djana says you were called. That your blood knew you were of the soil."

Jelani made a face. "Yummy."

"It is how she describes native people. They knew you were the key to the restoration. Even if you don't know how just yet."

"Right." Her head was spinning. A whole new history for herself and a family she'd never known.

"Jelani." Astan's firm voice brought her to the present once again. He seemed ready for business, a little sharper and firmer as he walked to the door, ready to leave. "Those under Bartolomey's command would take your life to keep themselves in power. There is a real danger every day, but not from Daven or myself."

She glanced at the door, as though she expected dark forces to be for her waiting beyond it.

"This is why I have told you as much of the truth as I know. And I apologize for the rough, blunt words. Daven might have been more gentle. But I think less effective." He studied her a long moment. "You are one of us, Jelani Marsh, child of the Vincent and our Linnea. I believe you can do this."

She gave an uncomfortable laugh. "Gee thanks, Tinkerbell."

Astan smiled, more at her tone than at her words. "As long as I don't have to wear the outfit."

Fidgeting, she hesitated, grateful for the warmth in his regard. "No, seriously, Astan. It means a lot that you told me the truth, even when you know I don't really want to hear it." She offered a wan smile. "I'd hardly figured out the life I had before you guys showed up. And now?"

"Now I have provided you with a whole new one. I know. It will take time to make your true life part of yourself." Though he stood several feet from her, Jelani felt they were very close. "If there is anything I can do to help you, I want you to tell me. I stand ready to make this easier, if it is possible."

"Thanks. I'll remember that. You want another beer?"

He looked as though he wanted to stay, but shook his head. "Daven will need me shortly. He is making connections with other humans who will be able to help us."

"Really? Who might they be?"

His face lit up with humor, as he opened the door. "They call themselves the Earth Liberation Front. ELF for short. Appropriate, don't you think?"

"Lane says those are bad people. Why are you getting involved with them?"

"I don't know where this Lane gets his information. We need people with very specific skills, humans who are familiar with the forests. We share a common purpose."

Jelani was pretty sure that Mad Dog, however he was connected to her father's death, was a member of that group, at least if Carolyn was to be believed. "You should be careful."

Astan actually laughed. "There's no other way to be." He opened the door and paused a moment before he stepped out. "Lock your door."

"No kidding, really?" She eyed him a minute. "I never leave it unlocked. I'm not an idiot."

"I'm counting on that." He grinned and vanished into the growing shadows.

Closing the door, Jelani locked it and leaned against it, letting the last hour slowly sink into her consciousness. Talk about too much information. She knew it would be a long time before she fell asleep.

And she was right.

* * *

CHAPTER 19

SHE was so very human.

Astan worried a bit about leaving the excitable young woman alone with so much to process. After all, he'd been through somewhat the same experience himself, and he'd passed through many stages. Disbelief of the facts. Anger at the lies. General overload from the eventual acceptance of his new truths.

He moved along the western outskirts of the city, and took the bend that led south away from Missoula into the mountains. The night air was cool with a hint of moisture. The gentle scent of wildflowers tickled his sensitive nose as he hurried onward, booted feet hitting the ground in a regular rhythm that soothed him.

His people often preferred not to use mechanized transportation, or many other human conveniences, even though they shared the same world. There was no need. Elven bodies were of the earth, and functioned at their highest and best level when attuned to the natural.

His people. And her people, too. Astan wondered as his body took in breath of the wind, pumped blood through strong vessels, whether she would someday be *of the people*, living with them in the forests. He hadn't expected to admire her so much. She had real spirit, a nature that did not reject what seemed impossible. He thought again about her jewelry, her comforts, her human needs, and he doubted it.

But how he would like it if she did.

His feet hit the trail that led to a familiar glade above the rim of the small canyon, a place where Daven and those others that Jelani had restored to life had chosen to live. After all those years of nothingness, Daven had said, they needed the earth beneath their feet.

Astan and the other young elves, who had been raised in the human world, had been invited to stay in the woods with Daven and his companions. He often chose to do so, seeing that time as a further opportunity to learn.

Some of his childhood friends were dealing differently with the experience, not so eager to accept the fact that fathers and others long thought dead had returned without warning. It wasn't even so much that they now had unforeseen family, but there was a general feeling of rebellion in the younger group as these lost family members asserted authority over the small band. Grigor, in particular, was affronted that his position as ostensible 'leader' of Astan and the others had been challenged by the newcomers.

Despite his personal resentment at the long-term deception, Astan had resigned himself to the fact that Daven and those brought back to life through the magic of the slipper had lived in those earlier, uglier times. They understood the full depth of Bartolomey's treachery. They knew those who had remained with him. They had personally met the human spoken so reverently of as the Vincent and the lost Linnea.

Somehow, it was fitting that they would lead the fight. He bore no resentments toward the restored. Perhaps one of them would even depose Bartolomey as leader of their people, if Linnea could not be restored. For now, he and his brethren were bound to come to grips with the new order of things. Fate would show them the next steps when all was ready.

Astan ran on softly.

The city sounds faded as he left the road and started cross-country. He traversed the ground lightly, his feet hardly bearing weight when he touched down. Gray-shadowed clouds cleared overhead, exposing a half moon that reflected enough light, even through the trees, for him to be aware of obstructions in his path. Miles passed while his active mind returned to thoughts of the girl he had left.

It was obvious that Jelani had the Vincent's intelligent mind, though without his bent for higher-level study. Perhaps she preferred the stimulation of contact and conversation with a wide group of people over the study of books. During the time she had watched over her at the coffee shop, Djana had said the girl seemed to thrive in such an environment. All the same, obvious in retrospect but mystifying to him at the time, Djana had pressed the girl to carry with her certain charms and other sacred items to protect her from discovery. Like the dreamcatcher with blue jay feathers.

Djana had said the Circle had been elated when they learned that Linnea's daughter lived, and that she had returned to Montana. At first, they had marveled at her courage, supposing she had returned to continue the fight. But soon they realized the young woman had no sense of her place in their community. Believing Bartolomey had no knowledge of her existence, they resolved instead to keep her safe and 'unseen', sheltered by elven ways, at least until her quarter-century anniversary. Once that had come, then she was of age and could rise to be leader of their people.

Though he was no healer, Astan could sense the girl had been hurt. Her prickly responses evidenced that. She'd lost her father and her mother. He could understand her rejection of the revelations he had given her. Hadn't he done much the same?

It had taken time to digest the truth, many bites at an overwhelming apple. But he had come to believe. He even had some compassion for the humans, though they seldom seemed to deserve it.

And now the future of his people rested on the unknown and untested abilities of a young woman, half-elf, half-human, who was only at this moment coming to terms with what that meant for her life.

She was not yet a princess, but Astan could see in her the underpinnings of what she might become. If he could put his trust in her, that is.

Daven seemed to believe that Jelani could be trusted, and one didn't argue with Daven. His charisma wooed both elf and human alike. Somehow he had persuaded the rabid environmentalists to help them protect Linnea. Based on their previous association from Linnea's time, Daven had volunteered himself, Astan, and a dozen of their companions for some ELF missions to "demonstrate their dependability as well as protecting the forest." ELF had been all too happy to have them.

* * *

WHEN Astan arrived at the glade, no worse for wear after a seven-mile run, Daven greeted him with the usual curt smile.

Several humans from the ELF group waited impatiently, but Astan didn't know them, not even the nicknames they cultivated to avoid identification by the authorities. Daven had promised that someone familiar with the history of their situation would be there this night.

When the ELF operatives went back to their truck for some equipment, Astan sidled up to Daven. "I have explained all to the Vincent's daughter," he said quietly.

"You what?" Daven's brow clouded. "She was not ready."

"She was. She is special, for a human." Astan gazed past Daven to the others, who were carrying paint cans, hammers, and other tools as they came back to the woods. "She seemed to accept the truth. She is made of stronger fiber than you imagined."

Daven studied him, eyes glittering in the moonlight. "You should have waited. I hope she is not frightened away. We need her."

"Humans seem to better prepare for the future when they believe their cup is half empty, not when it is half full. I believe when we see her again, she will be ready to do what we need."

"You boys coming?" one of the men called to them. "Lot of work to do by morning."

"We're on our way," Daven called back, giving Astan a warm pat on the shoulder. *All will be well.*

Astan shouldered a bag of tools and followed the others into the forest. Each team of elves was two, one elder, one younger, as they'd been selected by the tribe. Astan himself was charged with the duty of protecting Daven, chosen even over some of the stronger young elves to be his second. Tall, blond Grigor had initially protested his own assignment to Ansalom, a distant relative, believing that as the first among the youngers, that he should squire Daven.

Though Astan was aware of that resentment, he didn't let it affect his performance. He intended to prove the masters right in their selection, and served with honor, knowing there was something meaningful to his choice.

This night the ELF team planned to set up a warning section at the edge of an area of the forest that had some particularly large pines. By marking trees with paint along the perimeter of the section they wished to protect and then embedding metal bits in the trunks of the trees to deflect or chip loggers' saws, the group hoped to discourage the company from attempting to take any trees.

As they reached the top of the rise, a grizzled older man in a bright blue plaid lumberjack's jacket called out to them, his voice loud like those who were half-deaf. "You boys really made it, did you? Good for you! Daven, how are you?" He marched over and shook Daven's hand.

Human, then, Astan thought.

"I am well, my friend. And you?" Daven, too, raised his voice to an equal level.

Astan watched a moment as Daven turned on his usual charm, but his eyes also observed the area around the men, on alert in his role. Everything seemed calm enough, other than the hammering.

"Can't complain, can't complain. Though my back sure as hell does when I get home from a night like this." The man laughed. "Who's Silent Bob here?"

Astan snickered. Daven hesitated a moment, confused by the reference, then took his cue from his companion and smiled. "This is Hawk. Hawk, this is Mad Dog Mulligan, one of the guys who's been into preserving nature for as long as…well, how long has it been, sir?"

"Nigh on fifty years, son. I've loved this green land of ours just like the good Lord gave it to us." The old man grinned. "Nothing like seeing the history of our world through the majesty and glory of some of the living things that have watched all the years come and go. Despite the interference of us puny humans."

He gestured over their heads to the branches gently waving in the night breeze.

As Astan stepped forward, Mad Dog held up a hand to stop him. "Whoa! Wait a sec there, friend." He bent down to the ground and picked up a small ball of fur. He made soothing noises as he opened his hand to reveal a baby rabbit, shivering on his palm. "Must have lost his momma here somewhere."

He walked over to the nearest bush and bent down again, his knees cracking, to release the small animal under cover of leaves. "Now, let's shake," he said with a grin.

Astan nodded, pleased. "Very honored to meet you, sir," he said. He caught an envious look from Grigor and one of their childhood companions. What was he supposed to do? Be rude? Insist that the others meet him first? He was not the leader. He intended to follow Daven's instructions.

"What was that?" The man leaned closer, squinting a bit.

He spoke louder. "Honored to meet you."

The man shook his hand as well and draped a skinny arm over Daven's shoulders. "Now you said you had something important to tell me, son. Something about Vince?"

Daven nodded. "We've learned that the Vincent is dead. Has been for some ten years."

"Is that so?" Mad Dog pondered the revelation. He leaned down, scraped some mud off his boot, and then tossed it aside. "That would explain it. I called him last time Stinky got close to Quadrant-C. It's been years. About that long, come to think of it. He never showed. I was surprised as hell he wouldn't come, not with all he had at stake."

Astan frowned. This didn't sound like anything he'd heard about Vincent. Although Jelani had said the woman he'd married had never spoken of this. "His woman never told you he was dead?"

"Look, friend, all I knew about the woman was that Vincent wanted a cover, someone to show Stinky he'd moved on, forgotten all about what he'd left in Quadrant-C. He had other priorities, you know, that precious baby of his, just in case he never succeeded. It's all he'd have of her, you know?"

He removed his grimy cap and scratched his head. "He didn't want me to contact him unless there was a crisis, so as to keep that cover from being blown. When he didn't show that time, and the rest of my letters got returned unopened, I figured Vince was done with me." He shrugged. "When you boys appeared, I was just glad to get back in. God knows the forests thrive under a healthy watch, ain't that right?"

"And we're glad to have you," Daven said, with a pat on Mad Dog's shoulder.

Astan heard a rustling in the woods behind Mad Dog and his trained muscles stiffened. "We should get out of the open."

"Yes, boys, let's get to work," Mad Dog said, picking up his own bucket of spikes. "Over this way!"

A whoosh split the air from the same direction as the rustling. Mad Dog froze for a moment, and then tumbled forward. The moonlight shone on a beautifully carved hilt of a dagger that protruded from the center of his back.

* * *

CHAPTER 20

ASTAN let out several sharp whistles, very similar to calls of an angry blue jay, to alert his allies to the danger.

Pulling a dagger from his polished black boot, Astan dragged a protesting Daven into the shadow of some smaller trees.

"Stay down," he whispered.

"But my friend," Daven protested.

"These are my orders," Astan hissed in Daven's ear. "You are to remain safe." He stared Daven into silence. Then stepped aside and quietly scurried ninety-degrees around the open area to scout out a new angle. There he awaited the appearance of the attacker, because surely no one would leave behind such a well-crafted weapon. An Elven weapon.

He was correct.

Soon, the silence in the glade was punctuated by returning birdcall and the trill of insects in the wood. Heavy footsteps sounded from the north. A large figure strode into the glade, a dark hooded cloak concealing his identity.

Astan waited for the right moment.

The hooded one looked left and then right. Apparently satisfied his bold act had frightened away lesser beings, he planted a foot on Mad Dog's back, leaned down, and pulled out the dagger. After wiping the blood on the jacket of the fallen man, he tucked the elven blade inside his cloak. Then his hood fell back, exposing a rough-hewn face with sharp cheekbones under ragged black hair.

"Margitay! You remain a traitorous dog!" The voice was unmistakable.

Astan tried not to groan as Daven engaged the enemy. For one who wasn't raised with humans, Daven was most impetuous.

The hooded one, surprised, glared in the direction from

which the voice had come. "I know that voice, though it has been many years since I have heard it. You accuse me of being a traitor, Daven Talvi? I, who have remained with the leader of our people while you have disappeared and blown your duties to the wind? Show yourself."

Don't show yourself, Astan commanded silently, scrambling back toward the place he'd left Daven. If he returned to the city without his father, he didn't even want to think what Djana would say. He might be exiled to the forest in solitude.

He jumped over a dead stump, grateful Daven had not yet shown himself.

How could an assassin, elven or otherwise, have known of their meeting? There was a traitor among them. But who was it? Was that person waiting in the forest to attack as well?

When Daven didn't appear, the one he'd called Margitay once again brandished the dagger, its blade a flash in the faint light, the handle held comfortably in his hand and his gaze scanned the brush around the fallen trees where they'd taken cover.

"But our king will be interested to hear that you are not dead. How many others survived, Talvi? Where are they, all these deserters? I promise you, they will have the same end as this woodsman. And that of the accursed Vincent!"

Trembling with fury, Daven started to stand.

Astan grabbed his shoulder and shoved him back down. "Don't!"

Daven just glowered at him.

"How long do you think he was listening?" Astan asked in an angry whisper. "Haven't you given them too much information already?"

Astan saw Daven's first reply fade on his lips, followed by a nod. A moment later, he confirmed he had sent a telepathic order to disperse to the others of their band.

And our friend? Daven sent to Astan, his expression stricken with guilt. *Shall we leave our friend there in the mud? Won't the others believe we had something to do with it?*

"Then I'll find you!" Margitay roared. He started toward the grassy spot where the two were hunkered down.

"You'll think of something," Astan said, pulling Daven to his feet. "You always do. Now go!"

As Daven ran to the west behind him, Astan wondered how much damage had been done.

He stepped into the open to confront the killer. The clouds above parted, letting in bright slices of moonlight to lengthen the shadows around them while illuminating their faces.

"Now who are you?" Margitay stopped, studying Astan. "You're with Talvi, so you must be elf." He let his weapon sit loose in his hand, feigning ease as he stalked closer, stopping well out of reach. "But I don't know you."

Astan stood his ground, his own dagger in hand. "I'm fine with that."

He listened behind him a moment, counting the seconds needed for the others to get to safety.

Good travel, my friends. We'll meet when I'm finished here.

"The lines of your face are familiar. You could be." Margitay studied him. "Your father, your mother, were of our clan? But they no longer follow our king, do they? Turncoats. Like Talvi. Like Vincent Marsh. Like Linnea. And like them, you'll die!" He rushed the distance between them, slashing when he got in range.

Astan was ready for him, ducking aside with the agility of youth. He pivoted, turning the blade in his hand so it paralleled his forearm. The two blades caught, the vibration of the impact rattling Astan's wrist.

Pressing his advantage, Astan parried each attack as he tested the skill of his opponent, buying time for the others with each stroke. The sound of metal striking metal echoed off the trees, silencing every creature in earshot.

His opponent seemed weak for his size, and Astan felt him tiring as the fight drew on.

Margitay's weapon glanced off the hilt of Astan's dagger only once to deliver a cut to Astan's hand, but Margitay took at least three strikes. One on his cheek drew a faint trickle of blood.

This must be what Djana had meant, when she said the remains of Bartolomey's tribe had aged as humans. Astan knew that Margitay was not strong as an elf should be. Any of the youngers could have bested him.

Finally, having the sense that the others were safe, Astan knew it was time to end this little game.

Deflecting one last blow, he felt strength coil in his legs as he jumped into the air with the thought of lightness foremost in his mind. The trick lifted him high, as he'd practiced many times. He landed with both feet on a startled Margitay's back and then changed his focus to becoming extremely heavy. Margitay fell hard, and as Astan landed with him, he felt bones break under his boots.

Astan jumped off and watched for a moment, but the big man didn't move. "Take that news back to your false king, too." He listened for movement in the surrounding forest, waiting for accomplices to reveal themselves.

The only elf he saw was Grigor, who had apparently not left the area as ordered. After a long emerald stare Grigor withdrew, the expression on his face hard to decipher.

Astan waited ten minutes more, during which nothing moved but the clouds that covered the moon once again. Then, slipping into the darkness, he ran to rendezvous with Daven and the others.

* * *

CHAPTER 21

IT had taken Jelani over an hour to get Azrael to stop yowling at the door, after Astan had left earlier that evening. Finally, she had tossed the agitated cat into the bathroom, just so she could get some peace.

Now she sat at her laptop, scrolling through yet another internet search and hoping for something that made sense. Of course not, she, thought, because it doesn't make sense.

But, strangely, it did. Somewhere in her gut. Everything that Astan had told her, the reason why she had grown up without a mother, the respect they had for her father. It felt right.

That was the scariest part of all.

She needed something more solid, some sort of confirmation, and so she called Lane.

"Can you look up some things for me?" she asked. "I don't need an answer right now. I thought maybe I could pick up some bagels and come by in the morning for coffee. All right?"

"Sure," Lane replied. "Just don't get Crisp one with seeds. You know if he gets a seed stuck in his teeth, he's sure it's a government plot."

"No doubt."

"What do you want to know?" he asked. "Oh, and by the way, Crispy and Iris found some interesting papers in the boxes you left. I'll pull those out for you too."

More mysteries. "Okay, thanks. What I need to know is if my father had any connection to an organization called the Earth Liberation Front."

"ELF? Now wait a minute. Like your stepmother said, that's some bad business there. They're monkey-wrenchers. Eco-terrorists. Trying to stop the assault on Mother Earth by making it too dangerous for the loggers to proceed."

Somehow having Lane corroborate it spooked her even more, especially since that's who Astan Hawk said they were off to meet last night. Why would they be meeting with terrorists? Did this have anything to do with her father's death?

"Right," she said. "Those guys. Please get me the information on that. I'll be interested to see the papers. Hopefully, they'll tell us something so we can find some other way to help these guys."

"Jelly Bean, you shouldn't get involved with that anyway." His voice took on a fatherly tone.

"Hey, it's not my idea, okay? See you in the morning."

She let the cat out of the bathroom, and he stalked off, miffed, to hide under the bed. "Don't worry, Az, I think he's an okay guy, all right? I've just got some issues to think through right now."

The cat didn't reply.

Jelani soaked in a hot bath with blackberry amber bubbles as she sipped a cup of hot chamomile tea with knapweed honey, trying to slow the wheels spinning in her brain. Astan's story sounded like something out of a spooky movie. Could she truly have reanimated a host of elves? Where were the rest of them? What did they expect from her? How was ELF involved?

Why hadn't her father told her any of this?

That was the biggest question as far as she was concerned. The why of this left a trace of doubt in her mind. Vincent Marsh could have explained such odd origins to her, if the story was even true, at any time when the two of them were off in the woods together, or in his study with the photographs or many other times where he wouldn't have to tell Carolyn, if that was his choice. But he'd never even offered a hint.

Why not? Maybe the answer was in the papers. Lane had said there was something new she needed to see. The collection of papers might make more sense now that she had some idea what she was looking for.

Despite the soothing bath, she lay awake for some time. Finally, Azrael forgave whatever sin she'd committed and curled up beside her, his rattling contented buzz working to coax her into sleep.

* * *

IN the morning, Jelani dressed comfortably and headed out, leaving Azrael a fresh bowl of cat food with a little tuna as an apology for being short with him.

She warmed up the car, putting in some Lily Allen to set the mood for her day, and then stopped by *Bagels on Broadway* for half a dozen of their tasty round breads and a container of cream cheese, because the Boys never seemed to have any.

When she arrived at the Boys' place, she found Iris' bike parked out front. She balanced the bag, her purse, and a box with a few more papers in it as she climbed the stairs. The door opened even before she could give the coded knock.

"You're just in time. Sweet goddess, you won't believe this. Crispy went outside!" Iris was ecstatic, practically dancing on her toes with excitement.

Jelani glanced over at Crispy, who waited half-behind the door to the kitchen. "No kidding. What happened? The Four Horsemen pop by?" She smiled to show she was teasing.

"Stop!" Iris scolded. "I'm so proud of him. He went out on the front step to get the mail." She turned to her former client and beamed. "I'm so proud."

"Are those my bagels, woman?" Lane roared from the Cave. "They're getting cold."

"They're already cold, Lane. It's ten o'clock, for heaven's sake." Jelani walked into the kitchen and sat the bag on the uncluttered counter. Crispy watched her with suspicion. "What?"

"Were you teasing about the elves?"

"Believe me, Crisp, I wasn't. I didn't even believe till last night. A lot of things made sense after that."

"Come share all these edifying things with the rest of us," Iris demanded. "And then we'll show you the deed to your property."

Jelani poked her head into the other room. "My what?"

"Apparently your father left you some real estate up near Flathead," Lane said. "I pulled a satellite shot off the internet, but all you can see is trees."

"Trees?" Her heart jumped. Was that perhaps the place

where the tree that supposedly held her mother's spirit was located? Had someone tried to contact the owner, but hadn't been able to find him? Her? If she owned the rights to the property, then she could keep people off it forever. Problem solved. "Show me."

She watched as Lane pulled up the image on one of his computer screens, but acknowledged that a bunch of trees seen from overhead really didn't help. Astan had been much too vague about where this tree might be located for her to be able to give Lane anything more precise. She'd have to ask him pointblank.

Iris handed her the document, which announced itself by Old English-style letters across the top as a warranty deed. She understood that Vincent Marsh had transferred to her a piece of property consisting of five acres in Flathead County. There was a long recitation of measurements north, then east, then south along some property lines, then west, but they didn't mean anything to her. The rest blurred together in a jungle of legalese.

But it was definitely her father's signature on the last page, along with a separate inscription: "Keep this with you."

"Wow. I'm a real property owner." How had this escaped his estate? Shouldn't Carolyn have gotten it? Was that why she'd been so hateful just after her father's death?

At almost twenty-six years old, Jelani didn't have the faintest idea how the legal end of life worked. Instead of learning more about grownup responsibilities, what was she doing? Chasing elves. Elves, for God's sake.

She sighed, as Crispy placed a hot cup of tea in her hand, and turned to face her friends. "All right then. This is what Astan said. My mother is a tree. *That* tree." She pointed to one of the photographs, still propped against the wall from their sorting engagement the other day.

Encouraged by the incredulous looks on their faces, she warmed to her subject and shared everything the elf-man had told her the night before.

When she was done, they were respectfully silent for several minutes before Crispy muttered something she couldn't hear.

"What?" she asked. "What was that?"

"I want to belieeeeve," he said, at first very serious, then his dark eyes sparkled as he broke up into odd laughter. "The truuuth is out there. And so are you."

Oh great, now the craziest one among them thought she was the one who was nuts. "Shut up!" Jelani smacked him on the arm, but the rest of them were laughing by then, as well.

"You got to admit, Jelly Bean, it does sound like a cancelled sci-fi show of some sort."

Annoyed, Jelani gave Lane a pointed look. "But there's just something about them, guys. They're—I don't know. So believable. And Daven can read my mind. Really."

"A man that can read your mind," Iris said with a dreamy look. "Can you imagine?"

Jelani knew that's where Iris would go. "So, Lane, what about this group? The ELF group?"

"Classified as the top domestic terror threat by Homeland Security a few years ago. They started serious inroads into this area of the country just before the turn of the twenty-first century," he replied. "Then in 2002, ELF came right out and told folk up at the Bitterroot that if they didn't stop salvaging logs in burned out areas, that they'd take direct action."

"You mean, they'd protest?"

"That's how they started out, some good old Thoreau-type civil disobedience. But as the decade went on they got serious. I mean these ELF people have training manuals on fire-bombing and tree-spiking, and they encourage others to join in. They call it ecotage, short for economic sabotage."

"Tree-spiking?" Iris asked.

"They put nails in the trees, and not just your little hardware store dozens, either. Twenty-penny nails, preferably three-inch masonry suckers. The nails are hammered in at an angle where it's most likely they'll catch the blade of a chain saw. They beat the nails even with the bark, so they aren't obvious, sometimes one per tree, sometimes ten, some low on the trunk, some high, obviously trying to discourage the logging."

Jelani frowned. "You mean if they try to log the tree, the blades break on the nails."

"Exactly. With potentially deadly results. Even cut logs can still injure people once they're processed back at the log-mill."

"Holy cow!" Crispy said. "They murder people!"

"Hold your pants on, Crisp. The point is not to hurt people, but protect the environment. Tree-spikers traditionally warn the loggers that their spread has been spiked. The hope would be that they find it risky enough they set their sights elsewhere."

Lane rolled over to a second monitor and clicked on a bookmarked page. "They don't try to shut down all logging, either. There really is some life science put into the decision, depending on the effect that logging would have on a habitat. If a company intends to clear-cut a section, it would be fairly obvious that all the plants and animals in the area would be heavily impacted. Old-growth forests, too, tend to be more protected by the ecotage folk."

Old forest. That was the term Astan had used. Maybe this was the right sort of hook-up for them, Jelani thought. If it wasn't for the Mad Dog thing. "So is it legal?"

"Oh, hell no! It's a crime, big time."

"Your father was tied up with those evil people?" Crispy asked, on full alert, as if he expected troops to land on the roof once this information hit the government sensors hooked into Lane's webcam.

"Carolyn said he was. At least this one guy." Jelani sighed. Sure there was no evidence that this Mad Dog killed him, but otherwise it was rather suspicious. "Anything about it in any of the boxes?"

Lane shook his head. "We got through most of them. There was just a lockbox left and a couple of little bags." He gestured over at a small stack on the floor at the end of the stained coffee table.

"So why would Daven and Astan want to hook up with people like that?" Iris asked, concern in her voice.

Jelani stared at the papers in her hand for a moment. "They've got to find Linnea and engineer this release in a short time. Now that I'm of age." It was the one piece of information she'd held back. As she expected, they jumped on it.

"Of age for what?" they cried in unison.

"Apparently I can rule the, ah, elf kingdom. If they can't get my mother back to life."

Crispy looked desperate. "What will they make you do? Bleed on her tree?" He twitched just thinking about it.

"Eww. I hope not." Jelani frowned. "They weren't very specific about it."

"They need ELF for that? I don't see why." Lane leaned back in his wheeled chair, brow furrowed. "You better hope your guy talks as sweet to those people as he did to you. Sounds like he could sell ice to the Eskimos, though." Having shared his research, he grumbled as he shut down the browsers.

"Sure wish we could meet them," Iris said, still a little longing in her tone for the perfect man.

"I'm so glad you said that," Jelani added, fighting a smile. "I want to invite them over here for dinner so we can all meet. You all can help me make sure I'm doing the right thing. How about tomorrow?"

* * *

CHAPTER 22

THAT had sounded so easy, Jelani thought later in the day as she mixed a mocha latte with two percent and shook vanilla powder on top. The meeting would be an interesting one.

She could imagine their responses. The elves would be fascinated. Crispy would freak out. Lane would try to disprove everything the elves said. And Iris would drool over Daven, trying to get his cell number. *Fabulous.*

The coffee shop was about to close, and for the first night in weeks Daven and Astan had not appeared. Had Jelani done something to chase them off? Had the ELF people hurt them? Or had their goals been achieved by mere disruption of her life?

It was odd to miss something that had seemed more of a hassle than anything else. She had to admit there was something appealing in Daven's gentle touch and reassuring in Astan's no-nonsense approach. She hoped they were all right.

Jelani was the last one out the door, locking it as she bid goodbye to her co-workers and walked across the alley to the lot. The streetlights reflected off the other cars as they drove away one by one. She unlocked her car door and got in, her feet grateful for the respite after a long shift.

As she slipped the key into the ignition and started to turn it, a knock on her driver's side window startled her enough to evoke short scream. Annoyed, she saw who it was and rolled down the window.

Daven bent down to peer in her car. "I apologize if I startled you."

"If? You'd be sorrier if I carried a gun."

His congenial smile went a long way toward softening her heart. "Discussions with our new friends didn't go the way we expected. You are well?"

"My nerves are shot to hell. But, yeah." Studying his face, she thought the shadows under his eyes weren't only from the angle of the light. "Astan told you we talked?" She looked behind him, and for the first time did not see Astan.

"Yes. I had hoped to tell you these things myself, in time. The truth is not always easy to hear."

Jelani sensed that Daven craved companionship. She was tempted to ask him to come home with her to talk, but her natural instincts decided against it.

"Look," she said, "I've got some friends who are helping me look up things about my father and this whole situation."

He nodded with understanding. "The two men who are confined."

She raised an eyebrow. "No, they're not...I mean, not like *that*. Crispy, he doesn't go out. Long story. Lane goes out just fine, he just chooses not to." She shrugged. "Look, I've arranged for all of us to have dinner there tomorrow. They've been going through a bunch of my father's papers to see if there's anything helpful. Would you come? You and Astan? I mean, is there still time before whatever you have to do in the forest? It won't cause any trouble with this Bartolomey guy, will it?"

Daven straightened and took a deep breath, as he considered the invitation. "If there is a way to avoid ugly alliances, it would be best. Yes, Jelani Marsh, we shall come to dinner. Is half past six acceptable?"

"Sure. We'll be ready." She gave him the address of the storefront.

"You are most kind." He stepped back from the car. "Until then, you should keep up your guard. The situation is changing with the flow of information."

"Oh, yeah. Right," she replied, feeling as though he had just dismissed her. "No problem. See you tomorrow."

She gave a little wave and pulled out of the parking lot, thinking there was something he had not told her.

In her rearview mirror, she saw Daven walk toward the back of the coffee shop. Astan hurried out of the shadows to meet him, and they disappeared together around the corner of the building.

She could not help worrying about dinner tomorrow night. Better bring two bottles of wine, she decided.

* * *

CHAPTER 23

DINNER was supposed to be a simple affair.

Jelani had brought linguine and a jar of vodka sauce with tiny meatballs to cook in a pan on the side, so as not to offend any vegetarians. Two loaves of Italian bread, as Lane had warned her one wouldn't be enough, lay precariously atop the bag she carried into the kitchen. On the counter waited Iris' promised salad, magnificent and bright with julienne vegetables topped with orange nasturtiums.

"So," Iris asked as Jelani came in, "where is Prince Charming?"

"He'll be here."

Crispy hung back by the kitchen door, watching the activity around him. It would likely be too many people for his comfort level in this small space, but it was the only way Jelani could have arranged the meeting. She offered what she hoped was an encouraging smile.

"What's new, Crisp?"

He watched her with large dark eyes. "Three hundred and fifty people were poisoned in Japan last week on the subway."

"Always some cheery bit of trivia." Iris laughed. "Living these years with Lane has done you good. You're both fountains of totally useless information."

"At least mine has a constructive bent," Lane said, peeking out from behind a Creamy Cupcake crate.

"They probably heard you say that," Crispy warned.

Lane rolled his eyes. "They are so not listening. I told you!"

Jelani carried her load to the stove, where she found Crispy had set out the full range of appropriate pans and utensils for preparation of the meal. "Do you want to help?"

"They're strangers," he said without moving. "They're fairy

strangers."

"Not fairies, elves," Jelani said in a patient tone.

"Lions and tigers and bears, oh my," Lane murmured with a chuckle.

"Wrong fairy tale, Lane," Iris scolded, as she opened the wine to let it breathe. She eyed the label. "Is this that Holmes Pinot Noir from the organic grapes? The New Zealand one?"

"Smoky with ruby flavors, the guy said," Jelani said. "Supposed to be vegan, apparently."

Crispy frowned, scrubbing at the spotless counter. "Do elves even drink wine?"

"Do elves drink wine?" Jelani looked at him and pursed her lips for a second. "You know, I don't know. Astan drinks beer. Or at least he did at my place."

"I can't believe you let him in your place," Lane grumbled.

A knock on the door grabbed everyone's attention. Iris practically sprinted to answer it.

In a moment, she returned with the two men and a wide smile.

"He's too cute," she whispered, slipping past Jelani into the kitchen.

Astan came in first, doing his usual reconnoiter of a place before he'd let Daven follow him. He didn't smile at anyone but Jelani.

Daven, on the other hand, personified magnanimous grace, greeting Crispy with great warmth but never challenging him with an extended hand or other demand. He then turned to Lane, who was leaning out of the Cave to study his guests.

"Thank you for your hospitality," Daven said.

Lane got up, pulled down his black T-shirt that bore a picture of Gollum from *Lord of the Rings* proclaiming 'We shall find the Precious', and walked across to shake their hands. Jelani smiled as she caught him comparing himself to the others, noting Daven's superior height and Astan's tight suspicion.

"Lane Donatelli, Crispy—I mean Ron Mendell, Iris Pallaton, this is Daven Talvi and Astan Hawk." She set several glasses out near the wine bottles. "Anyone want a drink?"

Crispy hung back in the living room, but he couldn't take his eyes off the newcomers, particularly Astan who was near the Cave studying the set-up. Astan seemed particularly interested in the webcam Lane had installed. The device slowly began to move, tilting at a new angle until its lens pointed harmlessly in the direction of the wall. Without a hint of emotion on his face, Astan gave a simple nod. Crispy just raised an eyebrow and crossed his arms.

Daven turned his smile on Jelani and stepped toward the counter. "How can I help? Would you like me to pour?" Jelani was surprised as he filled each of the six thick-stemmed glasses just past half full with practiced ease as though he'd performed this particular human task all his life. When he was done, he handed them out to those who weren't at the counter.

"May I propose a toast? I don't want to be forward," he said in a warm and humble voice.

"Why not?" Lane asked, leaning against the stove. "Can't wait to hear it."

Ignoring the sarcastic undertones of Lane's comment, Daven proceeded as if it had been a gracious invitation. "To the return of our queen with thanks to her lovely daughter, who has resurrected us." He lifted his glass to Jelani.

"Oooo," Iris cooed, grinning. "He talks pretty, too."

Jelani blushed and took a sip, the red liquid tasty on her tongue. The rest drank, Crispy last, his dark eyes still suspicious.

Lane gulped down his wine, his agenda clearly on his mind, and then snagged a red pepper off the top of the salad. "So what's the news on ELF? Y'all got your bombs ready?"

"Lane!" Jelani scowled.

"Just checking, Jelly Bean." Lane studied them. "I'm from Missouri, you know. The show-me state."

Astan and Daven exchanged puzzled looks.

"It is not my intention that any human should be harmed in the process of this rescue," Daven replied. "Bombs, as you say, should not be necessary."

"But you've been working with them, right? They've got all kinds of weapons."

"These men and women are very devoted to their cause of protecting the environment in any way they can." Daven shook his head, when Astan opened his mouth to speak. "Their stated intention is not to harm anyone physically. Theirs is economic warfare."

"Isn't there a better way to do what you need done?" Iris asked.

Astan would have answered, but again Daven silenced him with a raised finger. "The issue is time. We have such a small window during which to secure that area of old forest so that we have the time to do what we need to without interference. ELF is prepared to move to protect that area from human incursion now."

"Yeah, well maybe so, but you know these guys got a pretty big chip on their shoulder. You get tied up with them, you're running with the devil. Whatever trouble comes after them, it's gonna come after you too." Lane eyed Daven. "And it's coming after Jelani. I tend to be pretty conservative where she's concerned."

Embarrassed, Jelani stepped over to the stove to stir the linguine in the pot and checked the temperature of the sauce containing the meatballs. She reminded herself that Daven was only looking out for her and not intentionally trying to piss off everyone.

"Jelani is blessed indeed to have such friends," Daven said at last.

Iris followed an awkward silence with a little wave of her hand and a shy smile. "Can I ask a silly question? I mean, it's not really pertinent to this mission thing. But I'm still a little new to this idea of elves being here in town. Elves, you know. So, what do elves do? Do you have an apartment? Jobs? Or do you just hang around the coffee shop all day?"

Daven did not seem offended. "Those, like Astan and his grandmother, who escaped to the human world, they have done what was necessary to provide for their needs and to blend into their communities. At least as well as the humans would let them."

"As for the rest of us, since our revival we have been consumed with the tasks at hand," he said. "Of course, we take rest, as must all living things. But we do not have an apartment or employment in the way of humans, no. Nature provides what we need."

"So you're homeless?" Lane asked.

"Not at all." The tall elf-man laughed. "Our definition of home is, however, broader than yours. We find comfort in the natural sounds, the canopy of trees overhead as ceiling, the rustle of pine needles on the ground as floor." He looked over at the Cave. "We each have our preferred milieu."

Jelani drained the noodles and set them out in a blue ceramic bowl, with the bread and the sauce on the small counter that separated the living room and kitchen.

"Let's eat," she said in a cheery tone, hoping food would defuse the growing tension.

She had hoped bringing the group together would serve some function. There was no reason to assume it would all roll smoothly. All she needed was a little proof that she was not going crazy.

Iris switched into people manager mode, one of her best, providing just the right amount of light chatter as she helped the men serve themselves. Astan and Crispy stood off to different sides, jaws clenched with nearly identical fretfulness. Lane, of course, was focused on the food, and ladled a thick serving onto his plate.

Daven came into the kitchen, and Jelani felt his intent gaze on her. She gave him an apologetic smile. "They haven't ever met an elf before."

"I wouldn't be so sure."

"What do you mean?" she asked in a low voice.

"Did you think we were the only ones?"

"You mean, you're not?" The idea rocked her.

He looked deep into her eyes and laid his warm hand over hers on the counter. Her vision filled with the picture of men and women walking among the trees in deep woods. *Our people have lived in these forests for hundreds of years, side by side with your world,*

Jelani. As humans have encroached into our space, so have our people visited yours, more and more frequently. Some live solely in the human world now.

An image of the coffee shop flashed into her mind, dark-haired Dee talking with coffee cup in hand. "Like my mother and her friends, Astan and his." He chose a piece of bread, sniffing it, then eating it with delight.

Iris made Crispy a plate and sat him down next to Lane before getting her own food. Jelani picked out pieces of salad for her plate and then ladled Iris's homemade raspberry vinaigrette on the salad.

"Dee certainly has gone out of her way to watch out for me, if what Astan says is true."

"The future of our people cannot be taken lightly."

"Every girl should have a...what? Fairy godmother?" She chuckled in self-mockery.

"Any of us would protect your life, Jelani." Daven studied her.

"What are you two talking about over there?" Iris fixed her gaze on Jelani's flushed face. "Come on, spill the gossip."

"Nothing." Jelani poked with her fork at the food on her plate, feeling something from Daven she couldn't quite identify.

"You shouldn't have secrets. Especially when you're talking about dangerous entities." Lane watched Daven with a suspicious raised eyebrow.

Astan took some greens on a plate, added some dressing after a long sniff at the bottle. "There are more dangers than you know."

"Astan." Daven sighed. "There will be time."

"Like there was time for your friend Mad Dog? They know. We cannot make those words unsaid again."

"Mad Dog?" This time it was Jelani, Lane, and Iris in unison. Jelani set the plate she'd filled aside, untouched.

Astan turned to Jelani. "Then that is the name you were told?"

"That's the man who called my father out here to his death." She felt a chill despite the summer warmth.

"He says he never saw your father after that call." Daven frowned, took some pasta, and chewed it slowly. "He thought the Vincent no longer wished to have contact with him."

"If you know where he is, then take us to him," Jelani insisted. "I have questions for him about what happened to my father."

"He's dead," Astan replied in a flat voice.

"Astan, is this wise?" Daven asked with a warning tone.

"They are human, Daven, not mentally deficient. She must know." Astan's agitation escaped in a sharp outburst. "Mad Dog was murdered before our eyes at our meeting last night."

* * *

CHAPTER 24

"MURDERED?" Iris gasped. "Oh, my sweet Gaia!"

Lane glanced over at Crispy, who had turned pale and retreated to stare out the window. "Maybe they should go," he mumbled just loud enough for everyone to hear.

"Not yet," Jelani said, trying to get the situation back under control. "We need more information. Who did it?"

Astan hesitated, casting a glance at Daven who said nothing. "One of Bartolomey's men." Astan watched Jelani's reaction, as if gauging her understanding. "That's not all. Before he was killed, Mad Dog and Daven discussed Vincent and the fact he had married that woman as a fiction to show a disinterest in Linnea. And that he had done it to keep you hidden."

"Son of a bitch!" Lane cried. "And this clown heard it all."

Jelani shivered, not liking the turn of the conversation. "What do you mean, a fiction? My father loved Carolyn. He would never have used her like that!"

She considered the likelihood that Vincent Marsh might have taken all sorts of steps to protect the baby daughter he had rescued from all but certain death. He was her father. He would have done anything to protect her. Right?

When she looked up, she found herself under Astan's intense scrutiny. "So you think that Bart knows? About my father? About me?"

Astan nodded, his demeanor grave. "I think we have to proceed as if he does. Margitay is likely dead, but he may have recovered enough to return to the north. Others may have been watching, too cowardly to come forth when they saw what happened to Margitay." Astan took a deep breath. "Frankly, I think Bartolomey and his people are at least as deadly as anything the ELF humans may have in their little warehouse."

"What kind of powers do Bartolomey and the others have?" Jelani asked.

Daven leaned his back against the counter, his long legs stretched out. "Bartolomey has a certain dark charisma that can pull others in against their will, wind his lying words through their minds. Malina, his mate, can stop an animal in its tracks, dead. Several of the others can slave the will of wild animals to their bidding. Rotiner can hypnotize, like a cobra waiting to strike when you are under his spell. Each of us has a gift. The question is how those gifts are used."

Lane glared at Daven. "Why didn't you just send these guys a freakin' map to Jelani's door, huh?" He walked over and put his plate in the sink. "Maybe you're gonna need this place in the woods to hunker down before they off you, too."

"Tell me about this cabin in the woods," Daven said, trying to smooth over the rough edges in the conversation. "Have you found something in the papers the Vincent kept?"

Since most of them had lost their appetites by that time, Iris persuaded the uneasy Crispy to help her clean up the dinner dishes, while the rest moved over to the small table to review documents.

Astan sifted through a stack of papers Lane had printed off the internet, including maps and other bits of information. He tossed aside most of them, as if nothing caught his interest.

"How are you going to find this place without directions?" Lane grumbled in obvious exasperation.

Daven gave a half-hearted shrug. "There are many known landmarks, other stories passed through tradition. We are well-versed in the marks of our kind."

Astan grinned and dug in his pocket, pulling out a handheld device. "Or GPS."

"Oh. Well, yeah. Duh." Lane looked foolish a minute. "Guess I hadn't thought that elves would, you know…. "

"Understand technology?" Daven smiled. "Our peoples have shared this earth for many, many years. It is wise to— "

"Know thine enemies," Astan finished.

"Spying on us!" Crispy blurted.

Jelani clicked her tongue. "Boys, don't make me stop this car." She turned a mock glare on them all. "Lane, can you get a satellite map printout or something if you have GPS coordinates?"

"Sure can. Lay 'em on me." He rolled his chair into the Cave and grabbed a mouse. As he moved it across the table's surface, a monitor flickered to life, its screen filled now with the image of a UFO above the words *I Want to Believe.*

"See, there's hope," said Daven, grinning as he read the screen. "They have open minds."

Astan gave the latitude and longitude coordinates to Lane, who dutifully typed them in. They gathered around like scientists awaiting the culmination of some chancy experiment.

"There. On the east side of Swan Lake." Lane tapped the screen, zooming in for a closer look at the roads and other access.

"Where was that property my father left me?" Jelani asked.

"Let's see." Lane reached for the papers Astan had cast aside, but Crispy ducked in and grabbed a couple of sheets, held them out. "Thanks." Lane studied the papers and reached for the screen again. "Here. Just off the highway north of Woods Bay."

"So, not the property where the tree is. But not too far away." Jelani, disappointed, looked up at Daven. "I'd hoped that title alone, and denial of permission for anyone to enter, might solve the problem."

"What kind of place is this cabin?" Astan asked. "Are there facilities there? Any supplies?"

"Honestly, I don't know," Jelani admitted. "I didn't even know the place existed, until I got my dad's things. He didn't tell me any more about that than he did the rest of this. Carolyn clearly didn't know, either. Daven, did he ever say anything about having a place in the woods?"

"Not to my recollection. But when he was with our people in the forest, he stayed with us."

"Maybe you should take a run up there," Iris suggested.

"Road trip." Lane's grin practically split his face in two. "I call shotgun!"

* * *

CHAPTER 25

"EVERYONE?" Jelani was a little surprised. "I don't have a van or anything." She raised a brow in Daven's direction, but she was fairly sure they didn't have a vehicle. At least she'd never seen them in one.

"Iris does." Crispy's morose revelation drew attention from all of them.

"Since when?" Jelani asked.

Looking uncomfortable, Iris shrugged. "Well it's not mine, per se. It belongs to the agency. But I can sign it out, if I'm transporting a client." She leveled her gaze on Crispy's thin face. "That means you'd have to go."

"Go out to the woods? No!" Crispy's eyes widened, filled with panic. "No-no-no! I couldn't!" He backed away from them, his breathing now fast and strident. "I'm sorry, Jelani, I can't. Oh, no!" He tripped over the coffee table and ended up on the sofa, where he curled up and whimpered. "I'm so sorry. I'm so sorry."

"It's fine, Ron," Iris said, casting a glance at Lane who stood silent. "No one will force you to do this."

His only response was to shudder where he lay.

"Is this the illness of which you spoke?" Daven asked Jelani. "Something palpable blocks him from life." He studied Crispy for a few moments. "A shadow on his soul. A darkness eats at him from behind the wall of his memories."

That was as apt a description as the psychological bits she'd picked up from Iris and Lane over the years. Now that the suggestion had been made, it seemed the only thing to do. "We don't all have to go," she said, hoping to console Crispy. "Maybe Daven, Astan, and I can— "

"No way!" Lane protested. "After the hole they've dug themselves so far, I'm not letting you go up there without me.

Who knows who they'll have waiting to get you?"

"Lane, I can't fit all of you in my little compact, not for a trip that far."

"Just because it's Japanese doesn't mean five grown people won't fit in it," Lane said. "Crisp probably wouldn't even get out of the car if they—hey! What are you doing?"

Jelani was distracted by a light buzz in her ears and then noticed Daven had crossed to the sofa, where he knelt on the floor at the opposite end from the corner where Crispy cowered. He moved slowly closer, by inches, the same way Jelani did when approaching a frightened animal at the shelter. Crispy reacted much the same way as those deer and rabbits, as well, wide-eyed and still as death.

Jelani watched, fearful that Crisp would lash out at Daven. Over her shoulder she could hear Lane complaining about the danger the elves posed to Jelani. She didn't react, feeling removed, almost as if she was in a film for a moment or maybe the camera recording the action of the film, observing the scene without being part of it.

From the corner of her eye, she saw Iris move in slow motion toward Daven and Crispy, presumably in an effort to head off an incident.

The man on the couch didn't move, his terrified expression peaking as Daven reached out and took hold of his wrist. Iris and Crispy both protested loudly, but Daven didn't let go. Instead, he pulled Crispy toward him, murmuring words Jelani either couldn't hear or didn't understand. She wasn't sure which. Protests fading, Crispy stared at his captor with an indefinable expression.

"What's he doing?" Lane demanded, breaking off his tirade at Astan. "Hey! Don't hurt him!"

Jelani felt she should do something, but the buzz in her ears interfered with her thought processes. She felt encased in gelatin.

"Make him stop!" Lane turned to Astan, but he seemed somehow frozen, as if watching the scene without moving. He then moved to Jelani. "Jelly Bean?"

She tried to reassure Lane that everything was fine, but she couldn't get out any words.

Lane then turned on Daven. "What the hell is going on here, you freak?"

Daven had Crispy's full attention now and gradually moved to sit on the sofa next to him, their gazes locked. He continued with the stream of words Jelani decided at last was not English.

Iris seemed unaffected by whatever dulled Jelani's responses, but all the same, she had simply stopped to observe when Crispy had ceased his protest, no doubt professionally fascinated at what was happening.

"Just leave them, Lane," Iris warned, as Crispy's roommate threatened to disturb the tableau. "Let's see what he's got to offer."

"He's screwing with Ron's brain, that's what," Lane accused.

"I need Ron's cooperation," Daven said without turning. "You must stop interfering." Daven's free hand flicked in Lane's direction.

Shocked, Lane stopped in his tracks, one hand clawing uselessly at his throat. He was breathing, but could not form any words.

Jelani could see by the clock on the wall only a few moments had passed, though it seemed much longer. Another five minutes ticked by as if she was submerged in thick honey, and then time slowly seemed to catch up and she could move again.

Daven sat back and released the man seated with him. "How do you feel?"

"A little dizzy," Crispy replied. He rubbed his wrist where a few red marks remained, an impression of Daven's fingers.

"Water," Astan said.

"I'll get it." Iris hurried to the kitchen, came back a few seconds later with a glass.

Astan crumbled leaves from his pocket into the water and handed it to Crispy. Jelani recognized the move, wondered if it was the same herb that Astan had given her.

"No!" Lane screamed, apparently free of whatever control Daven had exercised over him. "Now what are you giving him?" He reached for the glass, but Crispy was already drinking it.

"Crisp?" Iris asked, sitting lightly on the arm of the sofa next to him.

Astan sat quietly, and then glanced at Daven. Jelani looked to Daven, too, for some sort of explanation. The tall elf-man walked over to stand next to Jelani, close enough to touch.

The others might be alarmed if they knew what had happened, I think. His hazel eyes were warm with understanding. *Do you comprehend?*

She shook her head, marveling as their nervous and paranoid friend sat calmly, a faint smile on his face as he drank water he hadn't poured himself despite the foreign substance in it.

"I was able to follow a line of his strong emotion into his mind and begin to loosen his defenses around his phobia of leaving a known safe space."

She couldn't figure out, though, what had happened to her, why she'd been frozen in that odd way.

Our healers often draw energy from other living things nearby to aid the healing process, Daven explained. *The damage to your friend was grievous and buried deep. I was in need of assistance and life force greater than my own to begin to heal your friend so that the mission would not be jeopardized by his paralysis. I was able to draw life energy from you and from Astan, just enough that you would not miss.*

"That's real?" she whispered. "That's really real?" She remembered on the way to the airport Lane had suggested such a theory and she'd pooh-poohed him. "So, is he healed?"

"Healed?" Iris asked, surprised. "I've worked with him for five years and he's just gone outside today for the first time. You can't just heal someone who's that scarred in five minutes!"

"I would leave that term to the human medical community. But I think you'll find he's prepared to join us on an expedition north," Daven said with a broad grin directed at Crispy.

Lane's frown hinted of disbelief. "Crisp? Is he right? You're seriously going to go?"

His roommate finished the water, and then turned to face them all, his face aglow. "I think I'd like that, actually. But can it wait till morning? I want to go for a walk."

"Well, I'll be." Lane eyed them all a long moment, and then retreated to the Cave from whence issued the sounds of furious keyboard tapping.

"I'll go with you," Iris grabbed her bag.

"So, tomorrow," Astan said pointedly. "You'll have the van in the morning? Our time grows short."

"Sure. I'll call the office tonight and leave a message to reserve it." Murmuring in astonishment, she followed Crispy who was already halfway out the door.

"You fixed him? Seriously?" Jelani was no less surprised than Iris.

Astan spoke for Daven, who still seemed a bit pale. "His fear is assuaged, though likely not released. He will be well enough to travel on the morrow." His solemn gaze turned to his companion. "There is much to prepare."

"So there is. We should make our farewell." Daven gave Jelani a smile. "Thank you for introducing us to your friends, and for a wonderful meal together."

"Do you need a ride somewhere?" she asked.

"No. We'll be fine." Daven let Astan slip past him toward the door. "Good night!" he called more loudly to get Lane's attention but received no response. The two men almost seemed to fade from view, as they entered the shadows of the hallway.

"Daven?" Jelani stood there, feeling a bit abandoned.

Unsure what to do, she thought perhaps leaving wasn't such a bad alternative. "Lane, I'm heading home!" she said, but heard only the tapping of the keyboard. "Yeah, so I'll see you in the morning." No response.

Jelani left everything she'd brought except one bottle of wine, which, as keyed up as she was, she thought she'd need to get to sleep. Absorbing the night's events, she let herself out and padded down the stairs to the street.

Maybe tomorrow would bring answers, she thought heading toward her parked car.

* * *

CHAPTER 26

"WAS that really necessary?"

All the way back to their small enclave, Astan had mulled over Daven's restoration of Jelani's friend, the small man called Crispy. He seemed useless to the kind of scenario in which the elves found themselves. Because Daven was of that earlier generation, Astan was willing to assume he'd had a purpose in what he'd done.

"That human has endured more pain and suffering than any other I've encountered," Daven said. "I am amazed at their resilience. Truthfully, I had not thought it possible for humans to be so strong."

"Not all of them are," Astan agreed. "Are you saying then that this one is strong enough to help us?"

"I don't know. I only touched a portion of the pain-induced protection he had constructed inside his mind. If I had gone farther at this point I might have lost myself."

"Then why risk it?"

Daven laid a hand on his son's shoulder. "For the same reason we carry hammers and nails for ELF. To demonstrate our good will. Jelani's human companions must trust us as well or they may dissuade her from helping us. We need her to like and appreciate us. In the long run, her devotion to us is the ultimate goal. What happens to the human is a collateral benefit."

"She is the ultimate goal, then, and you will stop at nothing to secure her."

"The Circle has not said otherwise. There is also the possibility that we will not recover Linnea. Then we will need Jelani more than ever."

Astan assimilated the explanation with a nod, finding that his own personal priorities certainly matched. "Small steps."

Daven smiled. "You understand the way we must move. Some of the others— "

There was a frustrated growl from behind them and Grigor came into the light, approaching the meeting area. "Some of the others? You mean everyone but your own personal pet! The rest of us want to find the despot Bartolomey and reduce him to the dust from whence he came!"

Astan saw over Grigor's shoulder several other young elves he'd grown up with, all of whom held anger and dissatisfaction in the lines of their faces.

Daven didn't bristle at the hostile tone, instead sharing a warm smile. "Bartolomey's fate will be what he deserves, but it may not be for us to deal it to him. If so, we should seek the wisdom of the group as a whole. Come inside, my friends!"

He stepped aside to let the others enter, and to Astan's surprise Grigor led his group between the strong tree trunks without further comment. His raised eyebrow brought a wink from Daven, and the two of them followed the others in.

The small open space wasn't very different from hundreds of others in the Missions. The dark-needled pines would look nearly black from the lowlands, their shadows impenetrable from the human roads and byways.

Half a dozen large trees had fallen around the glade, long enough ago that small brush and grasses had grown up around their trunks. No signs of human interference were evidenced by them. Astan could not see traces of fire or scars from cutting saws. Yet here they were, fallen into a pattern that created a group meeting site, with places for all to sit along their ragged bark.

It had to be magic.

Daven crossed the open space, passing the low flames of the campfire to confer with a few of the other elders, and Astan drifted to the southern end of the glade to find an inconspicuous seat.

Another of his generation, a burly boy named Beckley, sauntered over to Astan, leaning against an upright tree trunk beside him. "So, is he going to bed her?"

"Who?" Astan felt a rush of indignation.

"Lord Daven. Isn't he the one the Circle has chosen for the princess?"

"I hadn't heard that." The news took Astan by surprise.

"Surely Djana wouldn't let anyone but her own blood have such a chance." Beckley's voice held a mocking note. He had been another of Grigor's restless ones, those unhappy to forfeit their leadership of the young men to the returned elders. "And with the enchanting Daven in pursuit, it's not like she'd consider you."

She wouldn't? Why wouldn't she?

Astan managed not to blurt out those questions aloud, instead taking a moment to compose a response, despite the turmoil inside him. "Our mission is to release the queen. The princess is not an issue at the moment."

Beckley smirked, as if he could read all the emotions he'd unleashed. "All the time you're spending with her, Astan. Word has it she's not partnered with any of those defective humans she cultivates. So if she's to become truly elf again, she'll need an elven mate. A mate who will become king." He pulled himself off the tree trunk with a dark smile. "Maybe Djana will find the rest of us have our own ideas about that. You've always been a good guy, Astan. You know we youngers have to stick together."

Beckley walked away to rejoin his fellows. As he spoke softly to them, they turned to look over at Astan for a moment and there were several encouraging nods.

Astan pondered a moment to figure out why Grigor's men would suddenly want to cultivate him. It wasn't hard to guess that his access to Jelani and Daven would be coveted and envied. Interesting that our people choose to experience all those negative emotions they complain about in the human world, jealousy and ambition, the same evils that twisted Bartolomey. He hadn't expected such from his own kind. Things were changing. For a while he had felt a darkness threaten to separate their resistance group.

Until Jelani.

Astan realized there was more to the schism between the

elder and younger than group leadership. Grigor and the others aimed to secure a firm place in the ruling class of the new elven order by placing themselves in line to become king.

Astan's glance drifted to Daven, who was his usual charming self with the uncles and others who had been restored, laughing as he regaled them with some tale. Was he also mocking Jelani's friends? Or telling them how he was placing ideas in the young woman's head to woo her, to bind her to his will?

The question of Jelani's destiny could drive a schism between Daven and himself, if Astan's heart had any bearing on the situation.

* * *

CHAPTER 27

JELANI found the ride to Swan Lake nearly interminable.

It took nearly two hours for Iris to negotiate the van through the stop and start construction traffic. With every jerk, the tension in the packed vehicle bubbled below the surface like a waiting volcano.

Mountains lined the vistas, only a few tops frosted with snow now this late in June. In sunlit spaces, the mountainsides revealed themselves as green-tan areas of grass filled in by dark green pines. Where clouds blocked the sun's rays, the ridges were blue-purple, the trees black shadows along their crests. Between the roads and the pines, tall grasses of the fields sported violet lupines that stabbed their way toward a bright blue sky dotted with mashed-potato clouds.

Jelani caught flashes of Montana's state flower, the low-growing bitterroot, for which the valley around Missoula was named. The bright pink flowers topped roots which were, as the name suggested, bitter to taste, although they had been a staple food for Native Americans in the area some hundred years before. Tradition dictated that the roots must be picked before flowering, when the taste would be much less harsh.

She'd practically had to trade her prospective first-born child to get two consecutive days off at the coffee shop so she could manage this mission of discovery. She carefully left out any insinuation that she was traveling with Daven and Astan to avoid the lecture from everyone. And the potential phone call to Richard.

For all the effort it took, she prayed the trip would yield something worthwhile.

Iris appeared lost in the Celtic music that flowed from the front speakers, seeming not to notice the worn upholstery and stained carpet of the agency van.

Lane, as promised, had co-opted the front passenger seat. "Need before Greed!" he'd told Jelani.

From the computer printouts he clutched like talismans, Lane had launched a steady stream of trivia about the land, the forest, and the potential location of the cabin.

Daven and Astan had taken the uncomfortable rear seat, allegedly to avoid inconveniencing any of the others. They sat with knees just grazing each other. From their occasional gestures and eye contact, Jelani guessed they were speaking telepathically.

Crispy's reaction to the journey fascinated Jelani the most. He sat at the window behind the driver's seat, nose pressed to the glass like a blind man given sight for only one day. He would sigh. Then giggle. Then open his eyes wide with awe at the passing scenery.

It must all be so new for him, Jelani thought a bit envious.

"Is that a hawk?' he asked with excitement, pointing up toward the mountains on their left. "Look, there are two!"

Jelani leaned down where she could see out his side. "Red-tailed hawk. Good call, Crisp."

"Yeah. See there, where his tail's spread out. It's great." Crispy stared for all he was worth, drinking in the soaring flight of the birds. "They've got to be, what, maybe four feet across the wings there?"

"They can get that big. He can probably see us as well," Astan said. "Their vision is eight times better than a human."

"It is a mated pair," Daven said. He turned to study Jelani with a gentle smile. "Hawks mate for life. Their existence is thus made complete."

Jelani looked away. Maybe male hawks were worthy of trust. What did they have to do? Kill some mice and toss them in the nest for the kiddies? That much was instinct for them. Not like human males. The sight made her think of Romeo back in the wildlife shelter and the other eagle that had tried to get close to him. Could it be that romance was just easier for avians than it was for humans?

"Man, another holdup," Lane complained, as a road worker

stepped in from of the van, brandishing a red and white STOP sign. "Cupcake?" He held one out to her.

"Do you even know how old that thing is?" Jelani asked with a grimace, the delay setting squarely on her nerves. She picked at a torn nail that threatened to bleed at the quick.

"Who cares?" He grinned and peeled off the cellophane, taking a bite.

As Iris started to speak, Lane raised a hand. "And don't give me that 'your body is a temple' speech, thank you very much. Right now I'm arranging to worship the false god of yellow cake and creamy filling goodness." Licking thick cream from his fingertips, he returned to his maps.

They had traveled north from Missoula on Highway 93, formerly one of the most dangerous roads in the state when it was a straight two-lane route.

Unfortunately, the state initiative to bring the highway to a four-lane status had moved slowly and occasioned frequent stops for construction vehicles. With everyone in the car absorbed in his or her thoughts, those stops drifted along in silence.

Finally, they reached the south end of Flathead Lake. As Iris turned east onto State Road 35 just before they came to Polson, they all got a glimpse of the lake's azure waters. It wouldn't be the last, because 35 hugged the east side of the lake as far as they were going and beyond.

The lake was huge, over two-hundred square miles, the largest fresh-water lake west of the Mississippi River. So big, in fact, it very seldom froze through in the winter. That much, Jelani remembered from her environmental science classes. The southern half of the lake was also within the Confederated Salish and Kootenai tribal lands, and many of the road signs were stamped in both English and Native American languages, an act that had occasioned a modicum of protest from both camps.

The entire area was a magnet for fishermen and boaters. Anyone who'd seen that Hollywood movie about fly-fishing had absorbed the natural beauty of the area and many came to check it out for themselves.

"I haven't seen Flathead since I was a little kid," Crispy

whispered in wonder. "It looks like a silvery ocean. You can hardly see the other side!"

"Sure you have, Crisp. We came here with the fosters when I was, I dunno, about sixteen? You were probably about fourteen. Joe and Maggie were fighting about the grill he wanted to set up, remember?" Lane shifted with difficulty to look at his roommate over his shoulder. "We were out there on one of the beaches, and Joe was yelling at Sammie, and— "

Lane stopped abruptly.

The sudden silence jarring Jelani from her nail-picking. She caught his stricken expression, and looked over at Crispy, who'd covered his face with both hands. "What?" she asked.

Iris reached over and smacked Lane's broad forearm. "Idiot! I can't believe you'd bring up Sammie," she growled, as she pulled over to the side of the road.

"I didn't mean to! It just came out!" Lane looked back at his roommate. "I'm sorry, Crisp. I wasn't thinking."

Astan leaned forward behind Jelani. "Why have we stopped?"

"I'm not sure. Some historical problem, apparently."

Iris got out of the car and yanked open the sliding door next to the seat where Crispy was starting to curl into a fetal position. "Hey," she said. "Hey!" She grabbed his hands and shook them. "Talk to me."

"What's the matter?" Jelani asked.

"Bad memories," Iris snapped, more concerned with her client. "Come on, Crispy. Ron, stay with us here! There's nothing you can do about Sammie now. Think about the day we've had. Think about the hawks flying free. Ron. Ron!"

"The fear has returned." Daven frowned. "I knew the measures we took last night were preliminary, but I didn't expect another roadblock so soon. He must be deeply damaged."

"You're not helping," Iris said, shooting him a look. She pulled Crispy from the van and with a steadying hand on his arm dragged him behind the vehicle to talk to him.

"Lane?" Jelani asked, straightening her yellow cotton shirt.

With a groan, Lane leaned his head back and closed his eyes. "Sammie was a kid that stayed with us at the foster home for nearly a year, I guess. Maybe more. Home life really sucked. Mother was a drunk or druggie or something. Sammie and Crisp were real close. His mother went to court to get him home. They finally let him go, because she'd done her rehab and they couldn't see how she'd be a threat to him. Not six months later, her boyfriend beat him up. Broke a rib. Punctured a kidney." He sighed. "Sammie didn't make it. That was the summer Crisp really got drug-crazy and then quit going out of the house. He was just convinced the real world wasn't safe any more."

"No wonder," Jelani said, turning to watch the two talking through the back window.

"Yeah. I should have known better." He fumbled for the door handle.

"No," Jelani said, holding out a hand to stop him. "I think they're coming back."

Crispy climbed back in his seat with a quick look at Daven and something that might have been a smile before it faded.

After studying Crispy for a moment, Iris closed the door and got back into the driver's seat.

Jelani smiled at Crispy, unsure what else to do. To her surprise, he reached over as the van started and took her hand. He said nothing and went back to looking out the window, as they rounded the corner to head north along the lake's edge. She glanced down at the hand in hers. She couldn't remember another time when he'd ever been free enough to touch her.

Daven's hand came up over the seat onto her shoulder, and she heard his voice inside her head. *You see, you have the power to comfort even the most troubled mind. Soon we will see what new wonders you can accomplish.*

Turning, Jelani met Daven's gaze. There were warm fires in those hazel depths.

With a nod, Daven withdrew his hand and then spoke softly to Astan, who relaxed back into the seat.

Jelani could not help but wonder if she would be able to give them what they wanted and whether or not she was willing to give it.

* * *

CHAPTER 28

TWO hours later, they threaded a dirt driveway through pine trees nearly half a mile before they found the property Vincent Marsh had left his daughter. Deep in the wooded lot waited a small log cabin, a weathered combination lock in the hasp holding the front door closed.

Jelani approached the building cautiously, studying the dilapidated wood structure. Two of the corner supports leaned precariously toward the diagonal. No log was complete. Missing chinks of wood gapped each uneven row. The window frames held a tenuous grip on their rugged openings. She guessed a strong wind would devastate the hulk.

"Oh man," Lane said, peering in the cobwebbed windows. "It doesn't look like anyone's been here for ages." He tugged at the door handle to no effect.

"It's a dump," Jelani said. "And I don't have a key. Anyone else have a key?"

No one did. Astan went to the door and pulled on the handle as well, but the door wouldn't budge.

A breeze rustled the overhead pine branches, releasing their scent. It reminded Jelani of the trips when her father used to take her into the woods, a much more pleasant prospect than facing what decomposing specters might await them in the cabin.

She turned to find Daven and Astan watching her intently. "What?"

"What is inside?" Daven asked.

"How do I know?" She walked up to the door and yanked at the lock. To her surprise the lock clicked open in her hand. "Whoa."

She slipped it off the hasp, studying it to see if she'd broken it. When it appeared to be sound, she pulled the door toward her.

The upper hinge tore away from the rotted wood, and the top swung heavily downward as it left its niche.

Astan leaped forward to support the door before it hit her.

"Are you all right, Jel?" Iris asked from the van.

Crispy extracted himself from the vehicle, looking around in wonder.

"Yeah." Jelani picked idly at a splinter in her finger, wincing as she removed it. "Ow."

Lane pushed past her. "Check this out!"

Jelani and the two elves followed him, discovering a rustically furnished single room, approximately fifteen square feet. Several small windows illuminated a narrow folding cot set up in one corner, a tall bookshelf packed floor-to-ceiling with multi-colored books and a framed photograph.

"Well, it must be the right place," Jelani said. "It's got the Tree."

Daven walked over to the cot and laid a hand on it for several seconds. "The Vincent has slept here."

"I wonder how long it's been." Jelani's father had been dead over ten years. Which of his many trips had brought him to this cozy hideaway for the final time? Was it his last?

They scoured the cabin, searching for secrets it might have to reveal but found nothing of immediate use. The cupboards had several cans of food of indeterminate date, the drawers around the sink held the sort of silverware and cooking utensils one might expect of a seldom-used hunting camp, and there were a few pieces of clothing in the small rugged dresser.

The inside of the cabin was understandably dusty, but clean and dry compared to the outside. Jelani had a fleeting thought that the decrepit nature of the cabin's exterior was perhaps contrived. But to fool whom? Bartolomey and his kind? And how could the interior remain so undamaged after all this time?

Lane seemed ill at ease without a keyboard under his fingers. "What are we looking for?" he asked.

"I didn't exactly have an agenda," Jelani replied. "I just wanted to know it was real."

"It is assuredly real," Daven confirmed with a smile.

She poked through the drawers of the wooden desk next to the cot, pulling out several stacks of papers before she found one of her father's carved wooden smoking pipes. Cradling it in her palm, she studied the blackened interior and remembered the faint cherry smell of the burning tobacco that seemed to permeate his office back in the house in Indiana. The old scent set off a round of memories from those times. She tucked the pipe into the pocket of her jacket to take home.

Turning to the papers, she could see that they were more of the same from the boxes they'd already gone through, letters exchanged with the Forestry Service and other logging concerns. However, there were several hand-scribbled notes in thick black marker from someone who signed the worn lined paper with the name "Squirrel" and two more from Mad Dog. The notes were in a similar mystifying half-code as the earlier ones, talking about safe zones, and bad guys with super-villains' names.

"Lane." She held the letters out to him.

He took the papers, scanning them with curiosity. "Whoa! I haven't heard of Headlok for years." He cackled. "You know, he's all a big mind-controller guy." When he received blank stares, he frowned. "Oh, come on. No one follows the comics? And the Taskmaster's Minions here? I think I love this Squirrel guy already." He flipped through the letters. "Wonder if he's still around?"

"Mad Dog said he's in prison," Daven said.

"Prison?" Iris gasped and looked at Jelani. "You mean like, for murder?"

"No, no, for his ELF work. His unit destroyed a fleet of trucks in Oregon about twelve years ago. He and another man were prosecuted by your courts." Daven leaned on the natural wood window frame, looking out at the forest.

"Dangerous, dangerous," Crispy murmured from the doorway, as he and Iris came into the cottage.

"Monkey-wrenching is a dangerous business," Lane said. "This must have been some previous time when the lumber guys were going to take that area of trees. There are several veiled references to threatened trouble and sabotage, though nothing probably that would be considered enough evidence to actually nail anyone." He handed the papers back, and Jelani showed them to Daven, who read them more slowly.

"So my father did have dealings with those groups before. The ELF people. And more than just that Mad Dog guy."

"Though I did not know all of Vincent's contacts, I know he tried many options in an effort to protect Linnea." Daven shook his head. "Some of these letters are from after our people went into hibernation. I could not confirm exact motivation after that."

"So, you know I've been dying to ask about that," Iris asked, as the others continued exploring. "How did that happen, exactly? And how did you suddenly get reconstituted like orange juice from that glass slipper?"

"There is no easy explanation," Daven began.

"You know what, pal? For you, there never is," Lane muttered. "You always seem to skinny out of anything meaningful. This could all just be a crock of crap, this ELF stuff. And you've dragged us up here to...." He stopped, as if unable to come up with an appropriate dastardly deed.

"Hey, wait! We came up here because I wanted to, not them. Because of the deed," Jelani protested. "And after all, he fixed Crisp, right?" She looked to Daven, who passed Astan a satisfied smile.

"He snookered Crispy into thinking he was okay," Lane grumbled. "That man hasn't been out of our house in years. He's been that way as long as I've known him. He's been through plenty of crap, honey. He's earned his neuroses."

As Crispy started to reply, Lane waved him into silence. "I love you more than my own brother. More than my mom, even. But so help me, I'm getting damned tired of all this hocus pocus crap!"

Lane was angry in a way that Jelani had never seen. It was odd to have Crispy demonstrating a spooky calm with Lane riled fit to beat the band.

"Lane, we mean you no harm," Daven said, his soothing tone pitched at a frequency that affected all of them. Hand outstretched, he started toward the heavy-set man who jerked back, knocking over an old camp lantern on the shelf.

Everyone stopped what they were doing and stared as the glass globe of the lantern, blackened with old smoke, shattered when it hit the ground.

* * *

CHAPTER 29

A BARE trickle of gas leaked from the fuel compartment, but there was no odor. As they all stared in shock at the sudden noise, they could see a folded piece of paper lying among the glass fragments.

"What's that?" Crispy asked, pointing. Astan bent down and picked up the paper, handed it to Jelani.

Before Jelani had unfolded it, she recognized her father's precise scientific handwriting. The letters were square and even for the first half of the letter, but more hurried and less meticulous as it concluded. It was dated October 8, and she realized with a start that it must have been written the week her father had died.

Sobered as she held perhaps the last words her father had written, she straightened the paper and read it aloud.

Dear Jelani: I trust you are reading this because I am gone and you have found the deed giving you ownership of this cabin. I never told Carolyn about this place. Indeed, never told her about much of my life in the West, including the story of how I met your mother. It was safer. For all of us. Please forgive me for keeping the details from you. Believe that I would have told you how very special Linnea was, had it been safe for you to know. The vessel that I hope to hide with this letter may be valuable if you encounter the right companions, those who will know what to do with it. I had hoped we would use it together, but the time was never right. However you draw on the vessel, hold it close always and it will keep you safe. I know not where you are in your life's journey. Perhaps you are long married, with a husband and family. Your childhood, and me, may be beyond your mind. If this is so, I wish you all the goodness life can bring, and hope you will be as happy as I was with your mother.

But if the stars have seen fit to bring you in search of the truth, then you will learn the explanation of your conception and birth. Jelani, you were created from the great depth of love between an incredible woman and a very, very fortunate man. The treachery of those who falsely proclaimed familial love for your mother may have destroyed her, indeed, destroyed us all. There remains a chance now, if you gather those to you who are gifted with understanding, and protect yourself against those who would do you harm, you may become part of a greater Adventure. Only those with this gift will be able to advise you on the wisest choices, and you should heed what they have to say. You will learn things you would never have believed could be true. You must leave your mind open to astonishing possibilities. Believe, my dear Jelani. Believe.

Mystified, she studied the last line once more, then at the end of the letter, the simple postscript: "Dad."

Why would her father put paper in an oil lamp? Wouldn't it burn up before anyone could notice it was there?

"He wrote this last part in a hurry," she said, puzzled. "I wonder what happened."

"May I?" Daven held out his hand, and she gave it to him. He scanned it, brow furrowed. "Our part of the clan had been in hiding for many years by then. Astan?" He passed the letter to his companion.

Astan took a minute to look at the words on the letter, and then continued to study the paper, turning it over and holding it up to the light. He began to nod as his finger traced something Jelani hadn't even seen. "Herc," he said. He blew on the paper, and the heat of his breath brought a faint color to words scribed in a delicate shade of red.

"Invisible ink!" Crispy said, pausing in his fastidious work.

"Elven work. He didn't want just anyone to see this." Astan, still carrying the paper, walked outside, held it flat in an area of bright sunlight. The natural heat brought the lettering to full development.

They all gathered around, amazed by the spidery scratches so different from Vincent's carefully defined English print.

"So what's it say? Or do you have to be a magician to understand it?" Lane's voice held an edge.

Astan shot him a look, and then returned to the note in his hand. "Jelani, may I read it aloud?"

"Sure." A thrill ran through her, a fear of what these crimson letters might reveal.

Her father wrote in Elven script. There was so much she didn't know about him. If she didn't know who he was, how could she ever know herself?

Daven could read the uncertainty on her face, and reached to take her hand. *Believe, Jelani. There is much to absorb, but it will make you whole.* He continued to hold her hand, and Jelani felt slow warmth and a wave of contentment move through her.

You're handling me, Jelani warned, studying his face.

Daven's hazel eyes filled with amusement.

Clearing his thought, Astan shifted his attention back to the paper in his hand. "Greetings, Guardian," he read aloud.

"Guardian?" Iris asked. "Who's that? Not Jelani?"

"Ah. So that's where this is going." Daven nodded. "The Vincent was very cautious. The paper was charmed, so it would not reveal its secrets unless the princess and the guardian…" His voice trailed off, as his gaze found a sharp focus on Astan. "You are the chosen guardian."

"You didn't know that before," Lane said with renewed interest. He paced several steps and then whirled around like a gumshoe tracking for clues, his sharp eyes fixed on Daven. "You don't like that. You thought you were the guardian." A slow smile spread across his face, as his gaze slid toward Jelani. "Guardian of the princess. Well now."

"Well what?" Jelani frowned as a cloud moved over the sun and the letters started to fade. "Just shut up and let him read, will you?"

Astan waited a moment. When no one else spoke, he continued reading. "Greetings, guardian. I offer my regrets that I cannot greet you personally. I expect to meet my end very soon, as Lorenz did before me. The treachery surrounds me, but I must do what I can, even if it takes my last breath, to protect Linnea and the sanctity of the Elven ways." He paused and glanced at Jelani, whose tears had begun to fall. "Are you prepared for the rest?"

She sniffed and nodded. "Go on."

Astan looked back down at the paper in his hands. "The burden now comes to you and your fellows," he continued. "If Lorenz is as adept as he believes, we shall leave a vessel that contains the power to heal the schism among our people. I beg you to protect and cherish Jelani as I would. Guide her toward her destiny, and help her embrace who and what she is. Give her the gift of faith, and show her she has nothing to fear by believing in magic."

As finishing, Astan appeared to read through the message once more. Then he folded it carefully and returned it to Jelani. "Your father is very wise."

"What does he mean about meeting his end? How did he know?" Jelani felt chilled even in the sunlight.

"The treachery to which he refers is no doubt Bartolomey and his men," Daven said.

"But what about Mad Dog?" Jelani was troubled. If one of Bartolomey's men had killed Mad Dog as a traitor, that didn't clear him of wrongdoing in her father's death. But Daven could read people. He would have known if Mad Dog was lying when he said that he never saw Vincent Marsh that fall. So if the ELF operative and her father never met, then Bartolomey could know exactly where her father's hideaway was. "Bartolomey could be watching us now!"

Iris looked around nervously. "Then we should leave."

"We must find the vessel," Astan said.

With Jelani close behind him, Astan returned to the cabin. Daven and Lane followed, but Crispy looked on the verge of a full freak-out.

"I'll take Crisp to the van," Iris said.

Jelani watched through the window, until Iris had him tucked safely inside the vehicle, and had half an inclination to follow them.

"A vessel," Jelani pondered aloud. "Whatever that is."

A vessel? Like a boat? A blood vessel? She knelt down, examined the detritus of the broken lamp. Then checked under the furniture to see if some part of the lamp had been lost in the destruction. The others did the same, except for Lane, who finally located an old broom with a cracked handle to sweep up the glass.

"Do you know what we're looking for?" Jelani asked Daven.

"I have never seen a vessel, though I know they contain powerful magic."

"Magic." Lane snorted, as he tossed the fragments into the worn metal trashcan and then slumped into one of the chairs. "Right. Here you go again. Come on, Jelly Bean. Stay real with me here, will you?"

"Remember all those D&D explanations you gave me? I was willing to believe those too, if they'd really had substance. I'm out of my league. And my dad says to trust the guardian." Jelani let a small intrigued smile creep onto her lips as she studied Astan a moment, before she returned to the search.

"What's that?" Daven asked, gesturing toward a shadow under the farthest corner of the rough-hewn table.

"Yes!" Astan said, drawing a soft cloth from his pocket. He bent down to retrieve the object and presented it to Jelani. She noticed his fingers didn't touch the thing at any time.

She opened her hands to reveal a small globe wrapped in the cloth. Approximately an inch in diameter, it at first appeared to be made of red glass. As she watched, the vessel filled out with vibrant-red liquid that contained myriad gold flecks of various sizes. Though solid, it was warm to the touch and almost seemed to pulse in her hands, as it slowly grew to the size of a baseball.

"What is this?" she asked, amazed.

Lane leaned close to peer at the thing, fascinated despite his earlier cynicism. "Epic drop. Score. Bravo. Looks like blood."

"Blood?" She nearly dropped the globe.

"Don't let it fall!" Astan commanded, and Jelani felt her fingers close tight on the cloth around the globe. "Wrap it up and put it away," he added more gently. "You should do as the Vincent has said. Keep it with you always."

Jelani wrapped it carefully and tucked it into her pack along with the deed, which she'd brought. Then she remembered that she was the only one able to open the door. Was it because she carried the deed?

"Can paper be charmed?" she asked Daven.

"Anything can be charmed."

"Well," Jelani said, "I guess we have what we came for."

"At least you know where the cabin is now," Lane said. "So if we need to come back, we can. Not that I can see much reason for it. No electric. And DSL is right out, I'm sure." His rueful tone evidenced his feelings of computer withdrawal already.

Jelani nodded and gave the cabin one last look. It was a big step toward finding out the mysteries of the past that she never knew she had. "All right, let's go."

When she stepped out, the lock re-clasped itself. She asked Lane to try to open it, curious about her theory. As she expected, it wouldn't open.

They started for the car, as the plaintive hoot of owls sounded in the trees above them.

"The owls are not what they seem," Lane said with a smirk, as they climbed in the van.

"What are they, then?" Iris asked.

Crispy rolled his eyes. "Just ignore him. He's being an ass."

But Jelani saw Daven and Astan exchange a troubled look. "What's wrong?" she demanded.

"Nothing for you to worry about, my dear," Daven said in his usual honeyed tone.

"You really need to stop treating her like a fool," Astan said. "She's not some silly sheep. I've warned her already that she's likely being watched." He turned to Jelani. "Our people often mimic natural voices of the forest to communicate. It would be unusual for owls to sound during the daylight hours. So what your friend says is possible."

"I was just kidding, actually," Lane said. "Bad reference to an old TV show. Um, sorry." He turned back to the front of the van, muttering to himself.

Nothing they could do about it now, Jelani thought. If it was something bad, there was no doubt in her mind it would surface when she least expected it.

Jelani climbed into the van, with Daven and Astan squeezing into the rear seat. She felt their tension behind her and guessed it had something to do with the identity of the guardian, and also Astan's little comment about how Daven was treating her.

What was this, Jelani thought, high school? Was she supposed to be some homecoming princess with one of them serving as captain of the football team?

* * *

CHAPTER 30

THE second day back to work at the coffee shop, Jelani discovered she had new stalkers.

A man with long white hair, accompanied by a thin birdlike woman with a scar on her cheek, inspected some of the herbal displays in the front area of the narrow shop. While one fiddled with the displays, the other kept sharp eyes trained on Jelani, like prey under a raptor's gaze.

"Are you wearing a sign on your back that says 'Stalker Bait'?" one of her co-workers asked.

"Must be," Jelani replied, trying to appear as unruffled as possible.

She debated calling the police, but that would mean dealing with Richard. When it came time for her break, she decided to confront them.

Jelani marched over to where they huddled, perhaps in their own idea of unobtrusive, behind the candles. With arms crossed, she stood in front of them. "Is there something I can do for you?"

The man smiled, but the woman's pained glare never faltered. "I would think there was something we could do for you, Jelani Marsh," he said.

Startled, she took a step back, looking from the man to the woman and back. "Who are you?"

"This is Malina." He gave a warm, almost seductive smile. "You look so much like your mother. We're very happy to meet you."

"And you are?" She felt nothing of warmth from the woman and tried to screen her out. As for the man, there was something about his eyes. She couldn't ignore him.

"Bartolomey."

Bartolomey! The leader of the evil faction was here? She stiffened and glanced around for help, but everyone was busy with normal duties. She turned away from 'those eyes' and started straightening the area around the espresso maker. Exactly what could she do? Call the police and tell them an evil elf lord was in the coffee shop threatening her? Ridiculous.

This time she was on her own. None of the other elves were present. As she scrubbed at the counter, she could feel the two moving closer, one on either side. It reminded her of some movie she had seen with hunting groups of dinosaurs. It wasn't the one in front you had to watch for, she remembered, it was the strike from the side.

She glanced to her right. The white-haired man stood there with hands folded before him, dressed in a dark jacket and slacks, an outfit that wasn't quite a human business suit. His pale eyes were almost violet in color. He didn't seem like a bad man, standing right there inches from her.

I was misunderstood, his voice whispered in her head. *I mean you no harm.*

"That's the best you can do? You're not going to tell me how surprised you are to find your long-lost niece? And isn't this great, maybe we should have dinner?" She tried to smirk.

Bartolomey gave a soft laugh, a gesture that seemed incongruous with the intensity of his gaze. "Vincent was always very resourceful. For a human."

His female companion continued to stare with eyes sharp as cut onyx.

Jelani heard Bartolomey's constant whisper in her head. *You should believe me. I am your blood, Jelani.*

"We wanted to warn you," he said aloud.

She blinked and tossed her wipe-cloth in a white bucket under the counter. "Warn me about what?"

"You're being misled by Daven Talvi and his servant. They are not as innocent as they seem. Indeed, they have quite the self-serving agenda. You may find they are leading you into a situation that is much too dangerous for you to understand."

Jelani eyed him. Astan as Daven's servant? Was Bartolomey's intelligence gathering really that far afield? She wasn't about to correct him. "Daven does seem to have a rather inflated self-image."

Bartolomey actually laughed. "You see. Malina, I told you the girl had my blood." He observed the other servers watching them. "Perhaps we should partake of the local products so we can have more time to chat."

"Sure," Jelani said, hoping he couldn't sense her heart racing, as she was trying very hard to maintain a cool front. "Mint tea? Herbal?"

He nodded. "Whatever you think is best."

How about Hemlock? Nightshade? She smiled at the thought, and then made them both a cup of simple herbal tea.

Bartolomey continued to watch her with a peculiar, intent gaze. She could only hope that the information Bartolomey had about her was as flawed as what he had about the others. And how dare they assume she would take advice from them? They were murderers.

Her thinking got fuzzier the longer Bartolomey stood next to her, sipping his tea like Miss Manners, a bland smile on his face. Maybe if she just played along for a bit one of the other elves would appear.

"No one's as innocent as they'd like to think," Jelani said. "Why should I believe you?"

"Because Linnea means everything to us," the woman replied with a twitch in her scarred cheek. "We would like to see her protected, just as your father would. We have many tools at our disposal. Perhaps you have some items in your possession as well. We could work together to save her." Her dark eyes studied Jelani like a watchful sparrow. "Do you?"

Did they know about the vessel?

The man's stare seemed to dissect Jelani's very molecules. "I know this is rather sudden, my dear. Or would you prefer to be addressed as the human girls do? Miss Marsh? If Vincent were alive, I'm sure he would have told you we could be trusted."

If Vincent were alive. So, he knew her father was dead. And he had not said 'the' Vincent.

She remembered Daven said Bartolomey had the power of persuasion. But the old elf sounded so reasonable, that she found herself wanting to believe him, believe that Daven was leading her astray and into danger. Bartolomey's gaze was warm and encouraging.

"I'm just working here till I can get back to school," she lied.

"That's very commendable." He set the half-full cup on the edge of the counter. "How long have you been back in your native lands?"

The sudden demand yanked an answer from her she hadn't intended. "Almost three years."

"So long!" Malina looked physically pained.

"As we thought." He stared at her. *Do you believe I am a fool? I know why you are here. To rule the clan. But if you intend to succeed, you'll have to kill Linnea. Vincent won't stand in your way, not any more. I've seen to that. We can help each other, girl.*

Jelani dropped her cloth, bending down to pick it up so he didn't see the expression on her face. She felt sick, knowing what his words meant. Not only did Bart know about her father's death, he'd practically just confessed her father's murder. It took everything she held within her to blank her mind and keep her face from showing emotion as she stood up again. "Thanks. My father always thought education was very important."

She started to turn away and noticed that one of the elves of Astan's generation, who had come with Astan to the coffee shop once or twice, had just slipped in the back door. He eyed the two with a judicious eye, and then nodded to Jelani.

Relieved, she excused herself. As she turned to leave, the scar-faced woman grabbed her wrist, holding on with a grip of iron. Nauseous and weak, Jelani tried to release her hand, keeping her mind a jumble, hoping like hell the woman couldn't read her thoughts. Why didn't that young man come forward and help her?

"Daven and his servant are dangerous, my girl," the woman hissed. "If you continue to deal with them, you will regret it."

"Malina," the man scolded. "You'll frighten her. She was coming along."

"Better to frighten her now before Talvi takes away our last chance for success!"

As they continued to argue, their hold on her weakened.

"Let go of me!" Jelani demanded, finding her voice again. She yanked away from the woman and tripped backward into the arms of someone passing behind her.

Of course, it was Richard.

"Are these people bothering you, Jelani?" he asked, giving them a cool once-over stare.

"We're old family friends, officer," the old man said, his smile ingratiating. He stood to shake Richard's hand, his gaze as intense as when he had been observing her. "We wanted to warn her about the two men who've been following her."

"You know them?" Richard brightened. "I've been investigating them!" His shoulders hunched a bit as Jelani turned a hot eye on him.

"Who asked you to?" she demanded. "Can't you just mind your own business?"

"Jelani, I wouldn't be doing my duty as an officer and a gentleman if I didn't look out for you here. Those men have no fingerprints on file. They have no driver's licenses, no identification papers. They could be terrorists."

"And you could be a horse's ass. Oh, wait. You are a horse's ass."

She growled and walked away. Richard followed her. She looked over her shoulder to see Bartolomey and Malina leave the shop through the front door. The farther away they got, the clearer her head became.

"You'll thank me someday, when I prove to you I'm right," Richard said. "And I will prove it, Jelani." He followed her to the counter, but she walked behind it and continued to the far end. "Jelani!" Seeing she didn't intend to listen, he turned on his heel and left the shop.

As she grabbed a pad to take the next customer's order, she watched with annoyance as Richard attempted to converse with the two people outside the front window of the coffee shop. She was pleasantly surprised when they blew him off. The man gave her a nod through the window, and Richard just glared at her.

"Horse's ass," she muttered to herself.

Stepping up to the counter, she put a smile on her face as she greeted the soccer mom who waited there.

* * *

CHAPTER 31

NO denying it. Jelani had been shaken by the appearance of the two elves from the woods clan in Butterfly Herbs and disgusted to owe thanks to Richard for chasing them off.

When she'd arrived back at her apartment, she'd pulled the curtains over the windows to make sure no one could spy on her.

The cat just gave her an odd look.

"What? I know it's barely dark. Astan's paranoia's getting to me, all right?"

But as the old saying went, you're not paranoid if they're really after you.

She checked twice to make sure the door was locked. Then made a cup of tea and settled into her papasan chair to try to read one of her old favorite novels. Several pages later, her attention drifted.

Reaching into the pocket of the maroon hooded sweatshirt she'd bought while she was a student, she took out the vessel they'd found at the cabin. While the blood-toned globe creeped her out a bit, it also somehow made her feel better.

She carried the vessel with her everywhere, either in her pocket or in her small backpack. At night she tucked it next to her pillow, where Azrael curled up around it with no qualms. From time to time, she would stare into it, wondering about its contents. Not actual blood, she hoped. That would be disgusting.

The vessel responded to her in various ways, the gold flecks inside coming to meet her fingers where they contacted the surface or swirling away in a mysterious dance. She never sensed that the globe meant her harm. Communing with it for several minutes restored her mental equilibrium, and she was able to distance herself from the thoughts of Bartolomey.

Once past the initial panic of being confronted at the coffee shop, she was able to consider the incident in more analytical terms. Lane's fears had been realized, and Daven's unfortunate disclosures had apparently revealed her to the bad guys. After everything this mysterious Circle had done to protect her. But now it couldn't be helped.

So Bart was proud of what he'd done. "Vincent won't stand in your way. Not any more. I've seen to that," he'd said. He really thought she would believe they could team up to set her on the throne as queen. What then? Would he move in as Regent? Or did he aspire to partner with her more intimately in his little fantasy? Certainly, she was younger and more attractive than that scary Malina.

How could he imagine she wanted her mother's place?

Because that's how he thinks. First get rid of the father, then the mother.

She cradled the vessel in her hand, thinking about her father. What must those last days have been like with a manic rush to fly west after Mad Dog's warning, waiting there alone in his cabin, knowing that the villains were coming? He'd have given his last breath to save Linnea, he said, even when he knew his chances against those elves were practically non-existent. Though Jelani had always loved him, she had never thought of him as that kind of stand-up storybook hero. The truth was a real revelation.

Believe, he had said in that last letter.

What was there to believe in? Fairytales?

Since her father died, Jelani had found it hard to believe in anyone. Her experience with Carolyn's daughters had been disheartening. Arik's betrayal confirmed that trusting people just led to pain.

Although her current three friends were dear to her, she tended to take them at face value. Iris she'd met as a student, when they'd both attended a so-called 'séance' held by a shady philosophy professor. Discovering it was a sham disappointed them both, but united them in friendship. Lane and Crispy, she'd met through Iris. She thought they were as close to her as they could get to anyone. She'd say the same for them. Would she give her life for any of them?

What about her new friends, these elves? They inspired a little more confidence, especially Astan. At least she could believe what he said. As far as she was concerned that was a big first step in a culture where men would likely say just anything to gain an advantage or get what they wanted.

She sipped her tea and laid back her head, closing her eyes. Tired as she was, she expected a nap wouldn't come easy. It had been weeks since she'd slept a night through, trying to decide what to do with her life. Some days she wondered if it was even hers any more.

What to do next?

One item on her agenda must surely be to notify Astan and Daven that Bartolomey had come to her. No telling what else the bad guys might know, if they'd tracked her that far. Then she realized she had no way to do that.

"Ha! What was I thinking? Just text them? Send an email?" She giggled at the ridiculous image that came to mind. "Does that tree have a landline?" She laughed more, letting all her feelings channel through the sharp release of hilarity, even when the humor had started to feel like it had an edge.

Azrael scrambled out of her lap and ran across the room to the kitchen counter, where he jumped up and eyed her suspiciously.

A second later, the ping of the doorbell sobered her.

Could they have followed her here?

She set her teacup on the small table next to her chair, wishing she had a fireplace poker or a baseball bat or anything to use as a weapon. After inching toward the door and resisting the impulse to look out the window, she squinted through the peephole.

It was Daven.

With a sigh of relief, she opened the door. "I was just thinking about you."

"How serendipitous." His smile was broad, convivial. He gestured behind him to Dee, waiting in his shadow. "I hope this is a convenient time. Astan was concerned about you."

"He was?" Pleased that Astan cared enough to worry, she

stepped aside and let the pair in, giving a quick look around outside for unwanted guests. "What was he worried about?"

If Astan was so concerned, why wasn't he there?

"Astan was told that Bartolomey has come to the city. Is this true?"

"Sure as heck is. He and his lady friend paid me a visit."

"Did he harm you?" Dee asked, distress etched on her face. Taking Jelani's hand, she turned her about in a thorough inspection.

"No. He was all slime, no claws. Malina, though. She gave me a chill and a half."

"Thank the Ancient Mother," the older woman said, surprising Jelani as she pulled her close for an embrace. "She is a dangerous being indeed."

Jelani pulled away, a little uncomfortable, and then moved into the kitchen area. She put the kettle on for tea, seeking something to occupy her hands. "Yeah, yeah, I'm fine. I'm glad Astan's buddy let him know, finally. I was kind of surprised he didn't say something."

"Who?" Looking up from the plant leaf he'd been studying, Daven moved into the kitchen and stopped close behind her.

"Astan's friend. I don't remember his name. One of the other local elves."

Dee frowned. "Astan didn't say how he knew." She hunkered down as Azrael ventured over to check them out. It wasn't ten seconds before he was rubbing up against Dee, purring.

"You all sure have a way with cats," Jelani said. "That's just what he did with Astan."

"We of the soil are of the same stuff as animals. We understand each other." Her eyes twinkled as she picked up the cat to pet it. "As you surely know from your work with the injured ones."

Jelani shifted her weight to the other leg, restless. "You know an awful lot about me. You know where I go, what I do. Daven said you're the one who put out the glass slipper."

"Over the time I've known you, I've discovered you have a wry sense of humor. It seemed like a creative way to persuade you to meet us."

"You didn't trust me enough to just— "

Daven laid a hand on her shoulder to set his answer within her mind. *Just tell you that elves needed your help? Tell you your blood would bring life to our numbers? Tell you that your mother's essence was confined inside the tree your father kept alive in his memories through photographs? Would you really have done anything other than report us to the authorities? Even your devoted admirer Officer Snyder?*

She bit her lip. "Insanity isn't any easier in small doses than in large. Astan's right about that."

Dee sighed. "I know the boy's having a difficult time. They all are. For years, they were protected from the truth, although they always prepared, always worked for the future. For our dream."

"Now that Bart's here, what are we going to do?" Jelani asked. Daven's hand still touched her as she recalled the faces of those who had warned her not to trust him.

"Poison!" Daven exclaimed, jerking back from her as if he'd been stung. "They try to turn you against us!"

"Yes. But thanks to you, I was prepared for his treachery. His mind is as powerful as you say. But he has me all wrong. I just let him believe what he wanted to."

"Probably a wise choice." Dee's troubled gaze searched Jelani's face. "They told you Daven was the one who intended you harm?"

"Not surprising, really. What else do they have to offer?"

"Exactly."

When the kettle boiled, she poured hot water into the china mugs and set out several boxes of tea bags from which to choose. "You know, it's ironic. All those years I wondered why I had no family on my mother's side, why my father wouldn't even speak of them. Now I find out that they're alive. And want me dead."

"I am sorry Bartolomey discovered your existence," Dee apologized. "We had gone to great pains to prevent that from happening."

"My lapse in discretion," Daven admitted. "I let emotion rule me, when Margitay challenged us there in the forest." He touched his mother's hand and they exchanged meaningful glances.

"Because of this, I shall redouble my efforts to protect you, Jelani."

"That's great, thanks." Jelani allowed a nervous laugh, as she slipped a teabag into her painted blue cup.

Dee selected an herbal blend, nodding thoughtfully. "Now that Bartolomey knows where he can find you, you are in considerable danger. You stand between him and his goal as well, Jelani. If Linnea does not survive, you will be her successor. You must choose a mate to govern the tribe with you."

"Whoa, whoa, whoa." Jelani's nerves twanged like a soured banjo string. "I'm not mating with anyone just yet!"

The other woman smiled. "Hush, little one. There is no need for haste, only caution. I bring the issue to the surface, because it is the way. Something we need to begin to think about."

"I disagree. I don't need to think about choosing a mate. Right now I've got enough to handle."

"Most important at this time is your safety," Daven interrupted, using a voice so soothing even Jelani could feel she was being 'handled' once again. "You should not speak to Bartolomey and Malina alone again. We cannot risk either their harming you, or the possibility that they could turn you to their own cause."

"Bartolomey has the power to control the minds of others not strong enough to resist him." Dee pursed her lips, considering the young woman. "I wonder if your status as half-elf leaves you more or less vulnerable to his persuasions." She glanced at Daven.

He reached for her hand. "If you would like me to stay with you, Jelani, I will."

"No!" She cleared her throat as she pulled back, feeling trapped, realizing she sounded rude. "Uh, no, you've got important things to do. Those ELF people, all that." Having someone violate her cherished privacy was the very last thing Jelani wanted.

"As you wish. We will be moving out with the ELF group again in a few days. I intend to have our relationship with them fully established in the event we need their help to ward off

Bartolomey."

"You're telling me this why? Because you want me to go?" Surprised, she set her cup on the counter, untouched. "Wow. I've always been against the rape of the forest, but never really considered being quite so radical."

"If you truly believe in your cause, no method will be beyond your consideration."

"I suppose. All right. You let me know when."

"We've decided to let this new development pass without much action. Then perhaps persuade ELF to go a little further north to the protected grove. There may well be a moment to liberate Linnea from her refuge at that time. And we expect that if anyone has the ability to transfer her essence, it would be you."

"I haven't the faintest idea how to do that, you know." She was confused enough by the unfulfilled work of her father. She still had not fully grasped the whole mother-in-a-tree thing, but they all seemed to be running with it so she decided to give them the benefit of the doubt. Also, she knew father wanted her to believe.

"Have you learned anything from the vessel?" Daven asked.

"Like what?"

He shrugged. "Sometimes these items are used as teaching devices. Have you carried it with you as the Vincent asked?"

"Yes." She was a little embarrassed to say how often she cradled it like a favorite rag doll. "But it hasn't done anything. No lessons. No changes. Just the same as it was."

"Perhaps Astan would have better rapport, Daven," Dee suggested in a soft voice.

"No," he snapped. "I'm not conceding that, Mother. It's my right." He set his half-empty mug on the counter and turned away.

Jelani retreated to get her empty cup, which she hadn't refilled when she'd given the others tea. She'd never seen Daven angry. He projected his emotion almost palpably, the same way he seemed to spread good feeling in a group.

The flowing emotional field disturbed her. What was his right? She studied them, reading their tensions. Her? Was she his right? Did he mean as a tutor, a mentor, or as more? Then remembered Dee's comment about choosing a mate. Would she be expected to marry someone? One of the elves? How could they presume such a thing? Did they think they could force someone on her? Daven?

She wasn't ready to marry anyone. Not yet. Not after Arik. No man was worth giving up her independence, not after she'd finally established her own life. She didn't need anyone. She could take care of herself. Involvement wasn't worth the pain it caused.

Apparently, it was not up to her anymore.

The realization hit her like a brick. Other thoughts tumbled after that one. Where would she go, once she'd hooked up? Would she have her little black and white apartment, or would she have to live in the forest with the elves? What would become of her relationship with her human friends? Would she have to leave them? What had her parents done to her?

She looked up from her contemplation and found two sets of eyes watching her. She didn't want to talk to either of them about this. She didn't know Dee well enough, and she didn't feel she could trust Daven at this point. Now, Astan was another matter.

"I think we should go, my son." Dee's smile was faint but intentional. "I wish you had more time to assimilate your life. Your reconciliation with the clan should have proceeded much differently."

"Me too. Guess that means the only choice is to revive my mother. Then I don't have to worry about it, right?" Jelani gave an echoing smile, but it faded as quickly as it had appeared. She shivered and crossed her arms. "Let me know when you need me," she said to Daven.

"I will." His emotions appeared to be back under control, and he was halfway to the door already. He held the door for his mother and started to say something further, but seemed to have thought better of it. "Take care of yourself," he said.

Then they were gone.

Jelani glanced at the clock. It was already nine p.m. and she had an early shift in the morning. She cleaned up the dishes, still pondering the future. Finally, she remembered the bottle of wine she'd brought home from the Boys' apartment. Now that might just help her sleep.

She uncorked the bottle, and then changed into comfortable blue pajamas before climbing into bed, glass in hand. Halfway through the bottle, her father's vessel in her hand, she finally relaxed enough to fall asleep.

The dream that came to her was a fantasy set in some perfect forest. Exactly the right amount of sun shone down through the overhead canopy to dapple the path before her. She was walking between wild flowers when a man appeared beside her. Despite his sudden arrival, she experienced no fear or worry, and when he turned she saw it was Daven. He spoke kindly, as he joined her walk. He took her hand. She felt very safe and secure, even as wild animals of the forest crossed their path, approaching Daven as though they were greeting him.

"You see, Jelani, I am meant to rule," he said. "You and I. We would make a delightful team." He beckoned a small deer over to them, and the deer bowed before her.

After he spoke, the dream felt less comfortable, the light fading, shadows appearing around the trees. Her thoughts disputed his words. She said nothing, but tried to put distance between herself and Daven, walking away slowly at first, then a little faster. Looking over her shoulder to make sure he did not follow, she ran into someone ahead of her on the path.

She gasped, but found to her relief it was Astan. He waited for her to become accustomed to his presence, and then walked on with her as the sun came out once again overhead.

When she awoke later in the night, the smile was still on her face.

* * *

CHAPTER 32

THE next night, Astan Hawk sprinted up the hill to Jelani's apartment and glanced into her curtained windows.

The lights were all out. By human reckoning, it was just after ten p.m., and the mountain air was cool and damp. He knocked softly on the door.

A few moments later, he knocked again, receiving no answer either time. Frustrated, he went down the steps and around behind the building, counting the windows until he found the one that had to be her bedroom window.

Humans had such different timetables. Under this bright moonlight, his people were still out and about.

And waiting for him to bring the mysterious Princess for a visit.

The jealousy Beckley had expressed about Djana's selection of Daven and Astan as Jelani's guardians had spread through the other young people of the clan. Grigor in particular had taunted him unmercifully about his exclusivity. They'd challenged him to produce her. And he had given in.

Astan wasn't proud of his decision. But Djana hadn't said anything against Jelani meeting the others. If she was going to be their queen, then they had a right to know her. Didn't they?

He found some pebbles on the drive and tossed them at the glass, hoping it wouldn't shatter. The second batch of rattling pebbles produced results. Jelani peeked out cautiously from behind the blind and then disappeared.

He returned to the door, finding her waiting for him, wrapped in a thin robe.

"Why are you here?" she said.

He tried to approximate Daven's charming smile. "Want to come out and play?"

"Are you kidding?" She gave him her best what-an-idiot stare. Her cat rubbed against her ankles and seemed to give him the same look.

"No." He waited, hands in his pockets. "Some of the other elves want to meet you. I thought you'd like to see the character of your future subjects." He added a trace of mockery to his tone, knowing her opinion of the opportunity to be queen. "Seriously, I think it would be good for everyone. Please?"

She appeared reluctant for a moment, and then shrugged.

"Why not? Might as well go full out crazy, huh?" Her smile was fleeting but sincere. "I'll get changed." She left the door open and disappeared inside.

Astan took a peek over his shoulder. The woman who lived in the main house came out to her front porch, skeptical of late night visitors. He waved at her and she went back inside. Knowing it was better not to be seen outside, he stepped into Jelani's apartment and bent down to pick up the cat.

"There won't be a lot of people, I mean elves, will there?" Jelani called from the bedroom.

"A dozen or so, I think." He hoped there wouldn't be more than that. He wasn't sure. The last thing Grigor had thrown at him when he left the forest was that he'd better be prepared to defend his preferred status.

"I think I can handle that." She came out of the back room, dressed in black denim slacks and a maroon hooded jacket. She wore a simple silver necklace with a leaf charm in lieu of her usual array of bangles and dangling earrings. "So, is this okay?"

He nodded his approval. "Might want your walking boots."

"Okay," she said amiably. "Going up to the big woods?"

"Just out past the Fort. We've got a small gathering place there, where those of us who lived in town used to meet and train. We can walk, if you're up to it."

She shoved her feet into hiking boots by the door and checked something in her pocket. "Let's go!"

He followed her out, making sure she locked the door. Their boots thumped in unison as they walked up Rattlesnake Drive toward the city, when she started laughing.

"Sweet mother Gaia!" She nearly tripped, she was laughing so hard.

He caught her arm before she fell. "What?"

"You're taking me to meet the parents!"

Parents? She'd met his father already and his grandmother. "Jelani? What do you mean?"

She giggled as they rounded the corner on Broadway. "Maybe you all don't do this. But we humans have the custom to take a boyfriend or girlfriend to meet our parents before we can, you know, seriously date." Still holding his arm, she looked up into his eyes, teasing. "Why, Astan, I had no idea you had such designs."

Could she read his feelings? "What? No!" he stammered, caught off guard. "I don't mean any disrespect, Jelani. That was not my intent at all."

"I was just joking, Astan. Really. I didn't mean to step on your pride or anything." She bit her lip and walked away from him.

Humans. So frustrating. He hurried after her and then walked beside her in silence. Maybe this had been a bad idea all around. He shouldn't have let Grigor pressure him into this. The Circle's priority was keeping her safe. On the other hand, there weren't many people out. He kept a trained eye for anyone who might be following or watching them, but didn't see anyone.

But she's with us. She'll be fine.

Meeting the parents, hmm? Seeking approval from one's family before making a commitment of time and energy to another. It seemed rational, not the sort of process he expected from humans. A course of action that would no doubt be a waste of time, since Daven had made it clear that *he* intended to be the one Jelani chose if the circumstance came to pass.

The thought rankled him. Jelani was young. Shouldn't her partner be of an age so they might rule together? Why shouldn't it be him?

Then Beckley's derisive words came back to Astan: "With the enchanting Daven in pursuit, it's not likely she'd consider you." They all knew well enough Daven's gift for persuasion, almost as good as Bartolomey. His feelings weren't likely to matter, if his father had truly settled on that course of action. Irritation picked up his pace.

They crossed the street and made their way up Higgins Street to the bridge that crossed the Clark Fork. Astan was pleased at the pace Jelani kept, showing she was fit and active. If she were going to live in the forests with them someday, that would serve her well. But who was to say?

The silence grew awkward after twenty minutes of walking. As they took the Brooks diagonal, Astan saw Jelani glance over at the restaurant where they had met weeks earlier. Had they seemed desperate trying to convince her of the truth back then?

"Seems like a long time ago," she murmured.

"A lifetime."

"A different life, that's for sure."

The conversation turned more companionable after the brief exchange.

They continued past the old Fort. Although the open fort had been a military installation in the late 1800s, now it served as headquarters for many governmental and environmental agencies, as well as a historical museum. Astan vaguely remembered a field trip there while he was still going to the human school. After that, he'd had no need for contact.

Approximately a mile past the main buildings of the Fort, they entered a wooded area that ran along a small creek. As they approached the stand of trees where he expected the others would be waiting, Astan gave the haunting alto *hoo-hoo-hoo* call of the boreal owl to let them know he was the one coming.

"The owls are not what they seem," Jelani said with a little laugh, echoing an earlier discussion.

"It's tradition. Less disturbing for the creatures with whom we share the path." He led her through the lightly worn trail into the training area, finding a group waiting for him that was slightly larger than he'd expected. They stood and sat in a semi-circle facing the entry where they'd known he'd come in, all eyes on Jelani. He gave her a little pat on the shoulder for encouragement.

"Geez, you'd think it was some rock star coming to visit," she said, stopping just inside the circle as the others stared without a show of emotion. "Hey," she said.

One of the young female elves, muscular and dressed in shades of gray, gave a disdainful snort. "She doesn't look like so much."

"I don't know, Elorra. You can't always judge from outward appearance." Grigor stepped forward and reached out his hand in the human way. "I'm Grigor, a distant cousin of both Linnea and Djana. I'm pleased you came to meet us."

Astan forced himself not to react at the elf-man's artificial courtesy, although it grated on him. Now he would see who intended to vie for the favor of the princess, Grigor being number one.

He stood out of the way and let Grigor make the introductions, deferring to the one who had always been the ostensible First of their group. He was pleased all the same that Jelani stayed close to him, as if he were her anchor and source of strength. Or at least wanted to believe that was why.

He watched her warm up to the group, hands in her pockets most of the time at first, but soon joining in discussion of topics like wildlife and the forests. She deflected questions about Linnea or her own personal status, for the most part, with a simple: "I really don't know."

Beckley sidled over to Astan, his usual smirk missing as he watched. "She is an innocent, isn't she?"

Astan shrugged. "She is not used to the ways of our people. Much of what we're experiencing now is new for her." He was careful to maintain an even tone, even when Grigor's closest associate Terzon monopolized Jelani's attention and personal space for so long that she pulled back. That's two. He counted three more in the next several minutes, provoked by the boldness of their compatriots.

"I think she'll do, Astan." Beckley gave him a sidewise glance. "You know, if one of our generation succeeds, I hope you beat out the old man to win her."

It took a minute, and a long look to see if Beckley was ridiculing him, but Astan decided the other was sincere.

"Thanks." He cracked a grin.

"Astan? Can we stay for the bonfire?" Jelani asked, surrounded on either side by young, solicitous men.

"Sure, why not?" Astan answered with a chuckle that was echoed around the clearing. "We don't have to get up for work in the morning."

"Funny. Very funny. Come on." Jelani marched over and took Astan's hand, drawing him into the group that had gathered around a pile of stacked wood.

One of the young elf-women picked up a long stick of wood. After speaking several words over it, the end of it popped into flame.

After the bonfire was lit, they all drew to talk as the night breezes picked up with a gradual chill.

* * *

CHAPTER 33

JELANI was overwhelmed at first by the sheer personal presence of each elf. Like Daven and Astan, each seemed to project a certain aura of self-confidence and power. They spoke among themselves in a language they knew was foreign to her, and she definitely felt they were judging her.

Why shouldn't they? After all, they've been commanded to accept the fact that Jelani might lead them. How could she be expected to lead a group of magical beings?

She studied them. Dark-haired Elorra, who could heal animals with her bare hands. Fontine, who had brought forth the fire that now warmed them. Terzon, who apparently had geokinesis, or the ability to control the soil and change it from dirt to rock and more. Elron had reign over the birds of the air and could call them to do his bidding. Little Max, whose elven name he said was unpronounceable by humans, could almost fly, making his body lighter than air when he wished. Others showed her how they could generate balls of energy and control them, or how they could make objects move just by power of mind.

The most persistent for her attention was Grigor, who demonstrated how he could dominate the flow of water around them by nearly flooding the little clearing where they all sat, but keeping the fire and their feet carefully dry. She wanted to ask him about that day in the coffee shop when Bartolomey had come to her, but there never seemed to be a good time. It was he who finally asked the difficult question.

"Show us what you can do, Jelani."

She glanced at Astan. "I'm not really sure, Grigor."

Elorra's eyes narrowed. "How can you lead us, if you have no power of your own?"

"She's the daughter of a human," one of the boys reminded

them.

"Human…human…human…." The word whispered around the group like a curse.

Astan stiffened, and Jelani wondered if she was safe. Her fingers closed around the vessel in her pocket.

"I don't think it's my fault that your clans are in this big power struggle," she said in tart tone. "You came to me asking for my help, not the other way around. I'm doing the best I can without having all the years of training you all did."

"Djana says she has demonstrated raw abilities in many categories," Astan offered.

The declaration didn't seem to satisfy the elves, and the rumble of discontent spread among them.

"Djana doesn't speak for us, perhaps." Terzon stepped forward, the fire reflecting light and shadow on his face. "None of those who have returned do. Daven the least of them." His cold look went to Astan.

"Agreed!" Grigor shouted. He stepped up onto one of the fallen tree trunks so that everyone could see him. "We are the ones who trained and prepared. Our generation will rule, not all those of a forgotten age." A cry of consensus went up around him.

"They went into hiding rather than save the queen when she was in danger," Elorra added. "How then shall they lead us into danger when they are cowards?"

Jelani realized the rebellion in the group was not so much against her, though she was the focus. They're just like any other teenagers defying their parents. All of them want the same end, but they are constrained to fight each other as well as the bad guys. She smiled. They're not so different from humans after all.

"You find this amusing?" Grigor said. He jumped down and grabbed her left wrist, pulling her to her feet.

Startled, Jelani heard Astan move beside her. Light flashed off a dagger blade in his hand.

"Let her go, Grigor." Astan's voice practically dripped with anger.

The others drew back, almost as if setting up a circle in which the two could battle it out.

Grigor's grip never faltered. "She's nothing special," he sneered. "Just another human."

Jelani's fingers closed on the vessel, finding as her emotion level rose so did the little globe's temperature. Some hidden impulse made her draw it out, holding it on her open palm, where it sizzled. That was the only word she could think of that described the outward heat, sparks, even little bolts of light that shot from it at the same time it remained cool enough not even to warm her palm.

Grigor released her, and the other elves drew back, as surprised as she.

"What is that?" Terzon demanded, not brave enough to try to snatch it from her palm, though she could see the temptation in his dark eyes.

"It is a vessel, a gift from those of my blood." She stared at the globe, wishing she could do something spectacular with it to prove she was more than just another human, like make it burst into flame.

A second later, it did. She held a flame about twelve inches high in her hand. Astan's pat to her shoulder urged her not to panic and drop it. As amazed as the others, she watched the flame and found it would obey her mental command to grow or shrink, to flicker or grow strong. When she thought she'd made her point, she wished it dark and shoved it back into her pocket.

"You shouldn't underestimate someone you've only just met," she said with a glare for Grigor.

"How very true that is." His eyes glittered with scorn in return. "Let's make sure neither of us does that again." He turned on a booted heel and stalked away, several of the other young elves following him.

Elorra and Max left last, after the broad-shouldered one called Beckley exchanged some quiet words with Astan. When Fontine stood on the edge of the glade and clapped her hands, the fire went out and the air was silent as they all blended into the trees around them.

"Well. Lane would call that a 'total party kill'." Jelani sighed.

"I'm sorry, Astan."

When she turned to him, she found him trying to stifle laughter, not frustration. He took her arm and led her out of the woods, waving a hand to put off explanation until they'd had some distance between themselves and the others.

"What?" she finally demanded when they reached the street. "What could possibly be funny? That sucked!"

"You, my dear princess, are a piece of work. A piece of fine, fine work. Handed their crap right back to them on a platter!"

He took her face in both hands, pulled her close, and then kissed her.

To her own surprise, she returned the brief embrace that followed.

After he let her go, she studied his gaze. "But didn't I just piss off all your friends?"

"Fabulously." He started walking back to Brooks, still chuckling. "They were so sure they knew you, and what you were about. You made me proud, Jelani."

Jelani felt her cheeks heat and hoped, as they neared the lights of the city, that Astan couldn't see her blush. "Well, gee. Guess you should thank my father. It was his vessel."

"How did you do that? Daven said you hadn't discovered how to make it work."

Cars passed by, catching them in their headlights.

Jelani found watching the ground was the best chance to avoid being blinded. "I hadn't. It's never done anything like that before. But they were starting to annoy me with that 'human' stuff, and I just wished it. And it did." With a little wiggle of pleasure, she relived in her head that moment when she held a bright flame on her hand.

"I wonder what else you could make it do."

"No idea." She had her hands in her pockets as usual, one tucked around the vessel, but now it was cool and unyielding to the touch. "I think I have to be wound up for it to do something."

He tossed her a quizzical look.

"It seems to respond to my emotions," she clarified.

"I see." He considered that in silence as they walked.

"By the way, he's the one. Grigor. He's the one I told Daven about."

"Told Daven about what?"

"When he and Dee were at my apartment the other night, I told him that Grigor was at Butterfly Herbs when Bart and Malina were there."

Astan grabbed her and spun her around, the streetlights hitting her in the eyes. "Bartolomey? Here in town? You spoke to him? No one said a word to me!"

"They said you knew. I mean, that's how the subject came up." Jelani told him the same tale she had told Daven and Dee. "I figured one of them would say something. Or else I'd have said something when you came over. He didn't hurt me. Bart's got oatmeal for brains, though, if he thinks I'm falling for that line."

Astan wasn't appeased. "If I'd known he'd accosted you, I never would have brought you out where you could have been a target." He grabbed her arm and started walking again. "We've got to get you home."

A little out of breath, she struggled to keep up with his quick pace. Her mind kept drifting back to his spontaneous and sweet kiss, which was so ripe with genuine affection. Maybe that choosing a mate thing wouldn't be such a burden after all, as long as she got to choose the one she really wanted.

"Astan, do all the elves have some kind of power?"

"All the ones I know do."

"What about your grandmother? I know she's got a talent for herb-lore, but that's not really a magical gift."

"Djana? She is a bringer of dreams. Uses them to prophesy. It's how she knew you were in town. A message came in a dream."

Did that mean Dee could control her dreams? Send messages to her as well? Like the one the other night? Jelani bristled to think Dee believed she was such a child.

Fresh irritation helped her pick up the pace, and together they arrived back at her apartment in record time, Astan still brooding.

She hoped for another of those kisses, but was disappointed

when he walked her to the door and looked up at the sky to get his bearings.

. "It's late. I've got to get back to Djana's. I'm going to have some words with her." He scowled. "We've got a date with ELF in three days. I'll come get you, but you'll likely have to drive somewhere up north."

"All right. What time?"

"I'll be here just before dark." His dark gaze searched her face as his hand reached out to hers. "You'll be all right here by yourself?"

"If I'm not, I'll let you know, all right?" She pulled him close enough to plant a quick kiss on his lips and then closed the door in his startled face.

* * *

THE next afternoon, Astan stood in the open door of Djana's house, blocking Daven's entrance.

"Bartolomey is here in the city," Astan accused, "and you didn't think it was important enough to tell me?"

Daven flashed his usual conciliatory smile and nudged Astan out of the doorway. "Won't you even let me get in the door, Astan? No harm resulted from the encounter." He crossed the room to give his mother a squeeze, and then turned to face his son. "We would have told you."

"When? When would you have told me? The next day? The next week? After you'd secured Jelani for your own?"

"Astan!" Djana's expression was disapproving.

"There was no emergency. The clan made sure Bartolomey skulked off to his usual territory," Daven said. "Why are you so concerned about my relationship with Jelani? We are supposed to be working for the restoration of Linnea."

Astan realized the situation had been turned on him. Now it was his motives and ambitions that were suspect.

"I am concerned, of course, for her safety," he mumbled, taking a seat at his grandmother's wooden kitchen table.

"Besides, she told us that one of your clan brothers was there with her. Did he not speak to you of the meeting?"

"I had not seen him in the interim. But we met last night." Astan didn't reveal anything further about the actual discussion, and Daven didn't enquire further. Djana poured them both some honey wine, attempting as she often did to smooth the way between them.

"Do you have that scribbled note we found at the cabin?" Daven asked in a casual tone that sounded a bit forced.

"Jelani took that with her." Astan picked up his glass and wiped a few beads of condensation off the outside of it. "I don't see where it would do you any good. You couldn't read it."

His father shot him an angry look. "If I had been given more time, perhaps I could have. The humans were in quite a rush."

Astan shrugged. "Perhaps. Besides, there is no endorsement in that letter other than that of the guardian. It says nothing about Jelani's future."

Djana started to speak, but Daven cut her off with a wave of his hand and then leaned against the counter behind her. "I am the senior of those who have returned. I am the one who was a confidant of both Linnea and Vincent, before the evil times fell. I speak for our clan, until the queen is restored! All of you will listen and obey." His face was flushed, and Astan wondered if he might have some sort of attack.

"Tradition prescribes that it is the queen who chooses her mate, not the other way around. I'm not so sure this young woman is so easy to command." Astan held back the smirk so anxious to break out on his lips, lips that had kissed Jelani and felt her warm response.

Djana stepped between them. "Enough! This young woman, as you say, will do what she must for the good of her tribe. The Circle has done what they can, setting objects around her to bring her to a better understanding of her place. I have done my part to assure she acts as she must. She has no choice." She paused to study Astan for a moment. "My grandson, I have raised you like you were my own after your mother was killed in the battle. I have taught you all you know of wood-lore and our history. You are a fine young elf. But you do not have the experience to handle this challenge."

"Nana— "

"No. Don't you 'Nana' me. Not on this point. The girl has been raised in the human world. She knows so little of what she will need. You, too, have grown up outside the life of the clan for many years, despite our wish for reunification. Daven is much more qualified to teach her what she needs to know to succeed as queen of the clan. The Elders have seen this. You and your brothers need to accept it as well."

Djana's fiery dark gaze caused Astan to look away. "Of course," he replied in a quiet voice.

She stared at him for a few more moments, and then took Daven's arm and went upstairs to speak with him in private.

Brooding, Astan drank the rest of his wine. Daven was a firebrand, stirring the hearts of their people to rally together, of that there was no doubt. Perhaps Djana was right about what was best, but that didn't mean Astan had to like it.

* * *

CHAPTER 34

AS promised, Astan appeared on Jelani's doorstep just before dark three days after her elven encounter in the woods.

He wore a leather jacket, black T-shirt with matching black pants, and the heavy-duty boots the ELF people had recommended. Jelani was similarly dressed and ready to go, feeling an awful lot like some clandestine spy with a double life.

For many hours each day, Jelani's life was just as it had been since she quit college. She went to work, paid her bills, and bought shoes and groceries.

But there were subtle changes. Now when she volunteered at the rehab, there would always be a familiar face waiting by the edge of the forest to make sure she got into the building from her car, and back when she was finished. She'd nearly gotten used to the feeling that almost everywhere she went someone was watching. Almost.

She just hoped they were friendly eyes.

"So ELF's still in, hmm?" Her hiking boots waited by the door and she slipped them on over two pair of thick navy wool socks. After that last escapade, she'd had blisters on her heels for two days. She wasn't going to let that happen again.

"After their operative was killed in our presence, they are reluctant to continue to help us," Astan admitted.

"I can't blame them there. But Mad Dog had to know he was at risk all along. It was just bad timing on everyone's part."

"That is how I understood Daven approached the matter when he spoke with the new commander."

"What was his name again?" She tucked her hair up under a local sport team's cap someone had left at the coffee shop.

"Spiderman."

Jelani snorted. "Spiderman. Fabulous. Out webslinging in the forests to save my mother, the tree." Without the luxury of a leather jacket, she chose instead a dark hooded sweatshirt with a pocket to carry the vessel. "How did your talk go with your grandmother?"

Astan looked away, uneasy. "She defended Daven. She always does. He can do no wrong."

"He's out of touch with reality, if you ask me." She smirked at him. "Oddly, they never do. Ask me, that is. Because they know I'd tell them what's what."

"You don't seem to have a problem expressing your displeasure, princess." Astan's laugh showed her he was teasing, and he held the door for her as they went out.

The night was clear, a perfect evening for wandering the forest. Jelani led the way to the car. "Daven's with them?"

Astan nodded. "I know where we are to meet." He sat in the passenger seat, staring straight ahead, at first, and she guessed his mind was already out there in the forest, working on details and preparing against eventualities. That was his way, she'd discovered in the more frequent contact they'd had over the last several months. "Take 93 north."

* * *

IF there had been any way Jelani could have been left out of this night's work, Astan would have argued for it, but Daven had been adamant.

Astan wasn't sure what specific area the ELF operatives intended to visit, but if by some draw of luck it was the right one, Jelani would have the opportunity to come face to face with the tree that held Linnea's consciousness. They couldn't miss that chance.

What if she did come face to face with that tree? No one was sure what would happen. The Vincent had apparently devised a plan. They had to hope by following his beginning they would continue to his conclusion. But who knew for sure?

He studied her when the lights of passing cars reflected on her face. As she rubbed her eyes, he thought she looked tired, her life force spent to a low point.

"What?" she asked with a sidewise glance.

"Nothing." He shook his head.

"That wasn't nothing. That was something."

With a grin, he reached over and squeezed her hand to reassure her. "I was just thinking you look tired. I should bring you some of Djana's restorative herbs."

Appearing mollified, she continued driving up the highway, the purple-gray shadows of the mountains barely visible on both sides, surrounding them as they went on into the night.

Astan settled back into the seat, wishing he was confident of her ability to protect herself. He knew he could not always be with her. In a situation like the one at the elves' fire, he was fortunate enough to be standing close when Grigor laid hands on her. To be fair, she rescued herself from that confrontation. What she really needed was the combat training the rest of the elves had been taught. Surely he could show her at least what he knew. If she needed more, others could contribute.

As they sped along the highway, he watched Jelani instead of the passing landscape, considering Daven's obsessive expectations about her. When the exiles had first returned, the conversations always evolved around resurrecting Linnea, the queen they had served a quarter of a century before.

But lately Daven had focused instead on the possibility of following the line of succession. His invocation of the tradition on several occasions made it clear he anticipated Jelani would choose him as her mate, if Linnea did not survive. Almost as if he'd already conceded the loss.

That determination had seemed to increase after the visit to the cabin, when Daven had not been able to read the coded writing on the Vincent's letter. His frustration over it seemed to be fueled by jealousy.

Astan had stood his ground on that point. The Vincent's own choice seemed clear to him. The subject had been revived during the argument he'd had two days ago with Daven and Djana over their failure to inform him that Bartolomey had approached Jelani in person.

He thought about that argument, and then remembered

walking Jelani home from the bonfire the day before that. Jelani
was fierce and passionate, when she mustered her intent. Most of
all when she was backed into a corner. Was it best for two
hotheads like Jelani and Daven to be forced together? In contrast,
Astan believed opposites suited. His calm mountain lake of a
disposition would be best to temper one who burned.

More to the point, he thought, watching Jelani in the dark as
she drove up the highway without hesitation to a new and
mysterious situation, he knew her better than Daven did. She
wasn't the kind to be dictated to. Once she got control of her life
and its new direction, he expected she'd be hell on wheels.

Astan settled back into the seat. So much remained to be
determined. If Linnea could be released, would she choose
another mate since the Vincent had been killed? Perhaps that
could be Daven's role, a warm and supportive follower with the
backbone to lead. Then Jelani would be free, at least for now.

If Linnea were lost, then the question of succession would
have to be confronted.

Until the moment that could be determined, Astan's chances
were still open. As far as he knew, his odds to win Jelani were
better than Daven's. Even Beckley had thought so. Moreover,
unlike his father, he was interested in Jelani as a person and not
only for what title she might hold someday.

He'd wait and see. He could be a very patient elf, when it was
necessary.

The landmarks he'd been watching for near the turnoff to
Turtle Lake came into the headlights.

"There," he said, pointing. "Just past the telephone poles.
Take the right, and head back toward the woods. And turn off
the lights."

She frowned. "Are you sure? No lights or anything?"

"That's the way these old boys like it. The darker, the better."

* * *

CHAPTER 35

THE dirt road wound back into the forest.

It was at least half a mile by the odometer, paralleling the foothills, but Jelani couldn't take her eyes from the rocky trail for fear she'd slide off into the mud on either side. There were three sets of tracks in the dirt already, reasonably fresh. It must be the place.

At last they came to a small clearing, where two small pickup trucks and an ATV waited in the midst of a beehive of activity lit by a couple of kerosene lanterns. She was amazed how much illumination the lanterns projected. Along with the light from a rising half moon, it was more than enough.

At least a dozen people in denim and black buzzed around an array of tools, including metal spikes, ladders, and other devices Jelani didn't recognize. They gave the new arrivals a passing glance and continued with their work.

Jelani pulled the car just off the path into a space between two trees, so people could pass on the road.

Astan's brow was furrowed with new lines of concern.

"Something wrong?" she asked. "I thought these were your guys."

"They are Daven's men, not mine," he said.

"Grigor was right, wasn't he? There's a real rift between his group and yours?" she asked, tucking her car keys into her left sweatshirt pocket.

He shifted, as he unhooked his seatbelt. "We disagree about many things."

Jelani noticed the long look he gave her and could only guess what it meant. "But you still follow him, and look out for him."

"I serve as his bodyguard. It is the tradition of the people. The Circle has decreed that I am destined to watch out for him and protect him. To be his adviser about the world, about humans, since I did not go into hiding with him."

"That must be hard, just to go along with someone else's plans."

"So far, our goals are on the same road. We both want the clan to be healed. We have the common enemy. I can put myself fully behind that, for now. Later, who knows?"

Jelani's further curiosity was squelched by Daven's impatient beckoning, so they got out of the car and walked across to join him. Daven escorted them to a cluster of three flannel-shirted men, and introduced the tallest of them as Spiderman, the other two Otter and Flounder.

"Funny," Jelani said, knowing the obvious pop reference, though Astan looked at her blankly. "Call me Ishmael."

"Ishmael?" Daven said, bewildered.

Astan smiled. "Perfect."

Spiderman looked from one to the other. "All right, folks, could we get on with it? We got a lot of territory to cover today."

"Of course," Daven said, soothing the ruffled feathers. He gestured to the man designated as Otter. "Hawk, if you would."

Astan looked over his shoulder as he left with the ELF guy, clearly reluctant to leave.

Jelani nodded in what she hoped was reassurance.

After Astan had gone, Daven turned to Jelani. "Spiderman has divided the forest into three sectors, one we will be protecting with spikes and blades, a central space that will not be touched, and another with some spikes. Random trees will also be posted with warnings, as will alternating trees around the perimeter of the sector."

Spiderman eyed her, clearly considering her an amateur, and started handing equipment to others of his team. "Just getting the first warnings set up this time. Won't be tree-sitting this round. Maybe when they actually come out to cut." He handed Daven a tool belt with a serious-sized hammer and package of railroad spikes.

"Tree-sitting?" Had Lane mentioned something about that?

The bearded protester eyed her. "You know, I'm not so sure

you belong here, little girl. You ask too many questions. I don't like people who ask questions." He picked up a set of bolt cutters and a heavy pair of gloves. Then glared at Daven. "Raven, you brought her along, you take care of her. And you're responsible if she gets hurt or spills anything, you got me?" Grumbling, he went off into the woods with the man called Flounder.

"What's up his ass?" Jelani complained. This might be new to her, but she wasn't an idiot. People just needed to explain what she should do. "I was just asking."

"Come, Jelani, we need these people to see us as their friends. They will likely be assisting us in a very important quest. We should do our best to be compliant with their wishes." Daven bent down and picked up an aluminum ladder from the pile. "We will need more spikes."

She obediently selected a pack of the heavy pointed objects and followed Daven into the woods. As she helped steady the ladder for Daven, who did most of the actual spiking, she watched others she could see in the trees around them.

Working mostly in pairs, they hammered spikes and some blades into the trunks of the evergreens, and then cut off the head of the spike so the tree trunk would grow to cover it. A few of them also chunked in the occasional small nail to throw off metal detectors if the loggers came in to survey the area.

Still others marked the spiked trees with blue paint, presumably as a cover-your-ass measure. Did the logger assume the risk if he went ahead and cut the tree, knowing it had been tampered with? One would have to believe so.

Time passed to the regular sound of hammering echoing through the moist air.

A man dressed in camouflage, wearing a wide smile and a ponytail, approached her and helped steady the ladder for a moment. "This is your first time?"

She grinned in return, embarrassed for appearing to be such a novice. "It's that obvious, is it?"

"Just a new face. We don't have many, especially not so pretty. Most of 'em look like Raven here." He gestured up the tree. "They call me Legolas."

"Of course, they do. What else would you call a long-haired, um…nice-looking ELF?" As soon as the words were out, she realized she sounded like a silly teenage girl. "I mean, you know, from the movie and all. Sorry."

"Don't be sorry! I'll take the compliment." Legolas checked Daven's work and gave him a little salute. "I'll see you around, hmm?"

"Sure. Take care" Jelani watched him walk away, and then stop to encourage several other workers. The exchange made her feel a little better. She wondered if he was one of Daven's men or one of the ELF regulars. She thought the latter.

"See? Not all these people are raging lunatics," Daven said. "Most, in fact, have a deep respect for nature and the forest and all the life within it. This is the reason why they break the human laws."

"I know. Even if Lane is paranoid about them, I understand the need to stand up for what you believe. What I still don't understand is how my father could have experienced these things twenty-five years ago and never told me!" She handed him some more spikes as he took three steps down the ladder.

"Linnea could never have loved someone who was not in tune with the rhythms of the natural world. The Vincent was very special in this. You have inherited their love of the soil. You will make a wonderful queen for our clan."

"Well I'm not looking to take that position for some time." She moved closer to the ladder. "Will we see it today? The Tree?"

She'd kept her eyes open, wondering if this was the particular area where the tree whose form was practically ingrained in her memory was located. From what she remembered of the meeting at the Boys' house, the Tree should be farther north. But then Daven tended to play it cagey.

What would happen when she finally came face to face with what remained of her mother? Would Linnea just emerge from the tree and come back to life? Would they have to have some sort of ritual? Would Jelani herself be unable to facilitate whatever it was they expected her to do? How would she know what to do?

To come so close and then fail would be the saddest of all.

"I know you are anxious to fulfill your destiny," Daven said. "Because Bartolomey knows you are here, we are reluctant to lead him to the tree. Better to enlist more friends, humans who have access to the forest, to increase our numbers before we have to confront him." Moonlight highlighted the compassionate expression on his face. "Soon it will be time. We must protect her first."

"You think this will do it?"

"Mad Dog told us when the metal is in a section of trees, and they are marked and posted with warnings, that the loggers will move on. In this way they hope to protect the area in which she rests as well."

She nodded, not really content with his answer, but it was likely to be the best she would get. She fidgeted, preferring a more direct approach. Patience? Not one of her more abundant qualities.

"But Astan said— "

"Hush!" Daven looked around, caution written on his face. He hesitated, surveying the area before coming down the ladder to stand beside her.

Jelani heard the rustle of more feet than she'd seen when she and Astan had arrived, hardly visible in their black clothing, moving silently among the trees.

"Our brethren have joined us," he said with warm satisfaction.

"Brethren, hmm?" She walked with Daven toward the center of the sector. "More ELF guys?"

"More elf guys," he said with a little chuckle, touching her arm so she could see the picture in her mind once again of the many homunculi rushing from the shattered slipper.

"So look. Isn't the whole objective here to get my mother out? Once we rescue her, won't the clan war come to an end? I mean, that would be— "

Her words were cut short by a sharp birdcall to the left, echoed on their right.

Daven grabbed her arm and pulled her to the ground. *Silence.*

After a few moments, she dared to look up.

Red lights flashed at the far end of the glade, and the bright white beams of flashlights reflected off nearby trees like arcing spotlights. The heavy sound of booted feet running came toward them.

He still held her arm. *Did anyone know you were coming?*

I didn't even know where we were going. She tried to make her mental tone as dry as possible.

"This is Homeland Security! We have you surrounded!"

Shocked, Jelani dropped her head again, hoping like hell it just was a bad dream. From what she knew of Homeland Security, those guys could throw people in jail without filing charges and hold them forever.

Shouts echoed through the forest around them, and some brighter lights, more stationary, glared into the night's shadows. Daven kept her down, and she was glad to stay there. There was more shouting and she could hear people being read their Miranda rights. Footsteps moved all around them, but somehow they were not discovered.

Our brethren have a way of concealing themselves from human discovery, Jelani. We will not be found. Daven's mental voice held definite disappointment. *Unfortunately the protection does not extend to those who are fully human.*

The yelling and running gradually faded away after a time, but not before Jelani's knees went numb from being curled up beneath her.

Distant car doors slammed. The glade remained silent for long minutes, until an owl hooted.

Detecting quiet movement around them, Jelani stood. She stretched her legs and winced through the pins and needles, until Daven urged her forward.

She and the others gathered in one area, where a small circle of sky peeked through the treetops. As the moon shone down in bright streams, she had a moment of déjà vu, remembering that dream of dark-clothed men moving through the woods on a secretive undertaking. She stopped to look over her shoulder at the faceless man from her dream.

Astan Hawk.

He nodded with encouragement and helped her over a fallen log, as they joined the others.

"Is everyone all right?" Daven asked, moving among his men.

Jelani could see that this particular band was comprised of more of the elder generation with only a few of the younger ones, Astan and Grigor among them. Some of the other more rebellious ones had not been included.

Satisfied none of his men had been taken, Daven turned to speak to Jelani when the human called Spiderman came running up out of the brush and plowed into him, knocking him down. "You bastard!"

Astan lurched into action and grabbed the man, pulling him away from Daven. "Calm down, friend."

Daven stood, wiping a bit of blood from his face. "Indeed. This is none of our doing."

"Bullshit!" Spiderman accused. "They've never been here before. Not until you started showing up. You know, you make it damned difficult to be sympathetic, you with your special tree to protect and your mysterious ways. You got Mad Dog wasted. And now there's what four, six of our new recruits just hauled away by Homeland Security? Screw you, man! We don't need your help! Take a damned hike!"

He yanked himself clear of Astan's grip and gathered several of his own people. After tossing what equipment hadn't been confiscated back into their vehicles, each sped away into the darkness.

Daven and Astan exchanged words Jelani couldn't hear. Then Daven and several others disappeared east into the forest, while Astan guided Jelani back to her car.

"That's it for tonight," he explained. "They'll be watching now. Your government men."

"Well, yeah. You don't want to mess with them." She needed no prompting to get her engine started. Using only parking lights, she headed for the main road, Spiderman's car the only one behind her. He drove close to her bumper as though he was trying to herd a wayward sheep.

No cavalcade of sleek black government vehicles awaited them at the end of the lane. Jelani sighed with relief. As they pulled up to the turn to Highway 93, Spiderman parked alongside her long enough to flip her off before he vanished in a hail of small stones.

Astan watched the spectacle. "Humans can be so rash."

She smirked. "I thought that was one of our better qualities. That and pissing off people."

Laughing, he relaxed a bit in the seat. Then his mood sobered. "I would like to say it is not our way, but surely the actions of Bartolomey show that all the evils we decry in humans exist as well in our world."

"So you're not better than us. Why would that matter? It's not like things ever turn out for the better in the long run."

"Jelani, how can you say that? If you didn't have hope for a better world, why are you working with us to rescue Linnea?"

She glanced at him, as she pulled out on the road to Missoula. "Because you made me. Not because I think anything's going to change. I mean, you know how people always use that quote about the glass being half-full or half empty? Some days I'm not even sure there's a glass."

Astan was silent as they continued down the road toward Ronan. Finally he laid a hand on her shoulder. "I understand how it feels to lose everyone that matters, Jelani. Sometimes the obstacles of the world seem to build to a point that it feels like nothing will ever come out from behind the shadow of the clouds. But you have to have faith that there is good ahead for you." His eyes welled up with tears, which reflected the light from a passing car. "If you don't, how can you go on each day?"

"You go on because that's what you do. The pain doesn't matter. The loneliness doesn't matter. You just live. Until you die." As she said the words, she knew how black they sounded. But after a frustrating night of little sleep, the unanswered questions surrounding her role in her new elven family, and the evil that felt like it was closing in around her, she was just about at the bottom of her pit.

Neither of them spoke for several minutes, the moment of

bared souls stretching between them.

Finally, she sighed and rubbed her forehead. "So, shouldn't you be guarding Daven? Since that's what you do?"

"He will be safe with the others. You are our primary concern now." There was warmth and amusement in his tone. "Certainly you're mine."

She was glad he couldn't see the blush that came into her cheeks at his possessive tone. "You don't need to worry about me. I can take care of myself."

"I wanted to talk to you about that. Just in case none of us are around next time Bartolomey shows up, I'd like to teach you some of the fighting skills we have perfected over the years."

"Hey, I took some judo at the university. I'm not totally helpless."

"I didn't say you were. Let's just say I'll sleep better, if I know that you know some tricks. Who knows? You may have some special skills of your own you haven't discovered yet. Are you game?"

As the first rays of a pale peach sunrise crawled over the horizon, she considered his offer. It couldn't hurt. Besides, she wouldn't mind spending the time with Astan. Somehow he made her feel like things would come out all right, even this new unknown future she had to deal with.

"Why not? I don't suppose I'll be the next kung fu kid, but for you? I can find time."

"How about we start when we get back? I know just the place."

* * *

CHAPTER 36

"DO you think they're outside spying on us now?"

Crispy looked like he wished he could hide behind his narrow lemonade glass. The thought of Homeland Security anywhere in the vicinity seemed to make him even paler than usual.

"I doubt it, Crisp," Jelani said, pressing her cool glass to her flushed cheek. "That's been a couple of weeks ago. I haven't noticed any guys in dark suits hanging around the shop."

The day had come on bright and hot, perhaps a record-setting day, the radio had said earlier. At Iris' complaint that Jelani had been neglecting her old friends, she'd asked Astan to suspend training for today. Besides, her muscles ached and she needed the break. All the same, she felt his presence somewhere nearby. Protecting her. A crazy notion.

"I want to get back to this thing about Daven being Astan's father," Lane said. "So if the oldsters were in hiding since you were an infant, then Astan must be about the same age as you. And Daven, too, if he was on ice all that time." Lane shook his head. "Man, just like Bucky Barnes."

Jelani gave him a blank look. "Bucky who?"

"Bucky Barnes. He was a sidekick to old Captain America back in the day. But he got put in suspended animation by the Russkies. And then thawed out and rehabbed to become the new Captain America."

"What is that, the life imitates art argument? Get real." Jelani handed Iris a glass of lemonade and then plopped down on the sofa.

"Now that you've booby-trapped the trees, what's next?" Iris asked. "That should stop logging in that area, in case that's where the Tree is?"

"Well, yeah, but Daven said the Tree wasn't in that area. May have just been a political move to cement that friendship after that Mad Dog got killed."

"Sounds like it backfired."

"I know. The Spiderman guy said something about tree-sitting when the loggers were ready to get serious. When they got raided, though, they dropped the elves like hot potatoes. Daven's big plan was to have the ELF people help them. Honestly, I don't know what they're going to do now."

"There's a bloody bright idea," Lane said. "People go and sit in trees. I guess they believe that the loggers won't cut them down if a human can get hurt."

"The government doesn't care about individuals," Crispy grumbled.

"They just climb trees. And sit there?" Incredulous, Jelani stared at Lane. "And what? For how long? Till nightfall?"

"No, Jelly Bean, these folk are serious. They sit there till the loggers agree not to cut the tree down." Lane rolled over to the Cave, pulled up some data, white letters against a dark blue screen. "I mean, this chick here, Julia Butterfly, stayed in her tree in California for two years."

"Get out!" Iris said. "How did she get a shower?"

"Or use the bathroom?"

"Or get food and water?"

Lane shrugged. "It rains. People get you buckets, bring you groceries, if they believe in your cause. Of course, all that means squat if you get pinched by the suits at Homeland Security." He looked at Jelani and shook his head. "So, you in it to win it, babe?"

"Ugh." Jelani stared at the fast-melting ice in her glass. "I think I'm losing my mind."

Crispy sat next to her. Taking her hand, he looked deep into her eyes. "No. You're losing yourself."

"What do you mean?" She wondered if it was crazy to have the crazy person diagnosing her.

"I'm still me, aren't I? Iris?"

The blonde shook her head. "Honey, of course you've changed since this all started. But that's to be expected. Finally you have a chance for a real family. Who wouldn't want that?"

With a wistful look, Crispy let go of her hand. "Sometimes it's not bad to lose parts of yourself that are unhappy. Iris says so."

"I'm happy. I'm happy! Oh, what the hell." Frowning, Jelani put down the glass before her trembling hand spilled its contents.

"The lady doth protest too much." Lane looked smug, and then rolled himself back into the Cave.

As the silence lengthened, she felt their eyes on her.

"There's more to it, isn't there, honey?" Iris said at last.

It might have been the hours she'd spent working with Astan, or the dreams that kept waking her at night, or just the pressure cracking her open, but once she began telling them what was going on, she finally broke down.

"Oh, my God," Jelani blurted. "That Bart guy showed up at my work the other day!" As Lane returned to listen, she shared the story of the visit by Bartolomey and Malina. "Dee and Daven say he's very dangerous. I felt like he crawled right inside my brain and filled it up with lies."

"That's him! The one Squirrel called Headlok! Remember, in those letters at the cabin? Said he was a mind controller, didn't he?" Lane returned to the Cave, tapping in queries that yielded information on both the comics villain and the problems he caused. Jelani just waved those off as irrelevant.

"But Daven and Astan are going to protect you, right, honey?" Iris' brow furrowed with concern.

"Apparently, they're going to protect the hell out of me, all the way to the altar." Jelani explained the ongoing conflict between Daven and Astan, and the insistence that she would have to choose a mate to settle things.

"What?" Lane rolled out and stared at her. "Our little Jelly Bean, getting hitched?"

"Which one do you like?" Iris asked. "You're going to choose Daven, right? Those eyes. Oh my sweet heaven, how can you resist those golden eyes?" She mock-swooned onto the sofa.

Jelani mentally kicked herself. She should have known they wouldn't be serious about this. On the other hand, she could certainly see the funny side of it, in that 'something you'll laugh about years from now' kind of scenario.

"Actually, no. I'm not ready to get married, mated, or whatever the hell to anyone." The words made her a little guilty, feeling disloyal to Astan as she said it.

"What's next, Jelly Bean, other than picking out elf china?" Lane teased.

"Very funny," she growled. "I guess now that ELF is out, we'll just have to go to find the Tree and pull off this rescue somehow."

"They haven't told you how to do it?"

"They all think I know. Or that I will when the time comes. But I don't have the slightest idea what I'm supposed to do or how!"

Disturbed, she reached for her purse and took out the vessel, still in the cloth Astan had used to pick it up. Then carefully unwrapped it and laid it on her lap.

Iris took one look and scooted back a foot. "Eww. I can't believe you carry that around with you. It's gross!"

"Makes me feel better. I sleep with it. Even Az likes it." She laid a hand over the top of the ball, felt it pulse. The warmth crept from the vessel into her fingers and then up her arm. With the warmth came a feeling of safety and a voice she could almost hear. It was there, just beyond the edge of her perception. Her eyes closed and she tried to concentrate on the whisper of a voice, following it down a darkened path somewhere in her mind. *I need a flashlight in here*, she thought. She was yanked back to reality by a yelp from Crispy.

"What?" she snapped.

He didn't say anything, just pointed to her lap, where the vessel had become a red, pulsing flashlight.

"Did I do that?" Startled, she took her hand away, and the object returned to its previous size and shape.

"My sweet Goddess!" Iris said. "Now you're magic, too!"

"I'm not magic," she said, annoyed.

"Magic," Crispy nodded with an expression hovering between fear and adulation.

"Not magic."

"Possessed?" Lane ventured with a grin.

"Shut up!" Jelani picked up the vessel and reached for the cloth to wrap it again, noticing the very distinct odors of deep woods and pipe smoke. She sniffed at the vessel, but the smells faded as quickly as they'd come.

Lane noticed her action. "What?"

"Nothing." The aromas wouldn't be any easier to explain to her friends than the fact she made the flashlight appear. The same way she'd made it spit fire to impress the younger elves. But she knew in her heart that they were right. It was magic. And she had done it.

Was this the gift Astan had prophesied for her? Was this vessel some sort of touchstone, something that could facilitate whatever it was she could do? What was it she could do? She'd changed the small round object into something she'd wanted, needed. Into what else could she change it?

She was losing herself, Crispy had said. Becoming something else. But what?

She cleared her throat. "Daven said we're going up again in a few days to get to the Tree this time."

"You're better off going without the ELF," Lane said. "Those freaks are frelling crazy. You could all get yourselves killed. Or at least arrested, especially if Big Brother has them staked out."

"We should support Jelani in this," Iris reminded them. "We would expect her support in any similar situation in our own lives. We're family. We'll go with you into the woods and stand by you."

"You don't have to."

Even Crispy seemed determined to be a part of this. "We should. Lane, maybe we can just go to the cabin. Wait till they're done."

Iris beamed. "I'm so proud of you, Ron. Volunteering to go up there, away from the apartment. You're just amazing."

As Crispy blushed, Lane seemed uncomfortable. "You don't suppose they've got wireless out that far, do you?"

"Be a man, Lane," Jelani scolded. "The service umbilical just doesn't reach the deep woods. If Crispy can drag himself out there, you should be able to manage."

"Fine, fine," he snapped. "I'll bring out a nice picnic and you all can stop for tea and crumpets before you go off tree-sitting."

"What do you wear for a tree-sitting?" Iris asked idly.

At the sheer ridiculousness of her friend's comment, Jelani felt her annoyance and confusion fade as she joined in the snickering. "Something waterproof, I'd guess."

"Well then. I'm in." Iris' smile was faint but encouraging.

"You guys are great," Jelani said, taking one more squeeze of the pulsing warm ball before wrapping it in its protective cloth once more and tucking it back in her purse. "I guess we'll just see how it goes."

"One day at a time. Iris always says that," Crispy added.

Lane just sat in his chair, brooding. "I'm gonna write a book about this. Someone might as well make a buck off the insanity."

"Just spell my name right, will you?" Jelani felt like a weight had been lifted from her shoulders with the burden now shared among the four of them.

As they drove back from the forest debacle, Astan had seemed to understand, even if he disagreed.

Everything could still turn out all right, couldn't it?

* * *

CHAPTER 37

THE next afternoon, Jelani had just come back from a break at the coffee shop when Astan burst in the back door from the alley, clearly searching for her. The other girl on shift gave Jelani a smirk and rolled her eyes, this odd cloak and dagger sort of stalker thing somewhat old news by now.

"I'm not sorry," she warned him.

"Go on, honey," her co-worker said, as she stepped over to take the waiting customers' orders. "I'll get these ladies."

"Thanks, Bee." Slipping on her apron, Jelani tied it and stepped from behind the counter to speak to Astan.

"Not sorry about what?" he asked.

"This morning Dee brought me some elixir to help me sleep. I told her no thanks." Jelani bit her lip, thinking she'd actually been a little too firm with the elf-woman. *Stay out of my dreams,* she'd told Dee, *or else I leave town and disappear into the world.* Dee had stepped back as if Jelani had slapped her.

"Oh. No, I haven't seen her. Haven't been home, even. Something more important on the radar, I'm afraid."

"What's happened?"

"We must go," Astan said, voice tight. He glanced over his shoulder to the door.

"Is someone after you?" She studied his face, noting his troubled gaze. Something had him rattled out of his usual stoic calm. She leaned closer. "What's happened?"

He did the same, speaking softly. "Legolas contacted Daven. The ELF people have apparently called in their big guns to help."

"Really?" She frowned. "I got the idea that old Spiderman was done helping you. Us." She gave a little shrug. "Whichever."

"As had we. Daven had nearly given up hope. But then news came in of a logging effort to be made in the old forest. ELF is riled enough to set aside what happened last time in order to defeat the loggers. If they're willing to go with us, we need to make one last-ditch effort." He took her hand. "Jelani, this may be our moment. We can't do it without you."

She sighed. "I am so going to get fired."

The other girl just shook her head. "Go. Just go. You owe me this weekend. I need Saturday night for a hot date."

"Really? You're a saint!" Jelani gave the other girl a quick hug and shrugged out of the apron. "Are you riding with me?" she asked Astan. "I promised I'd take the others along. They're going to wait at the cabin, though."

"Do you think that's wise?"

"I think I need all the help I can get." She looked sidewise at him. "I know you all hang together, but it might be nice to have a few humans on my side of the board. Besides the crazy ones."

Astan hesitated before surrendering to her wishes. "If we must, then stop and get them."

Taking out her cellphone, she called Iris and Lane, both of whom agreed to be ready in fifteen minutes.

She and Astan drove out of the parking lot behind the shop just as Richard's patrol car pulled into the alley. "Whew, that was close."

She could feel his stare burn into her face. "I believe the uniformed one truly cares for you."

"Yeah, I know," she admitted. "As much as it irritates me."

"I can hardly blame him. You are worth caring for, Jelani."

No matter how soft his tone or how tempting it might be, she couldn't openly accept what he had to say. Then she'd have to tap into her own feelings, which were much too tender where Astan was concerned. Business first, she scolded herself.

"We've got somewhere to be." She concentrated on her driving, and a few minutes later, pulled into a spot in front of the Boys' apartment and marched up the stairs, closing her mind to the chance that she could have her heart torn open again. *Beyond this point there be monsters*, she thought, remembering the lines of danger drawn on the olden maps.

Crispy had the door open before she could give the standard

knock. He looked excited, the way he'd looked in the van driving up to the cabin, more like a puppy about to go for a car ride.

"She's here!" he called over his shoulder.

"Game on!" Lane called from inside.

"Are you ready?" Jelani fidgeted on the steps, looking down behind her, but Astan hadn't followed.

"Let's go." Lane crowded into the doorway, a heavy black case hanging from a strap across his shoulder. He wore a bandanna on his head and sported a heavy black leather jacket with matching boots.

Jelani frowned, as she looked him over. "Who are you supposed to be, Elvis goes urban commando?"

Lane shook his head, as he put several cloth-wrapped items into the case. "Let's just say I don't intend to get caught with my pants down." He nodded.

Crispy leaned close. "You better hope not. There's no bathroom there. Just an outhouse. You know how you feel about spiders."

"Shut up, you!" Lane pushed past Jelani and then headed down the stairs.

She heard him greet Astan, and then Iris' voice joined the mix. Turning back to Crispy, she gave him an encouraging smile. "Are you sure you're up to this?"

"Ready to go out in the world. Thanks to your Prince."

"Prince?" She stepped down a few stairs as he came out and locked the door. "Oh, Daven, right."

If Daven was Prince Charming, what did that make Astan? One of the mice? A footman of sorts? A really hot party guest? If she hadn't broken the plot of the Cinderella story, she'd at least bent it a good deal.

Couldn't she do anything right?

"Jelani?" Lane called up the steps. "Get your sweet ass down here. Astan's about to shit a brick!"

"All right, all right. I'm coming."

She and Crispy hurried down the stairs, and they all climbed into the car. It felt like one of those clown cars at the circus. The air practically reeked of adrenaline.

* * *

AS Jelani sped down the highway, Iris tried to provide small talk on the way to the cabin, but eventually the growing anxiety about what waited ahead reduced her words to silence.

Soon she turned off the main road and headed down the long driveway. In a few minutes Jelani stopped the car in front of the little crooked shack.

"Are you sure you don't want us to come out into the forest with you?" Iris asked.

Jelani glanced at Astan for a response.

"We will move faster without you," he replied, with no hint of insult in his voice. "If they are only expecting us, it would be best that we are the only ones who show up."

Lane grunted. "Yeah, last thing you want is for some crazy with a shoebox full of C4 to get nervous."

"C4?" Crispy said, uncertainty showing for the first time. "Isn't that dangerous?"

Astan gave Lane an irritated look. "Life is dangerous. We live it anyway, the risk giving us meaning."

Jelani remembered she had to let the others in the cabin, so she bailed out for just a moment, the deed tucked inside her jacket like last time, so she could open the door. Astan seemed fretful, so she hurried across the small space between the car and the cabin to lay a hand on the door. It opened easily at her touch.

Sharing a brave smile with Iris, Jelani felt like she was off to war. "We'll see you guys in a bit, huh?"

"You be careful." Lane's brow furrowed, and he pulled her close for a big bear hug. "I'll get the crumpets ready."

The echoes of Iris' voice scolding Lane faded, as Astan hurried Jelani back to the car.

They climbed into the old sedan and drove further along the highway to the entrance to the backwoods.

"Daven's going to meet us up here?" she asked.

"This is what he said." Astan peered out the front windshield, shading his eyes with his hand. "There!"

She looked ahead and saw Daven, Grigor, and Legolas

standing together, while several others milled about.

"Where are the loggers?" she asked, frowning as she parked the car. "I don't see any trucks or a skidder."

"I'm not sure," Astan said, sounding a little puzzled. "But the ELF man is there. They must be serious."

They hurried out of the vehicle and jogged across the open area.

After several flannel-dressed men broke out of conversation and walked away into the woods, Legolas greeted them with a warm smile.

Daven reached for Jelani's hand and held it. *Legolas says the loggers have penetrated the central area. We must move quickly.*

Jelani's confusion over what she was supposed to do was foremost in her mind, and Daven picked it up.

Have you brought the vessel?

She looked into his eyes and nodded, realizing he was intentionally conducting this conversation in silence. There was someone he did not trust. She glanced at Legolas and Grigor, who were already following the others.

"Come on!" Legolas called. "There isn't much time!"

If Linnea is in danger, we must go. Daven nodded to her and turned to follow Legolas.

Astan urged her forward and then came on her heels, as they trotted deeper into the woods. Jelani concentrated on not tripping over brush and fallen limbs, wishing she'd had time to go home and change into her hiking boots. They'd been a real blessing the last time.

"Spiderman called out Team-B this morning, because he was sure someone would be specifically heading for the mid-section!" Legolas yelled over his shoulder. "They should be there by the time we arrive. Which way?"

Daven ran for another fifteen feet. Then slowed and stopped. He held up a hand and gave quick finger signals to Astan, who pulled Jelani aside and stepped in front of her. Legolas realized they weren't following him and stopped, too, turning to face them with his arms open.

Grigor came back to stand with them. "What's the matter?

Spiderman said the ELF unit would give us all assistance. Did the princess hurt her ankle?" He tossed a solicitous look at Jelani.

"I'm fine," she said, slipping her hand into her sweatshirt pouch, the presence of the vessel there lending some comfort. She watched Daven, knowing something wasn't right by the way he held himself and way his gaze darted around the trees.

"Spiderman would have told you the area we had staked out," Daven said.

"I know, Daven. That's where we're going. Into map sector A-6." Legolas shoved his hands into his pockets, too, perhaps unconsciously echoing Jelani. "I'm waiting on you."

"Where is Spiderman?" Astan asked, suspicion creeping into his tone.

With just a moment's hesitation, Grigor gestured ahead of them. "He was going to meet us there. Right, Legolas?"

Jelani looked from one to the other, paranoia eating at her gut. Something wasn't right. What were they not saying? If there were loggers in the area, why couldn't they hear chain saws or yelling or anything?

"Well if you won't go, at least let her come. They need her." Grigor reached for Jelani's arm.

Jelani ducked away, not trusting him, not liking the posture of either of her elf friends. "Just hold on a minute, pal," she said. "I don't go without them."

An authoritative voice came from behind them. "I've got a better idea, Jelani. How about you don't go at all?"

* * *

CHAPTER 38

NO way. This isn't happening.

Jelani turned to confirm her identification of the voice: Richard Snyder.

He wasn't in uniform, but he strutted across the space toward them, wearing a cocky expression and looking like a lumberjack from the Klondike. As least he came alone and not with the entire Missoula police fleet.

"Richard! What are you doing here?"

"I told you, I've been checking up on you. You're making a mistake here. I know you don't see it." Richard's gaze dripped with pity, as if she were a child who'd been caught with her hand in the cookie jar. "I heard through the grapevine about Homeland Security bust the other night, and I've been keeping an eye out ever since, me and a couple of guys on the force." Smirking, he gestured toward Astan. "I heard this one had come to the shop and you'd gone with him. So I got right on your trail. You never even saw me following you, did you?"

He looked past her to Daven, Grigor and Legolas, who watched with frozen stares. Then leveled his gaze back on Jelani. "I've just got to put my foot down. You're going to get hurt. Come on, now. I'll drive you back." Richard smiled in what he must have thought was a 'real world marvelous boyfriend' way and held his hand out to her.

"Leave me alone," she groaned, refusing his hand. "I'm fine. I'm perfectly fine."

"I'm serious about this, babe. I'm not taking no for an answer." Richard's eyes lost any warmth, and he reached inside his red plaid jacket and pulled out his service revolver. "Come on."

"You'd shoot me?" Jelani stared at him in disbelief, taking

several steps backward. "You've got to be kidding!"

"Useless humans." Grigor stepped up beside her and yanked her away from the others. "Enough of this time-wasting absurdity. She's coming with me. I have my orders." He jerked her close to him, while his other hand groped inside his jacket.

Jelani heard a heavy click beside her ear and saw sunlight glint off a gun barrel very close to her. It was pointed at Richard. Grigor with a gun? What was happening?

Her first reaction was to try the defensive moves Astan had taught her, but there were too many other targets at the moment. Astan and Daven both wore the same shocked looks, the realization slowly sinking in that they'd been tricked.

"Hey! She's supposed to be my prize!" Legolas burst out. "Bartolomey promised."

"Silence." Grigor's eyes were as cold and unfeeling as a reptile's.

What was he saying? Bartolomey had enlisted both elf and human allies to get her? She tried to pull away, but Grigor snatched her back, pinning her against his chest with his left arm around her neck.

"You let her go now!" Richard cocked his weapon and aimed it at Grigor.

"Like I said, I have orders."

A bright flash and the loudest sound she'd ever heard signaled the discharge of Grigor's pistol. She covered her ears by reflex, wondering if she'd popped an eardrum. She thought Richard's gun had fired, but he must have pulled back at the last moment, afraid he might hit her. As she opened her eyes again, she saw a splash of red spreading across the front of his brown plaid shirt.

"Richard?"

Her desperate whisper did nothing to stop the officer's fall. His expression was puzzled, as he hit the ground hard. A long groan escaped him. Then he didn't move again.

"You killed him!" she shrieked, pulling against the arm that held her. "Bastard! He wouldn't have hurt you!"

Setting aside what Astan had showed her, she went back to

the basic self-defense she'd learned on campus. If she'd just sway a little sideways, she could get some power behind her fist, and aimed right at the elf's crotch.

As she'd hoped, he moaned and bent forward. His hold loosened, and she quickly leaned forward to kick Grigor back, pushing away from him. She jumped to take Astan's outstretched hand, not looking at the body of her fallen admirer until she was safe behind Astan.

Astan made a sharp bird call to warn his fellows, never taking his eyes off Legolas, who was behind Grigor and to his left. He appeared to be watching for an opening to retake Jelani.

Grigor, his face red, gradually got to his feet and raised the firearm.

"I'll have her one way or another. Bartolomey doesn't allow failure. You should know that." He pointed the weapon at Astan, who remained solidly in front of her. "You should have opened your eyes, Astan, seen where the ultimate power lay. Now you'll be destroyed with the rest of the Circle."

"Bartolomey will have to get used to the fact that he won't be giving orders any more," Astan said.

"He's very powerful, friend. You all underestimate him. Mad Dog did, too." Legolas moved closer.

Daven took hold of Jelani's hand and tugged her back, while Astan stayed between her and the gun.

"Elves are powerful. Humans are weak," Grigor said. Turning to Legolas, he gave a dark and unpleasant laugh. "Bartolomey enticed you to betray your friend and leader in hopes of what? Riches? Power?"

"Mad Dog betrayed us, turning in some of our people to the cops," Legolas said. With an uneasy look, he gestured toward Daven. "Just like these led Homeland Security to us."

"Humans believe anything," Grigor snarled at Legolas, while still pointing the gun at Astan. "We needed Mad Dog to learn where Linnea resides, when Vincent failed to be helpful. I'll tell Bartolomey you served your purpose admirably. But now we no longer need you."

As the gun barrel shifted to point in his direction, Legolas seemed to understand his folly.

Then the gun fired, and Legolas dropped dead not far from the place where Richard lay.

Grigor's gaze swung over to Jelani. "But now we have our princess, who will help us finally succeed."

"I'll never help Bart do a damned thing!"

Astan twitched as she yelled from behind him, and she could sense his worry, but it wasn't for himself.

"I can't save you all," Astan muttered. "Go!"

Astan raised his hand toward her, his ability shoving her toward Daven.

She stumbled into Daven's arms, and he pulled her away from the others. She looked over her shoulder just in time to see Astan leap into the air.

But Grigor had anticipated the move, firing twice into the space where Astan arrived.

In what seemed like slow motion, Astan twisted away from Grigor, his back arching in pain as he fell backward to the ground and lay still.

Daven stopped, his grip on her loosening, and she could feel the flood of emotion rush over him, over them both.

"Astan! No!" She ducked under the probable line of gunfire and ran toward the collapsed Astan, the thought of losing him terrifying her.

All those people dying because of her? How big was the conspiracy? Humans and elves both. *I'll kill Grigor, myself,* she silently swore.

Lunging forward, she knelt beside Astan and heard his ragged breathing begin to slow.

Daven pulled Jelani to her feet and tucked her behind him. *Fool! You cannot allow the traitors to capture you!* His thoughts broke off, as he turned toward her with a stunned expression. *You choose Astan.*

"What?" Caught by surprise, she stumbled. The emotion behind Daven's thought was rife with jealousy and disappointment mixed with a deep sense of loss. "Astan needs help! Help him! Do what you do to heal him!"

Get down! I will protect him! Daven shoved her aside, and Jelani just caught a faint trail of a thought as he let go. *The traditions of the clan must be served.*

He launched himself over Astan's fallen body and straight at Grigor, who fired the weapon twice more, striking Daven mid-chest.

Her last defender down, Jelani scrambled to her feet and fumbled frantically in her jacket pocket for her keys, where she knew a small sprayer of mace awaited.

He won't kill me. He needs me alive. I hope.

After the staccato sound of the gunfire, all the natural sounds had stopped. She and Grigor faced each other across four bodies laid out in the grass. The cold determination in his dark green eyes spooked her, and her trembling fingers couldn't get a solid grip on the mace as she withdrew the keys from her pocket.

"It's time to go, Princess. Someone has a task for you to complete." He reached for her. It was almost as if he made a shortcut through the air, suddenly at her side, hand tight on her arm. "You won't need those where you're going." He shook her until she dropped the keys.

With a jerk, they sped through the forest like the Santa Ana winds, the passing trees reduced to blurs.

* * *

CHAPTER 39

ASTAN awoke, lying face down in the grass. The only sounds were birdsong and wind in the trees. His shoulder ached. What had happened?

He sat up with a groan, red stains on his shirtfront grabbing his attention. The stains were blood, his own. Through alternating dull and sharp pain in his wounded shoulder, he started to get up, to call for help.

Where were the others? The police officer who'd tried to rescue Jelani lay at his feet, the ELF worker near him.

Jelani!

Then he saw Daven.

What had happened?

He stumbled over to his father, wrenching his shoulder as he tripped across a fallen branch. The last moments of consciousness were beginning to come back to him. Grigor. Legolas. The gun. Jelani. The sudden pain after the echoing shot. But how long ago?

"Daven? Father!"

Astan knew at the first touch that it was too late. His father's stillness went straight to the elf's very core. Fire burned there no longer. Daven was gone. Astan had failed to protect him.

But there was still Jelani.

His priorities clicked back into the forefront of his mind. The glade was empty. No loggers, no ELF workers, no elves. He sent a mental call for his brethren, but after several minutes, none responded. Gone. With regret, Astan considered how Daven had been the one with the gift for communication, not he.

Frantically, he looked about for some clue. The only trace he found was Jelani's keys, tossed into the brush.

Astan glanced in the direction of her car, still parked where she'd left it. He could just see its silver paint downhill through the trees.

He knew very well what happened. Bartolomey's traitor was Grigor.

He castigated himself for never suspecting that such discontent would rise to the level of treachery. They had spirited her away for the nefarious purposes of Bartolomey.

What now?

Looking for direction, he searched the entire glade where they'd met Legolas, ignoring the ache in his shoulder and the sticky blood that trickled onto his shirt.

He was alone. The humans were dead. Daven was dead.

He fought back waves of emotion, as he stared down at his father's still form. He'd grown up without paternal guidance and companionship, and then suddenly had regained the opportunity to establish that lost relationship. Somehow, having grown up among humans, he'd imagined they would bond and that his father would become a wise adviser and friend.

Sadly, that had not come to pass. His father had been a grown elf, who'd picked up with his prior life, regardless of the fact he had a son. Astan had been a baby, when he'd been taken into hiding. Daven, dealing with the clan war at that time, had trusted the women to do what had been asked of them. When he'd been restored, what Daven required from Astan was his training as protector and, occasionally, an insight on the human world. Neither had anticipated they would become rivals for the affection of Jelani Marsh.

He shook himself free of the life-sucking regret that threatened to freeze him. There wasn't anything he could do for Daven. But Jelani might still be saved.

He had to act quickly. But what could he do alone?

The forest was huge. Did Bartolomey know where Linnea was? Had that been the precipitating factor of this ambush? It did not seem to be a move to force either he or Daven to reveal information with Jelani at stake. Grigor had dispatched them all with cold disdain. Or at least he believed he had. One point in Astan's favor.

Any chance Astan had of tracing Jelani at this point depended on getting help. He looked at the car again and started toward it.

He'd never driven an automobile. He understood machinery to some extent, and he'd seen it done. Where would he go? He might drive back to Missoula and find Djana, have her summon the Circle together. But how cold would the trail be then?

The others were closer.

Would Jelani's human friends be of much help?

Astan was sure they understood nothing of the depth of the schism between the two elf factions, but he knew that they cared deeply for Jelani.

And if they didn't fully comprehend the danger, so much the better. He needed them in motion, not paralyzed with fright.

He'd carry the fear inside, for all of them.

* * *

ASTAN struggled to carry Daven's lifeless body. It just didn't feel right to leave him in the woods.

His own injuries tearing open again, fresh blood stained his shirt as he hefted Daven across his shoulders, stumbled to the silver vehicle, and laid his father as gently as he could in the back seat.

Then he slid into the front, put the key in the ignition, and turned it as he'd seen Jelani do.

Learning to use the manual transmission, coordinate the timing of the gas pedal and clutch, was a painful adventure. Each rough, jerking failure made him more determined, and his jaw ached from the gritting of his teeth.

After nearly thirty minutes, he was able to navigate slowly, if inelegantly, along the back road and then navigate the long lane to the cabin.

As he turned off the rattling engine, he leaned forward and laid his head on the steering wheel, feeling like his heart would burst.

Iris erupted from the dilapidated cabin door. "It's about time you...." Her eyes widened as she saw Astan in the driver's seat. "What's happened?" Then she turned back to the cabin. "Lane!

Get out here!"

As Astan swung open the car door and stood, she hurried toward him with a little scream. "My sweet goddess! What happened, Astan? Where is she? Jelly?" She looked frantically into the back seat and grabbed the car door handle, weaving on her feet, clearly shocked by what she'd found. "Oh, no. No-no-no…."

Lane peered out the door before coming at a labored run.

Astan pulled himself from the car, dizzy from the loss of blood. He could barely hear the sounds of the forest around him, feeling only emptiness.

"What the hell?" Lane exclaimed, horror scrawled across his face. "What happened?"

Iris whimpered next to him. "Is he dead?"

"Who's dead?" Crispy leaned out the door, his nervous gaze flitting from the car to the trees and back.

"Dead?" Lane growled. He looked into the car, frowned, and then leveled a steely gaze on Astan. "Where's Jelani?"

"Come on," Iris said, struggling to regain control. She took Astan's hand, the one opposite of his wounded shoulder, avoiding the blood-soaked shirt. "Let me see what I can do for you."

Lane planted himself square in their path. "Where is she?" His eyes blazed with a thousand reproaches.

"They took her," Astan gasped. "They took her!" Agony ripped through him, the loss like knives in his flesh. His knees started to buckle.

"Lane!" Iris' voice was dangerously thin. "Get him inside. Now." She leaned close, slipping an arm under Astan's left shoulder to keep him upright.

Astan had the odd thought that Iris was much stronger than he had expected, before the mental puff trailed off into a haze. His ears buzzed. He fought to keep his eyes open. He felt Lane prop him up on the other side, and the two of them half-carried him to the cabin door and over the threshold.

As they entered, he sensed them pass the twitchy angst that was Crispy Mendell.

"You need the healer," the skinny little man said. "The other one is the healer."

Yes, Daven was the healer. Daven had all the skills. He had the answers. What did Astan have? Nothing.

"We must hurry, if we're to find her," he mumbled, eyes closed, jerked this way and that as Iris and Lane sat him on a rickety chair and removed his shirt. He heard Iris gasp.

"Get me some water," she said, sounding stronger and more capable after she'd absorbed the situation. "And something to bandage that with."

"That's a GSW," Crispy muttered. "Definitely a GSW."

"A what?" Iris asked.

"Gunshot wound. Who the hell had a gun? Is this more of that Homeland Security crap?"

Astan shook his head, wincing as it hurt his shoulder. "Betrayed by...elf."

"Well, no shit, Sherlock. I told Jelly Bean to stay the hell away from those ELF guys."

"No." Astan tried to put force into the word, but he was fading. "One of mine."

His eyes closed. Voices floated around him. They puzzled over his injury and the body in the car, but most of all Jelani's whereabouts. Astan found that forcing some mental distance made it a little more tolerable, especially Iris' ministrations which were hellishly painful no matter how necessary he knew they were.

Underlying his lassitude was a small driven voice. The minutes were ticking, ticking....

He was jerked back to full consciousness by a sharp burning smell under his nose. Blinking, he pushed away the bottle of Tabasco sauce that Lane held. He looked down to see he was bandaged, an unfamiliar shirt hung on his shoulders.

"No time for dreamland, pal," Lane warned. "Now, where is Jelani? How much trouble is she in? Bart's guys have her, right?"

Astan took a deep breath. "Legolas drew us in."

"Who? Get out." Lane's voice dripped with sarcasm. "Legolas? Really."

"Human. Bartolomey had subverted him. But Grigor shot him and the officer. He shot me. He must have shot Daven, too. Jelani was gone when I woke up." He fastened the buttons on the shirt, fingers awkward on the right side. Iris helped him slip into a sling made from a torn bed sheet.

"What officer?" Iris asked. Then she froze. "The Homeland Security people were back?"

Astan shook his head. "The officer from town. He followed her out to the forest."

"Richard?" Lane said, incredulous. "Did he head back to town?"

"No. He's dead."

"They killed Daven and Richard?" Iris' face was pale.

"And they have our Jelly!" Lane paced, dripping outrage.

Crispy hovered just in sight, picking at his sleeve. "Where did they go?"

"I believe he took her to the Tree."

"Isn't that where you and Daven were going?" Iris asked. "You were going to take Jelani to release her mother from the tree. She wanted to do that, to let Linnea be the queen." Iris gave him a faint smile. "She wasn't sure about having to marry someone just yet. Even someone as special as you."

Astan raised an eyebrow, distracted by the personal note. "She cares for me?"

Lane growled. "Could we get back to the crisis here? Our Jelly's in the hands of a killer!"

"Bartolomey wants to destroy Linnea," Astan said, still watching Iris and gratified by her nod of encouragement. "He will use Jelani to do it. She is likely safe, until they find where Linnea's been hidden."

"Well," Crispy said, after a moment of thoughtful silence, "I guess we're going to the Tree."

* * *

A proper burial for Daven would have to await their return. Lane, Iris, and Crispy wrestled the body from the back seat and carried it into the cabin, laying it gently on the floor.

"Now let's go get her," Lane said.

"Do you know where?" Iris asked.

"Yes," Astan said. "About thirteen miles, as the eagle flies."

"Thirteen miles?" Lane's dismay spread through the group.

"We have the car," Iris suggested. "Do you think we'll be able to get close enough? Can you walk?" She frowned, as Astan shifted awkwardly in the sling.

"I will do what must be done," Astan replied tightly.

"Then let's go!" Lane opened the door and grabbed a heavy backpack, practically shoving the others toward the car. "Iris, you drive. Looks like maybe Lucky here ran into a few things on his way to the cabin." He gestured toward several bumps and scratches along the front fenders. "Jelly Bean's going to have a cow."

"I've never operated a car," Astan said apologetically. He waited for the other two men to sit in back, and then he climbed into the front passenger seat just as Iris slipped behind the wheel.

Astan directed Iris in the direction of the sacred spot, along some back roads hardly wide enough for the vehicle to pass, until they came to a clearing. The trip took much longer than he'd hoped, but there was no direct route.

Iris pulled the car right up to the edge of the trees, where the shadows would help disguise the vehicle.

"Stop," Astan said. When Iris had parked the car, he pulled himself out of the seat. "We can walk from here."

"All right, just hang on a minute." Lane yanked the backpack out of the car, unzipped it to reveal a huge pistol with a long barrel.

"Oh my God, Lane!" Iris gasped. "What is that?"

Lane gave her a faint smile. "Home defense for Cave Dwellers. Mark XIX Desert Eagle, 44-magnum, ten-inch barrel." He displayed it proudly.

She studied him with a doubtful expression. "Can you shoot that?"

"Do I look like an amateur? Just because I play a shaman on the Internet doesn't mean I'm a complete idiot. I've been to the firing range. A couple of times." He shrugged. "I've read the directions thoroughly. Don't worry about it." He stuck the gun in his belt with handle in easy reach, and then turned his attention to Astan. "Well?"

Astan stood several feet ahead of the car, only half listening to the humans chatter. Wind brushed the treetops. An owl flew toward them, dipping low as it approached before flying into the woods.

An owl? In mid-afternoon?

The longer the group stood there, the more silent the woods grew around them.

Something was about to happen.

"Quiet," Astan warned in a hush. "There's someone out there."

* * *

CHAPTER 40

THE journey through the forest passed in a blur, but finally Grigor dropped Jelani against the thick trunk of a large tree.

That Tree, she wondered with some part of her brain, though she didn't dare twist around far enough to see. The bark scraped her back even through her sweatshirt. *Jerk.*

A few minutes passed before her inner haze cleared. A quiet conversation was going on behind her, near enough for her to hear at least two male voices but not close enough to understand the words. One of the voices behind her was definitely Grigor. He continued talking to someone whose voice wasn't familiar, but who sounded young.

Maybe that Beckley fellow. Or Terzon. How many others had Bartolomey planted as spies in the Circle?

Without moving, she assessed what she could about her surroundings. The tree that propped her up wasn't the only tall tree here. The forest on all sides was thick and green, an occasional butterfly flitted through the air looking for something sweet. Mottled shadows drooped from the waving canopy.

So. Middle of the woods. Somewhere.

Taking into account the surreal speed at which he had moved, they could have traveled a hundred miles, for all she knew. Several people paced in the space in front of her, looking anxious as they stared at her.

She allowed evil thoughts of revenge to swirl through her mind. What would ELF do when they realized one of their own was a traitor? Had ELF even known Grigor had been planted there by Bartolomey and his group? How long had Bartolomey's poison tongue worked on Grigor's mind, opening the way for his duplicity? Is that why he'd said nothing to Astan about seeing Bartolomey at the coffee shop? Had he engineered that meeting as well? Were there others who had not yet been exposed as traitors?

She shifted a little and found she was not restrained in any way. The short grass tickled her wrists and hands. Her fingers closed around a smooth pinecone, but it would not be of any use as a weapon unless she could use it to put out someone's eye. Wasn't that always the threat? It's all fun and games till someone loses an eye. Sadly, it was clear that the fun and games were over.

In the movies, this was where the heroine always came up with some dynamite plan that routed the villains and saved the day. All she needed was a vampire slayer hat and she would be all set. Even in her head, the words had a wry twist.

Jelani Marsh was no movie heroine. Most of her life she had run away from everything that was hard. She left home after her father died, rather than stand up to the bullying of her evil stepsisters. She allowed Arik to slip away, after leaving her at the altar. She dropped out of college, when it became too much work. In truth, she just existed, making a little money at the coffee shop and sponging off people when necessary. So where did that leave her?

Alone in unfamiliar woods in the company of enemies.

Daven was dead. Richard was dead. And Astan might be dead, too.

As that memory fell into place, she felt a sense of loss not experienced since her father had died. Astan's face came to the front of her awareness, in a montage of expressions, and then that smile he shared so rarely. They'd gotten closer in the last weeks. She felt like she'd really been able to see inside him. They were very similar in the way they dealt with the world, both a little prickly and distrusting. He had worked all those years so he would be able to protect Daven and the others when they emerged.

And her.

She closed her eyes, pain zigzagging through her. That protection had come at the cost of Daven's life and probably Astan's, too. How could she ever repay that debt to a tribe of elves she barely knew? Especially when it looked like she would now be forced to betray them?

Over my dead body, she thought, but really hoped it would not come to that.

Someone grabbed her arm and dragged her to her feet.

"Come on!" a gruff voice barked. "Bartolomey has wasted enough time on you!"

Jelani stumbled forward, clutching her thin sweatshirt close.

Her captor was thick and broad-shouldered, not as tall as Daven. Gray streaks in his hair indicated he was one of those who had lived the years in real time with the false king. His heavy boots crunched the underbrush as he half-dragged her some fifty feet, releasing her at last into a semi-circle of men and women. "Here she is."

"Thank you, Erdest." The almost-melodic voice belonged to Bartolomey, who stood in the center dressed in pants and a long jacket of dark green, the light breeze ruffling his silver hair. He looked as relaxed, as if he was at a vacation resort. "Jelani, my dear niece, I'm so pleased you could join us here. We have much to do."

She glared at him. "I don't have anything to do with you." Her hot stare turned to Grigor, who stood behind Bartolomey, to his right. "He's killed my friends."

Bartolomey reached for her hand, squeezed it gently before she yanked it away from him. "But my dear, those two were never your friends."

"I told you as much when we met you," chimed in a tight alto Jelani recognized as that of Malina. She too, stepped up from the group behind Bartolomey. "They want to continue a war that has no need to be. We seek peace. You can bring that to our people."

"You lie!" Jelani tried to back away from them, but the brawny elf planted himself behind her, blocking her escape. "You just want to rule the tribe, regardless of the tradition. You wanted to kill my mother and take her place for yourself!"

Was that a moment of uncertainty on Bartolomey's face? If so, it was quickly erased.

"That's what they told you? Oh, sweet goddess of the woods. No wonder. Poor child." He smiled at the other elves around him, and they nodded with understanding and sympathy. He stepped toward her again with arms extended to embrace her, but pulled them back as she struck out at him, catching his face with her fingernails.

He seized her wrist, but held her away from harming him further. "Don't you see? They are the ones intending to usurp the seat of power, Jelani. Through you. They wanted to use you to place Daven Talvi on the throne. They set the mechanism for his revival in your path. They placed him before you, so you would become attracted to him. They probably set out other charms for you, to spin you into their false web." He shook his head with a pitying look. "They knew that as time passed you would be drawn to him and take him into your confidence, into your bed."

"When he had charmed you, then the Circle, those old witches, intended to use their ELF allies to destroy the place where Linnea rests safely. They would kill the true queen, so that you would be forced to rule with Talvi at your side."

Bartolomey's soft voice dripped like drizzled syrup into her mind. She revisited the events he mentioned: Dee's dreamcatcher, the glass slipper left for her, Daven's clear interest in her, both of them disappointed at her growing attachment to Astan. Could it be possible?

She wrenched her thoughts free and pinched her leg hard through her sweatshirt pocket. Of course it wasn't. They were lying. They were trying to control her somehow. That voice, that hypnotic voice.

Her hand cupped the vessel in her pocket. The simple touch of the device, warm and pliant against her skin, gave her the ability to resist the powers of voice Bartolomey directed against her. Maybe she could use their tactics against them.

"But he's dead now," she said, trying to sound as though she was being slowly pulled into his thought process.

"An unfortunate loss. He could so easily have joined me. His mother, too. All the elves, those who hid from me in enchantment, as well as those in the human world. We should be one tribe again."

Bartolomey stepped closer and caressed her face. It took all the self-control she had not to claw him again, but she sensed she was safer to make him think she was going along with him, as she had at the coffee shop. Even the skills Astan had taught her in a few short weeks could not take on so many. The group had started with maybe a dozen and now there were perhaps thirty-five elves gathered round. They seemed to draw closer to the two of them as Bartolomey continued.

"You can make that happen, Jelani. We can make that happen. We can work together to reunite this fractured clan, to bring strength and vitality back into our numbers."

He tipped her chin up to look into her eyes. "If we cannot save my sister from her fate, you must answer tradition and take her place, dear child." With a smile, Bartolomey released her.

"I understand that Vincent deprived you of the education you needed to be able to assume your position, but that is no matter. Blood is thick, and I will stand by you. Teach you. Help you in any way you ask."

Bartolomey had taken no hostile action toward her. The words sounded like they made sense. He was just a sweet old man, deprived of his cherished family all these years. She gripped the vessel, and her heart warmed to protest, crying foul.

"All you have to do is show us where they have concealed Linnea."

There it was. The final nail in the coffin.

"But I don't know. I really don't. Daven never showed me. He was always afraid you'd find out." She hoped her voice was as sincere as her words. She had no idea what they would do, could do to her. Could they pull the information from her, against her will? Surely not, or they would have done it already. All the same, she was not aware of the breadth of the elf skills across the clan. What she'd seen had certainly been very diverse.

"Nonsense!" Bartolomey's calm slipped. "It was that fool's only reason for bringing you up to these woods."

Jelani flinched at his anger, and then focused on the small vessel in her pocket. She was a little surprised they had not bothered to search her. Maybe they thought she was just a human of no threat to them, although Grigor must have known better.

She cradled the vessel in her fingers and let its familiar touch reassure her. "We came up to spike the trees the one day. You can ask him," she said, pointing a finger at Grigor. "Or that ELF operative, if he's not thoroughly dead. They were there. He saw everything we did. We never went hunting for that tree."

Bartolomey turned to Grigor, who shrugged noncommittally. "It was never mentioned when we were in the forest, other than it was some kind of tradeoff for protecting Linnea. The ELF guys didn't seem to hold much stock in it. They wanted to use our skills for their own purposes without need to know anything more."

Striding to one side, Bartolomey spoke heatedly with Malina. Frequent glances were tossed in Jelani's direction, and she could see the earlier attempts to gain her cooperation through benevolence had failed. The looks aimed at her were increasingly cruel.

She perceived a momentary opening in the crowd behind her, and suddenly cut to the left, diving for it. The large elf behind her grabbed her shoulder, digging his fingers into the skin next to her shoulder blade till she moaned with pain. Then he dragged her back into the circle with one hand.

Bartolomey walked back to face Jelani and stopped a mere six inches from her. She wondered if he could hear how fast her heart was beating.

"I'm not buying this last-minute innocence. Why did you come back to the Northwest? Why did you settle in Missoula? Why did you arrange to meet Talvi and the others? Clearly, you're in on the conspiracy to deprive me of my fair right to rule!"

She blinked. "You're a few beans short of a coffee pot, you know that?"

His eyes blazed, and he slapped her across the face hard enough to knock her back into the large elf, who pushed her forward again, hands clamped on her arms so she could not move. "This is no joking matter," Bartolomey snarled. "Let me tell you what's going to happen. You're going to find Linnea for us. Now. One way or another, I'll finish my business with my sister."

His face suffused with dark hatred. "I will rip her soul from that tree myself and scatter her to the winds!"

"That won't be the end," Jelani said, her own face burning with the anger building within her, bolstered by the power of the vessel.

"No. Indeed it won't." He eyed her with deep hostility, the honey vanished, no mystery to his meaning whatsoever. "Once she is gone, there remains one last roadblock to my succession. I promise, Jelani, your death will be quick and painless, if you assist me. If you will not, then I promise you will die as your father did."

* * *

CHAPTER 41

JELANI stiffened. "So you admit it? You killed him? Were you courageous enough to do it yourself, or did you toss that off onto one of your peons?"

That characterization caused displeasure to rumble through the crowd.

Bartolomey's face morphed into a smile, cold and jagged as a Bitterroot mountain peak. "My dear child, you haven't learned that truth yet?" He trailed a finger down the length of her arm, the edge of his sharp fingernail scraping her skin. "The self-important arrogant fool Daven Talvi didn't see fit to share that information with you?"

Jelani watched him, repulsed. "He wasn't here when that happened."

"No. No, he wasn't." A gloating look of victory became Bartolomey's mask. "He ran away to hide from me. As did so many of my disloyal subjects." He paced before her. "Humans. They are so easily led." He stopped and studied her. "Vincent's human allies thought they were helping when they called him here. But they were only leading him into a trap."

"Mad Dog?" The connection was finally coming together. Jelani felt sick to her stomach. As Legolas had called them into the woods only to be deceived, so had the elder ELF volunteer thought he was helping Vincent Marsh. "He tried to warn my father, and instead— "

"Instead, I intercepted him. I tried to make him see reason. I wanted him to understand that the clan needed to be united, not split. We were dying, our small band. Our young men had so few females from which to choose. We had no idea when we could move ahead to a next generation. I needed them back, all of them."

Malina laid a hand on his trembling arm, but his rage was in full flight.

"Vincent and Linnea took everything from me! When I could have ruled the clan, they splintered it, sent the others away. I cannot move on until she is dead, and I can prove it. When the clan understands that there is no other choice, they will have to accept me as their leader. Don't you see?"

Jelani looked away, frightened by the depth of Bartolomey's fury. The elf's vengeance had been brewing for twenty-five years. His face was flushed and the growl in his voice. He walked up to her and grabbed her chin again, looked her in the eye.

"All he had to do was tell me where Linnea was, so I could end this farce of a life," Bartolomey snarled. "But no. The oh-so-noble human held steadfast to the end. His misguided loyalty forced this to continue for another ten years until we nearly died out. Do you want to know what I did to that traitor?"

He smiled again and reached into his pocket, taking out a deep red cloth bag slightly smaller than a softball. Jelani wondered for a moment if it was another vessel, like the one she had, but what he did next showed it was quite different.

A tap on the top opened it. He reached inside with two fingers and brought out a pinch of what looked like inch-long pine needles. He slipped the container back in his pocket, and then dropped the needles into his palm where she could see them.

The needles didn't appear to her to be so dangerous. She was about to toss off some comment when she looked at the faces around her, surprised to find fear and loathing there.

Biting her tongue, she struggled a moment with Erdest who still had a firm hold on her. All she could do was wait, tensed and ready.

"Her hand," Bartolomey commanded.

Grigor stepped forward to grab her left hand and stretched it out so she could not move her elbow. He smiled at her. "You should have considered your options when you had a chance," he said.

"Silence!" Bartolomey took one of the needles, whispered

something to it, and suddenly jammed it into her hand, an inch from the junction between the pinky and ring fingers. She screamed as it burned like a hot ice pick. Before she could hardly grasp the extent of that pain, he whispered to another needle and stuck it parallel, at the base of her thumb. She thought she would pass out.

Erdest and Grigor held her firm. Bartolomey leaned close, his eyes glittering. "Now, my little princess, tell me where my sister waits."

"I don't know," she gasped.

He waved his hand over hers and the agony started to spread. It felt to her as though the needles began to burn a larger area, moving toward one another. "Tell me!" he demanded.

The pain was excruciating. Hearing the echoes of her own whimpers, she fought to maintain rational thought. Her father had endured this? Carolyn said he had been tortured.

When it seemed that time had stretched interminably toward infinity, Bartolomey pulled the needles from her hand and slipped them back into his red pouch. Her skin burned, now red and blistered as if it had been held in an open flame.

"You bastard," she muttered. "You did that to my father?"

"All I wanted was information. He could have saved himself at any time. But he wouldn't tell me the location. He lied. And lied. And lied. Every time he lied, I gave him another needle. They all burned, like those." He gestured to her throbbing hand as Erdest released her. "I think he may have had a hundred or more when his heart finally gave out."

He tucked the pouch away as she considered the enormity of her father's sacrifice, a devotion she'd never suspected in him. Bartolomey had stolen her father, her mother, her childhood. Her whole life.

"You don't deserve to live, you monster!" she screamed.

An answering fury built inside of her, and she launched herself at him, trying to be first light and then heavy as Astan had showed her. Her first foot planted solidly in his solar plexus, and she brought up the other toward his chin.

He groaned and doubled over. Malina spat some words in

Elvish.

Grigor swung a fist, which hit Jelani in the side of the head, knocking her to the ground. He stood over her a moment, as if daring her to get back up. "Do you really think you know our ways?" he mocked. "How could you use them against those who have lived these ways their whole lives?"

Jelani expected another attack, but Bartolomey shook his head. With less rage than before, he turned and stalked away from her, Malina and the others following close behind.

"Bring her!" he shot back over his shoulder.

The sun had shone through the branches overhead when she had been brought to the clearing. Now the skies had clouded over, as the wind picked up. The shadows under the trees deepened in the fading light. She had no idea what time it was. Perhaps it would even be night soon. Erdest reached for her arm again.

"Don't you touch me," Jelani snarled. She glared at him hard enough he pulled his hand back ever so slightly. Satisfied, she started walking after Bartolomey, her eyes watching side to side for some break, some hint of how she might escape.

She thought it would sure be a good time to have a gift like Grigor, some sort of quick getaway movement. Or even Astan with his ability to stop people mid-air.

The reminder of Astan brought sadness to her again. Everyone had an agenda around her: Dee, Daven, Bart, even Grigor and the youngers. The only one who seemed truly to be interested in her for herself had been Astan.

It was just like her not to realize something was good until she'd lost it. Lost in thought, she tripped over a log and fell hard on her hands and knees. Mooning about an elf lover? She had allowed herself be captured and lost all her companions. Maybe Astan was better off without her.

Her usual dark outlook swooping in to re-establish her low self-esteem, she shoved Erdest away when he tried to help her up. Brushing herself off, she slipped her hands back in her pockets, considering her dilemma, wondering how long she could draw comfort from the vessel before it dried up and left her on her own, too.

Even if she managed to escape whatever death Bartolomey had in mind for her, her future was unclear. Iris had said she'd changed, but if Astan and Daven were gone wouldn't everything return to the way it was before: pinching every penny, barely able to take care of herself, determined she was better off without a man, without caring about anyone, her life in the vicinity of a good time, but never being able to actually find it?

Astan's words, shared between them that night coming back from the forest, came to mind: "Sometimes the obstacles of the world seem to build to a point that it feels like nothing will ever come out from behind the shadow of the clouds, but you have to have faith that there is good ahead for you."

Was there really good ahead? Remembering Astan helped her believe she didn't have to settle for what life gave her, nor bow down to the hurt and pain. Something deep within urged her to fight, to face the challenge. Something fueled by the vessel in her hand. She knew, though she couldn't have explained how, that the time for change was about to arrive.

As she marched onward through the forest, surrounded by the other elves, she tried to keep her mind open to possibilities.

Though she had lost the others, she was not alone. Soon she would be put to the test. Did she have the courage and the ability to survive the coming trial?

* * *

CHAPTER 42

"HUSH," Astan said.

"Are you sure we shouldn't call the police?" Iris whispered. "Surely they'd come if we told them about Richard."

"They'd think we had something to do with it," Crispy said, his shoulders hunched. "We'd be locked up forever."

Astan could see how the day's events had hurt Crispy's gentle heart. But there was no time to deal with that pain, even if he had been a healer.

He listened with a keen ear, sensing activity in the forest ahead. Elven activity.

"Hush," he said again.

As they fell silent, he was grateful for the bandage and makeshift sling they had crafted for his arm. While it hampered his movement, it also lessened pain that could diminish his concentration. He mentally reached out again to sense activity in the vicinity of the Tree that housed Linnea's soul.

"This way," he said.

He loped awkwardly into the woods, mindful that the humans could not move as fast as he could.

As they traveled, he tried not to dwell on how Daven's body had looked, how lifeless it had felt. His purpose now was not revenge. Instead, he prayed that Jelani had survived her encounter with Bartolomey. He suspected the false king would do nothing to his captive at first, at least until he got what he wanted from her.

Dee had often explained to all her Circle that once the Tree was located, Jelani would be able to facilitate Linnea's release. But she had expected, no doubt, that they would have many months to train her, to teach her, so she was able to perform the necessary magic. They had also expected Daven and his men would have helped to contain Linnea's soul and restore it. There was no doubt that Bartolomey would release it to permanent obliteration.

And once Jelani no longer served a purpose, Bartolomey would dispose of her.

Daven had brought Astan to the area where the Tree was located several times over the few months since he had returned to this plane. Astan believed he could find it on his own. He moved as quickly as he could past trees, through thickets, aware of the life around him, the age of the trees, their wisdom too slow moving for him to absorb, though others of their tribe could commune with them. Animals, too, paused to regard him, and then ran in fear as the humans came noisily behind him.

Astan fought to summon up the way in his memory. He'd lost the GPS somehow in the confrontation with Grigor. When he'd left in the car, it was only with thoughts for Jelani and not worries about his equipment.

He would just have to do it the old-fashioned way.

Daven had given him landmark points to help him. A tree branch shaped as an arrow. A sapling with branches only on the right side. A large granite rock set at the head of a small stream. They passed each of those, as he remembered them.

Movement ahead alerted him to trouble, and Astan slowed to a walk, raising a hand to get the others' attention. Then he stopped.

"Oh, man," Lane moaned, gasping for breath as he leaned against a thick tree trunk with Crispy holding his elbow as best he could.

"I told you living in that Cave would be the death of you," Iris scolded in a whisper. She broke out a water bottle and gave Lane a drink.

"Don't have a heart attack. Not now, man." Crispy fidgeted, his agitation growing. "Lane, come on."

"Is he well enough to continue?" Astan demanded, edgy now that a confrontation was imminent.

"Just give me a minute, will you?" Lane sat down his bag and bent over, hands on his knees, taking deep breaths. Finally, he nodded. "Let's go."

"Stop!"

They all turned to see a tall blond man dressed in dark green and brown camouflage, blocking their path forward. "You've gone far enough," he said, his unusually pale gaze moving from one of them to the next.

"Rotiner," Astan grumbled.

Here was one of Bartolomey's prime advisers, out in the open. But Astan knew this one was dangerous, having the cobra's gift to paralyze an opponent with fear until he could strike.

"Astan Hawk. We were told you had not survived." The color of the elf's eyes seemed to fade to near silver. "You are stronger than we anticipated. Margitay took some weeks to recover from the injuries you gave him."

"Pity he survived at all," Astan replied, wary. He raised a hand, prepared to launch Rotiner into the brush, but in the blink of an eye Rotiner stood before him. Insidious silent whispers filled Astan's brain, taking over his will faster than he'd ever expected possible. Astan started to speak, but his voice faded to nothing. He could neither speak nor move to stop whatever was going to happen next.

"Yours is the survival that is a pity, traitor. But no matter. That omission can be rectified." Rotiner turned his attention to Astan's companions. "You bring humans here? For what purpose? Surely you don't imagine they can be of help to you?"

"Shows what you know, buddy," Lane said, pulling out his weapon. He planted himself in front of Iris and Crispy and aimed at Rotiner, the barrel angle remarkably firm. "Now why don't you just move yourself aside and we'll just go get our shit done, huh?"

"Do you defy me, human? Pitiful, fat, useless human?" Staring at Lane, Rotiner started to move toward him. "Do you imagine your kind superior to us?"

"Look, pal," Lane started, but he seemed to waver, the barrel of the gun drifting out of aim.

Lane! Astan wanted to yell. *Don't look in his eyes! Don't watch him!* But the words remained trapped in his frozen body.

He looked desperately to Iris, but found her entranced, too.

Crispy, however, remained twitchy and antsy. With hands clenched into fists, he hung his head and did not looking at the oncoming elf.

Astan wondered what he was thinking, hoping he did not intend to retreat into some sort of trance. Jelani had explained that was often his reaction to stress.

Rotiner would make fast work of someone like that. They would all die with Astan helpless to aid them.

"Pasty, worthless flesh. You have no reason to live. You steal the resources of this world and produce nothing worthwhile! You deserve nothing more than death!" Rotiner came right up to the man with the gun, poking at him, taunting him.

Lane's hand dropped to his side, eyes focused on Rotiner. The big elf slapped at Lane's arm, grabbed his solid jaw, and then full out punched him in the stomach, sending Lane to his knees in misery. "How could your kind rule the forest? You offer nothing. How could you think anyone would ever care about you? You worthless piece of— "

"Noooo!"

Astan was startled as Crispy howled, the agony in his voice piercing the air.

"Not again!" The thin man's dark eyes practically crackled with emotion as he flung himself at Rotiner, fists flailing. "You're not going to hurt anyone, not any more. No hitting! No name-calling! You won't get him."

Rotiner staggered back. Astan could see he didn't know what had hit him and kept on hitting him. Crispy, a madman out of control, finally knocked the bigger elf off his feet.

When Rotiner was forced to turn his concentration to Crispy's attack, the others left his focus and began to recover.

Astan moved to intervene, but Iris took his arm.

"He doesn't even realize who that is," she whispered. "He thinks it's someone from his past. He's taking revenge for those years of abuse he suffered."

"I'm not so thrilled with the guy either," Lane growled, "but I could shoot him if Crispy would move his skinny ass."

Crispy never stopped, never looked at Rotiner, just stayed on him. "You bastard! You killed Sammie! You never loved him! You never let anyone love him!" He kept punching the fallen elf, who finally got a hand free to reach for Crispy's throat.

Astan studied the trees around them to see if anyone else had heard the racket, but no one appeared to come to Rotiner's aid. They must all be clustered with Jelani and Linnea. They had to end this quickly and move on.

"Crisp, get the hell out of the way!" Lane yelled, as he cocked the gun.

On pure adrenaline rush, the former shut-in was not to be stopped, as Crispy grabbed Rotiner's collar and bashed his head against the ground over and over. "You'll never hurt him again. You'll never hurt him again." Tears poured down his face. "You'll never hurt me again. Never, never again."

"Oh, Ron," Iris said, hugging her arms to herself.

Lane finally moved, tucked the gun in his belt and crossed the short distance to where Crispy knelt over Rotiner, weeping as if his heart had broken open. He yanked his friend off Rotiner, and brought him to his feet. The blood on the ground told them there was no need for further action. Rotiner was dead.

Lane tossed a quick, guilty look at Astan. "I don't think he meant to. Oh, man."

Iris grabbed Crispy and pulled him aside, hugging him through her own tears, speaking softly to provide what comfort she could.

"Rotiner would have killed any of us to prevent our interference," Astan said. He walked over to the body, knelt down, and confirmed its lifeless status. "He thought humans could not stand against him. His arrogance saved us."

Iris put her arm tight around Crispy's shaking shoulders.

"Jelani?" Astan reminded them.

"Right." Lane looked at Crispy and took a deep frustrated breath. "We're in no shape to help you just yet." He handed the gun to Astan, who tucked it into his sling. "Take that and go on. We'll deal with this. You watch out for more crazy guys."

Astan did not wait for a second invitation, but dismissed them from his thoughts as a problem solved and hurried on through the forest. His shoulder ached now, despite the sling, his whole body jarring his injury with every step. He wasn't sure how he would defend himself or Jelani when he arrived, he only knew he must go.

He would save her if it cost his own life. He had failed Daven, but he would not fail Jelani.

After an interminable few minutes, he arrived in the clearing Daven had showed him. He recited the points of the winds and turned to the south, walking one-hundred steps into the woods. There it was. The Tree where Linnea had remained protected from the enemy for more than twenty years.

He walked up to it and dropped to one knee for a moment, respectfully. *My Lady*, he thought, picturing the elf woman as Dee had described her over the years, dark and delicate, with a sharp edge that could turn to wit or to defense.

A twig snapped behind Astan, and he barely got to his feet before one of Bartolomey's heavies seized his sleeve and hauled him aside. He looked around the group that followed, sickened as he saw Grigor and Malina.

Then Bartolomey stepped forward, his hand firm around Jelani's wrist.

"Betrayed by her own defender. How beautifully ironic."

Astan moved to defend himself and the large elf behind him shoved him hard into the tree trunk, making his ears ring. He blinked in confusion as his thoughts rattled back into place, seeing a stricken look on Jelani's face.

What Iris had said was true. Jelani cared for him. He could see that now.

Then Astan's thoughts turned to dark revenges, as he saw signs that Jelani had been mistreated.

Bartolomey, his long white hair blowing in the breeze, smiled up at the tree. "Sister dear. Time for a little change in regime. But don't worry. I'll let your daughter help before I dispatch her, too. Keep it all in the family." He turned to Jelani. "Your turn, half-breed. Call her out. Now!"

* * *

CHAPTER 43

JELANI couldn't say which shocked her more, finally coming face to face with the Tree she'd seen in photos a thousand times or seeing Astan alive.

She studied his face, sure she saw lines of pain, and noted the red stain of blood starting to show through the sling. She had so much she wanted to say. She could feel he did, too. Neither of them spoke as Bartolomey started to pontificate, though she could see Astan felt the guilt of being the one to reveal Linnea's hiding place to the enemy.

Why did every good intention get twisted by these people? Had she stepped on her karma someplace? Short-sheeted it? Couldn't she catch a break? Not one?

Astan tried to move, but was slammed into the tree.

A bolt of anger rushed through Jelani and into the vessel she held in her hand inside her pocket.

How dare they? How dare they hurt him? Or Linnea?

To her surprise, she felt a responsive burst of heat come back to her from the vessel, so strong she nearly pulled away.

Bart slapped her across the face. "I said, call her out! You know the kind of pain I can give you! Or perhaps you would prefer I take your defiance out on your queen's defender!"

She felt the blood drain from her face, and Bartolomey didn't miss it, either.

"Ah. That frightens you. You don't want to see him hurt. You care for him." He laughed. "Wonderful."

He glanced over at Astan. "I wonder if that feeling is reciprocated. We could spend the night finding out. If I had the time or patience to deal with this nonsense, which I don't."

He grabbed Jelani's arm and shook her until her teeth rattled. "Produce Linnea now!"

Her face stinging, Jelani saw Astan's hand twitch toward the sling. Blood ran from the corner of his mouth, but he stood firm. She wondered what he was thinking and hoped she could be as strong as he was, as strong as Vincent had been in protecting the queen. It all came down to what she did next.

And the Tree.

The absurdity of the situation finally caught up with her.

"Yep, there it is. The Tree," Jelani announced with a laugh. "The tree that ruined my childhood. Could have been cocaine for all it did for our family. My father died for this tree a whole lot of years before you actually killed him. We all did."

Bartolomey tossed her a bewildered stare.

"You know, I keep telling you I don't know what to do," Jelani reminded him. "You know why? Because I freakin' don't! Because no one ever told me about this craziness. Not my father. Not my stepmother. Not my wacky elf friends. Not anyone." She looked Bartolomey right in the eye. "I can no more get my mother out of this tree—are you listening to this? My mother is in a tree! Do you know how crazy that sounds? I can no more get her out of this tree than I can build a rocket and fly it to Venus. So screw you! And the Tree!"

A murmur ran through the watching elves, and she could see Astan jerk as if he'd been hit. Bartolomey's face flushed, his gaze growing even more hostile.

Jelani supposed no one dared speak to Bart like that.

That must be how he made others do his bidding. He put it in their brains that he was the most reasonable guy, and they should comply with his wishes. She preferred his anger to that cloying compulsion. At least pissed-off was honest.

"Perhaps you don't have an answer in your conscious mind. But it's there, somewhere." Bartolomey looked at Astan. "You and Talvi failed to instruct her in the most important ritual of her pitiful half-breed life? You expect me to believe that she is feigning ignorance? Please. She may not know the extent of my powers, but I am sure you do. Shall I give a demonstration?"

* * *

ASTAN shifted his gaze to the ground, listening for the tones in Bartolomey's voice which were used to exert control.

"You should admit you have been defeated and surrender gracefully," Astan said, forcing the words out through bruised lips, despite the retribution he knew would come.

He was not disappointed, as the bulky elf next to him slammed him into the tree again. The movement dislodged the firearm from the sling and he barely caught it with a stab of pain in his shoulder. Adjusting it in his hand, he trained the barrel on Bartolomey.

"Perhaps you did not hear me," Astan said in a steady voice. "Let her go."

"Astan Hawk, you misunderstand me," Bartolomey said in that fake honey-sweet tone. "I don't intend harm to the elf population. I want to unite them. I want to bring peace to our people."

The gun quivered in Astan's injured hand. Having seen such weapons used but never firing one himself, he brought up the other hand to steady the aim. Wasn't there something called a safety?

"You're a liar," he countered, struggling to remember how the gun worked. "You want only to promote your own cause, increase your power. You want to subjugate the clan to your will instead of letting us all participate under the traditions!"

Unfazed, Bartolomey continued in the same gentle tone. "I want to see the clan prosper. I want to see us come together, for the betterment of each and every elf. All your rebellion does is destroy any chance we have to survive. Your friends saw that. See them here? Grigor? Fontine? The others? When they listened to me, they understood how important it is that we unite or die. Is that what you want, Astan? Do you want the humans to win? Shall they drive us from the face of the earth?"

Astan tried to shut out the voice that choked off reason as efficiently as a constrictor snake. "You're the one who— "

"Put down the firearm. We don't need human weapons between elves. We should deal with each other openly as we always have. Astan, I'm welcoming you back into the fold. Put

aside this alliance with the humans. Rejoin your people."
Bartolomey took a step toward him, hand outstretched as if he
were offering friendship.

As the last of his own thought vanished, Astan felt the gun
get heavier, so heavy it weighed his arm down until the barrel
pointed at the ground. Then the gun fell from his limp fingers.
He looked at Bartolomey, at the others, and finally at Jelani.

It was time for action, and Astan couldn't do a thing.

* * *

JELANI stiffened, even though that voice wasn't turned on her.

"Astan, resist!" she screamed. "Don't listen to him!"

She needed a weapon. A rock, a knife, anything. She had to
save Astan. Watching him die again would surely kill her, too.

The vessel in her pocket seemed to come to life, and she
drew it out. The color had brightened to that of fresh blood, and
its surface markings swirled at a furious pace.

The elves collective gasp caught Bartolomey's attention.

He turned back to her, eyes on the vessel. "I can't say I'm
surprised. You do have your magic device with you. You really
should have been honest with me." He broke into a smile
without mirth. "Give it to me."

"Not on your life, pal." She took a step back, her way clear as
the elves behind her moved aside, clearly awed by the talisman.

What the hell was it and what could she do with it? Why
hadn't anyone left her any directions for the darned thing? All she
knew how to do was make it into a flashlight or make it spit fire.
Would blinding anyone be real useful? Could it save Astan?

"You will give it to me, and you will give it to me now!"
Bartolomey marched toward her with his hand out and a
determined look on his face.

Yeah, I'll give it to you, she thought, wishing it was a gun or a
knife or anything she could use as a weapon.

The vessel moved in her hand, as he came close to her. The
round shape elongated inside her fingers and the other end form
a bright-red blade.

As Bartolomey came close enough to take it from her, she

grabbed his right shoulder with her wounded hand and pulled him toward her, thrusting the vessel between his ribs.

That part she almost understood. What happened next left her speechless.

Bartolomey stumbled backwards, the vessel now turned dagger still in his body. He froze, back arched, feet askew, arms outstretched. An eerie stretched-out scream ripped itself from between his parted lips.

Several of the elves practically tripped over themselves to get away from the spectacle. Terrified, Jelani could only watch. Astan remained between the Tree and Bartolomey, bleeding but standing his ground.

From the handle end of the vessel/dagger came a cloud of smoke that hovered in the forest mists for several seconds and then divided into two parts. While Bartolomey continued to scream, the clouds coalesced into two male forms. One Jelani had never seen. The other was Vincent Marsh.

"Daddy?" she croaked, wavering on her feet.

"My, you've gotten big," Vincent said warmly, as he came over to hug her. He left one arm around her shoulder to help support her sagging knees. "Shhh. Just wait, little one," he whispered in her ear. "Lorenz, your grandfather, has a few things to say. He's waited a long time to be heard."

* * *

CHAPTER 44

ASTAN recognized the white-haired man, from Dee's descriptions over the years.

He was Lorenz, Linnea and Bartolomey's father, who had reigned at the side of Linnea's mother Ele. Although he supposedly had died thirty years ago, Lorenz stood tall and strong like the tree trunk before him, snow-white hair hanging past his shoulders. Like Vincent, he wore a simple black robe.

Lorenz spoke as soon as he was fully formed, a voice rich and deep that echoed through the glade. "Bartolomey, my son, the years of your treachery have run long and hard. You have suborned the will of good elves of our tribe and made a mockery of the traditions of our society."

The white-haired man surveyed the gathered, many of them now on their knees.

The unnatural sound coming from Bartolomey's throat turned into a shriek of protest.

"You conspired with others of our kind and with humans to destroy your sister, whom the traditions sat on the throne as queen of the clan," Lorenz accused. "You murdered her chosen mate, and would kill her daughter, the one who would follow her on the throne. All to glorify yourself. How do you answer these charges?"

Bartolomey never moved. His mouth was petrified into a grimace. However, clear defiance showed on his face.

"What? No answer?" Lorenz moved closer to the doomed elf, eyeing him with displeasure. "Very well. Then I pass judgment on you. You, Bartolomey of the wood people, are banished forever from the comfort of your hearth and home!"

Lorenz clapped his hands. The vessel/dagger slid out of Bartolomey's body and floated across the space between them. It landed on Lorenz's open palm and re-formed into a round ball. The vessel then split open across the top.

"Nooooo! You ccccannott doooooo thisssss! I sshall ruuule! I shall ruuuule!!" Bartolomey screamed, but it no longer mattered.

Lorenz waved a hand and Bartolomey was lifted from the ground. His body bent and twisted at impossible angles. Then he was sucked into the open vessel, which closed on him with a snap.

The old man tossed the vessel into the air. The blood-red ball hung there for a few long moments, flushing and fading with color, as if fighting for its existence. Then it vanished.

* * *

THE glade was silent for what seemed like several minutes. Then Jelani heard soft weeping from the back of the group.

She turned to see Malina crying with a few of the others comforting her. Grigor and the other youngers looked dazed, unsure why they were even there.

"Oh, my God," Jelani gasped. "What happened?"

Vincent smiled. "The traitor got what was coming to him." He nodded to Lorenz. "And now the magic really begins."

Lorenz held out a hand to Jelani. "How beautiful you are. Like your mother. I have missed you both, as the years have passed."

She took his warm hand and discovered his acceptance of her therein, though his exact thoughts did not come through as Daven's always had.

"Dear Jelani," Lorenz said with a sigh. "It pains me that you were not able to live here, in the forests, among people who should have welcomed you, cherished by your mother and father. Instead, Vincent was forced to hide you far from these trees and rocks that nourish us." His eyes studied her, and she noticed she couldn't tell what color they were. Their shade changed as she watched, surging through dark tones of blue, violet, and gray as his emotions flowed.

"When I saw the discontent in Bartolomey, as my rule came to an end, I created the vessel for such a time as this." His warm smile spread to include Vincent. "Your father kept the vessel safe for many years, until he reached his own end at the hands of my false son. Its magic was able to save his essence before it was lost to the winds, and it was placed where you could find it."

"At the cabin," she said softly, looking back to Vincent.

Her father nodded. "I knew you wouldn't come there unless you had the deed. And you wouldn't have that unless something had happened to me."

"So are you back?" she asked, the enormity of the situation was beginning to sink in. "Will you stay with me? Or Carolyn? Or what exactly?"

Vincent's smile didn't leave his face, but it faded a notch. "The next few minutes will determine the answers to that, my child."

Puzzled, Jelani turned back to Lorenz, who just nodded. He turned toward the tree, where Astan waited in a defensive position, blood drying on his face and on the sling.

"You have brought yourself much honor today, Astan Hawk," Lorenz said. "You have protected both the queen and her daughter against unspeakable evil. The gratitude of our people knows no bounds." He laid a hand on Astan's injured shoulder.

The glade filled with a soft golden light that faded after a few moments. Astan looked amazed and stepped aside, removing the sling. His face and shoulder were whole again, the blood disappearing even from his clothing. He fell to his knees in gratitude, and Lorenz lifted him to his feet again.

Jelani couldn't help thinking it was like a super-hero comic book, where everyone had some wacky power. Then she remembered an epic novel where the king was the healer of his people. Maybe that was just the way of these things. Or maybe just with elves.

Lorenz stopped next to the tree and turned to face those gathered in the clearing. "We are one people. I know some of you were led astray by one who shall forever remain nameless among us. Some of you have committed unspeakable acts." He looked particularly at Grigor, who glanced away in shame.

"While our hearts cry out for vengeance, we know your will has not been your own. If you will commit yourselves to the reformation of the clan, to its strength, I beg you to rejoin your brothers and sisters, who await you with open arms. All shall be forgiven."

There were some startled looks and expressions of disbelief among the elves, which had traveled with Bartolomey. Those closest to Astan gradually reached out to touch him and to speak soft apologies in his ear.

"And now, your queen," Lorenz said with a look of approval.

He reached his right hand to the trunk of the Tree, laying it flat against the ragged bark, and then extended his left hand to Jelani. Vincent urged her forward, and she took the old king's hand.

"I don't know what to do," she murmured in apology.

"You have already done so much, child," he said.

The memory of the morning with the shoe came back to her. Maybe reconstituting dried elf guys was a power. Of some kind. Not much call for that on the open market, though, was there?

She tried to focus as Lorenz intoned some words in a different language, speaking to the tree. After he finished, there was a long moment of silence in the woods, even the birdsong coming to a halt, and the sun broke through the clouds overhead, filling them all with warmth.

"Now. Use your gift, child."

"What gift is that?" she asked.

"Reach within yourself. Consider what you can do."

Jelani concentrated on her talents. Running an espresso machine and matching clothing in different shades of black was probably not what Lorenz had in mind. She reached, laying her palm flat on the Tree. She felt the life within it. Sap running up and down the trunk. Leaves pulling in the carbon dioxide. The deep roots drawing up water. And she knew.

She took a deep breath and spoke to the plant.

"Tree, you who have stood strong and firm against the winds, against the weather, you who have sheltered a lost Lady these many years from harm, now become yourself again, and release her essence from within you!"

After several moments of silence, a large crack echoed as the base of the trunk split open to reveal a dark cavity.

"Come, my daughter. Greet your people." Lorenz reached into the opening.

His hand emerged with a small hand in his, followed by the entire body of a woman dressed in a robe of white. Her eyes were the color of love, and when she smiled the very air about them felt lighter, and the hearts of the souls present were cheered. The elves all around them fell to their knees, but Lorenz held Jelani to her feet.

"No, child, your mother will want to see you." He nudged her forward, and Jelani and her mother Linnea beheld each other for the first time in twenty-five years.

As soon as their eyes met, Jelani knew it was right. They embraced, and Vincent joined them. Jelani thought she was handling the sheer insanity fairly well, using the Zen approach Iris always urged, to live in the moment.

She had her beloved father back. She had a mother who was no longer an evergreen. She could feel the love that radiated between Linnea and Vincent like a palpable heat, as they rejoiced in their own reunion.

Jelani stepped back, letting her parents have their moment, while she considered what was going to happen next. Everything had been focused on the improbable task of Linnea being restored to a real life existence outside a tree, and here she was. Linnea would rule the elf clan with Vincent at her side. Astan, Dee, and the others would move back into the clan territories, one big happy family.

She glanced over at Astan. Was everything all right now? Could they go home? Where was home?

Looking at her parents together, she saw something that had been missing all her life. She was so happy for them. What her father had gone through, what all the elves had suffered, surely the outcome outweighed the torment.

Astan moved up to stand beside her, and she slipped her hand in his, wanting to feel something solid. "So, all's well that ends well, huh?"

He nodded, giving her hand a little squeeze. "We have each played our part in restoring the order of our small world."

She studied his face, now healed by Lorenz, her heart full. "I thought you were dead."

"I might have been."

"Did Richard survive? Or Daven?" She knew neither of them had come with Astan, but she'd thought perhaps they could have survived. Until she saw his face. "Astan, I'm sorry. You did your best."

He spoke quietly. "I failed him nonetheless."

"They tricked us all." She recalled Daven's last words, the disappointment in his tone when he realized she didn't have the feelings for him that he'd expected. He'd read her emotions then, raw and without interference. He had the truth of it.

But it didn't matter. Linnea was back. "So, what do we do next?"

A huge crashing came from the west, behind a clump of thick brush. Everyone came to alert, wondering if some of Bartolomey's people had been hiding to ambush them.

As the brush parted, Lane stumbled through, out of breath, followed by Iris and Crispy Mendell.

"Did we miss it all?" Lane asked. "Where's Bart? Is there a fire or something?"

Crispy gasped in awe. "That's the Tree!"

"Isn't that Jelani's dad?" Iris was watching the larger group.

"Bummer! We missed it all," Lane complained. He plopped down onto a broken stump.

Linnea and Vincent watched the entrance with amusement, and spoke to each other in low voices.

Jelani let go of Astan's hand and went to hug her friends, reassuring them she was fine and that Astan had showed up in the nick of time.

"Did Astan shoot Bertha?" Lane grinned. "I sent her along in case she was necessary."

Jelani glanced over at Astan, who was in conversation with Lorenz and a few of the other elves. "No, he had some other issues by the time he got here."

"Is he all right?" Iris asked. Her concern for them both was obvious, and she held Jelani's hand for an extra few seconds, offering support.

"I think so. Lorenz healed him."

"Is that the wizard guy? He's the spitting image of Merlin. He's a good guy, right?" Lane took a long pull on his water bottle.

"That's my grandfather."

"Really?" Clearly curious, Crispy hung back.

"That's my mother there," Jelani said, nodding in the direction of her parents. "She actually came out of the tree. It was pretty awesome."

"You're going to have to tell me all about it in detail, for the book." Lane nodded. "In detail. Full debrief mode. You bring the bagels."

"All right, Lane," she said. She excused herself as her father beckoned to her. When she rejoined her mother and father, Vincent gave her a gentle hug.

"I can't believe you're here, Daddy," she said. "All these years, I never knew what had happened. Now that you're back, we can— "

"I'm not back." His face took on a serious cast.

"What do you mean, you're not back?" She felt a sense of panic. "I just found you after ten years, and you're leaving me again? What about Linnea?"

"Jelani, I've been dead for ten years. Some of my essence, what we call the soul, had been trapped in the vessel, but that's all there is." He tightened his arm around her. "It's been a gift, a real blessing, to be able to see you all grown up."

"I don't understand." She looked at Linnea. "I thought when you were set free, everything would be back to normal."

Linnea smiled. "I could not have hoped for a better child had I been there every day of your life. You have fulfilled every hope I ever had for you. Vincent did all he could with the help of his friends."

"Have you stayed in contact with Carolyn?" Vincent asked

Jelani.

"Ah, not really. Well, I did go back in May, that's when I got all the boxes. She seems happy now. She lives in a new condo with no trees."

Vincent laughed. "That would thrill her, no doubt. She never understood why I loved the forest so much. But then, why would she?" He squeezed Linnea's hand. "She did what I asked of her. I'm glad she's happy now."

Jelani turned to Linnea. "You're leaving? You can't go now."

"I've spent twenty-five years without your father, child. I don't intend to be alone any longer. We're leaving, together." She looked at their clasped hands. "Our time is past."

Lorenz approached them, solemn look on his face. "What I have learned in the past few weeks while I have been in contact with you through the vessel, Jelani, has made me confident that our clan is in good hands. You may not know everything about your heritage, my child, but you have come so far since you've begun to learn. There are many fine clan members who stand ready to help you if you need their wisdom."

"Me? Now? No, guys. Really. It's not me." Jelani's eyes filled with tears, as she turned to Vincent. He looked so happy, not the worn and worrisome person he had been back in Indiana pining for his lost love. "Daddy?"

"You can do it. Think what you have accomplished. You have made it possible for your mother and me to be together for eternity. We will never be able to thank you enough."

Her mother leaned forward to hug her as well. "That means you will lead our people now." She took Jelani's hand, her fingers smooth and soft. "And the heart of the queen chooses the one who shall be king." With a twinkle in her eye, she reached for Jelani's hand, placing it in Astan's. "As you have chosen, so shall it be."

"Oh my God!" Iris gushed. "That is so romantic. Jelani, you'll be the best queen ever!"

Jelani turned to Astan. "You couldn't know he'd go after Grigor that way, Astan. Daven knew this was my choice," she said. "That's why he gave himself up to save you. To save us both."

"So it's true," he said. "You did choose."

She looked away, blushing. "When I saw you get shot, it felt like my heart was the one torn apart. Daven touched me, read me. You know, like he does. Did. And then he knew."

"He did?" Astan seemed a bit dazed by the speed of events, but Jelani could certainly sympathize. "Then he is at peace."

The king joined them then, having finished his leave-taking with the other clan members. "You shall be at peace as well, my children. The blessings of the wind be upon you."

Lorenz spread his arms toward those in the clearing, and all were awash with a sense of well-being. Before the feeling faded, the former king had diminished to a faint column of wispy white smoke that dissipated in the light wind.

"Rule wisely and well, and you will heal the wounds of our people," Linnea said, stepping back. "We love you, daughter."

The last words were a whisper as Linnea and Vincent vanished in the same manner Lorenz had done, there one moment, gone the next in a whisper of smoke.

A few silent moments filled the space between Astan and Jelani.

Then Lane spit out his gum and scurried to them. "Man, did you see that? What the hell was that? Did those guys just get beamed up to the mothership or what?"

* * *

CHAPTER 45

IN the minor chaos that followed the departure of Linnea and the others, Jelani watched Astan step in and take charge.

Once Lorenz had dispatched their leader, Malina, Grigor, and several of the others had disappeared.

Astan introduced Jelani to the remaining elves, who had been with Bartolomey but now chose to remain with the clan. They certainly knew who she was, but he suggested one-on-one contact would help them move past the destructive clan rift.

She felt uncomfortable accepting their good wishes and the new deference they showed her. Something of her mother's voice remained with her, reminding her she had to act like a queen now. Diplomacy and restraint were not at all her style.

Lane sat on his stump with some kind of handheld electronic device, typing something in as fast as he could. "Okay, okay. The good guys win. The bad guys get disintegrated. The heroine falls in love and gets a prince. No, a king." He frowned, trying to get it all down. "The diplomats pull off a huge negotiation success. Reunite the lost tribes. And even Crispy gets himself cathartized. This will make one hell of a novel." He looked up, brow furrowed. "Hey! You didn't lose my gun, did you?"

"No. Didn't use it, either." Astan let go of Jelani's hand for a moment to retrieve the heavy weapon and return it to Lane.

"She's still a virgin," Lane said, caressing the barrel. "Saving the first big bang for the right occasion, I guess."

"Lane!" Iris made a face at him. "I don't need to hear that." She leaned down to brush pine needles from her pant legs.

Jelani saw her and shuddered at the thought of needles. She looked at her red and swollen hand, remembering the excruciating pain.

The Boys filled in Jelani on their trip through the woods,

while Astan spoke to some of the other elves, giving them orders. The elves gradually all disappeared into the shadows of the trees.

"Did they beam up too?" Crispy asked wide-eyed.

"No." Astan grinned. "They have some thinking to do. We will all meet again soon, when Jelani is ready." He noticed her hand and took it in his. "Did Bartolomey do this?"

She nodded. "He said this is how he killed my father." She recounted the story as her friends listened and Lane typed as quickly as the small device could process the characters.

"Oh, Jelani, what an awful man," Iris said, looking around the glade with tear-filled eyes. "He's gone, right?"

"He's gone," Astan confirmed.

"This thing is gonna sell a million," Lane cackled as he typed in the details. "Two million."

"I hope you'll give something out of those millions to charity," Iris said.

"Charity? What?" Lane looked up from his work, a shadow of guilt passing across his eyes. "Umm, sure. Why not?"

Astan had continued to hold Jelani's hand, massaging it until she realized it didn't hurt any more. With a raised eyebrow, she studied her hand, thinking about what Lorenz had done for Astan, and now what Astan had done for her.

Crispy looked up at the trees, and then all around at the landscape before giving a nod of satisfaction. "I like it here. I think I'll stay."

"What? You can't stay." Lane frowned. "There's no DSL out here."

"That means you can't stay, not me. There's no webcams here." With a smirk, Crispy bent down, picked up a pinecone, and took a deep sniff. "I think I can. I could take care of the woods, make them happy. Can't I, Iris? Wouldn't that be nice? Out here in nature?"

The life coach looked puzzled, but pleased. "We'll see, honey. Maybe Jel will let you stay in the cabin sometimes."

"Yeah. See? Iris says I can."

"But you can't go without me, Crisp." Lane looked forlorn.

Crispy gave a hearty laugh. "Then you better look into

satellite. You've really got to learn to get out more."

"We've got to get back to the cabin now!" Jelani exclaimed, staring at her hand.

"What's the rush, honey?" Lane started packing his things into his backpack.

"Astan is the king now. He has the healing power." She held out her hand. "Look! We've got to get back to Daven."

They all looked at her, as if she were crazy.

"It has been much too long," Astan finally said.

She grabbed his hand and started to run. "You don't know that. How long have you been the king, huh? Fifteen minutes? What do you know from being king? Isn't it worth a try? Come on, get the car!"

They started cross-country, careful to wait for Lane when he slowed, and watching for traps that Bartolomey's people might have left.

Safely arriving at the little silver car, the others climbed inside while Jelani stood still next to Astan for a moment.

With her eyed closed, she listened to the forest, inhaling deeply. "Is all this true?" she asked.

"Let's test it," Astan replied.

A moment later, Jelani felt Astan's arms encircle her, as his lips fell protectively on hers.

"True enough?" he asked, after breaking the kiss.

She smiled and opened her eyes. "Very much." She kissed him again.

Lane nagged them from the car. "Oh, get a room."

Torn, Astan looked away. "Daven."

"I believe in you, Astan. You can do this." Jelani kept her fingers interlaced with his. "He deserves your attention now."

His smile was faint. "Then your father has reason to be proud, Jelani. At last, you believe."

Well, damn, she thought. *He got me. Even from beyond the grave.*

"Let's go," Jelani said, climbing into the driver's seat.

* * *

JELANI stopped the car in front of the cabin.

Everyone piled out, and then hesitated near the door.

"Do you want some help?" Lane asked.

Astan squared his shoulders. "No. I can do this alone."

"You don't have to," Jelani said, following him inside.

The reality of his loss hit her, as she looked down on Daven's body.

"I can't imagine telling Djana that Daven's been killed," Astan said.

"You can bring him back," Jelani said with confidence. "Just try. Please."

Taking a deep breath, Astan knelt down, laid a hand on his father's chest, and closed his eyes.

Jelani held her breath, listening for any sound, watching for any moment.

After a long moment, she gasped when she saw one of Daven's hands twitch.

"You did it!" she cried. "Astan, he's alive! You're the king! You have the healing hands!"

Astan stared down at Daven, who looked up at him, seemingly as surprised as they were. His wounds faded slowly from view.

In a few minutes Daven pulled himself to his feet and leaned on the back of one of the rough-hewn chairs.

"Father, I don't understand," Astan said, looking down at his own hands.

Smiling, Daven clasped one of Astan's hands and then one of Jelani's. *All is as it should be. Linnea has been released, reunited with her heart's choice. The new queen has been anointed, and she has chosen her king, as tradition sets forth.* His mental tone hinted of amusement. *Fate often teaches us we don't always know what is best for us and those around us. Even my pride can be pricked.*

Then Daven smiled at Jelani. "Congratulations. Please excuse me." A little wobbly on his feet, he sat in the nearest chair.

"I don't know anything about being a queen," she said with a little frown.

"But you have learned much about life, how precious it is, and how we have to open ourselves to it to experience the best of what it has to offer." Daven nodded. "You've discovered who you really are. Can there be a greater gift?"

Crispy stuck his head in the door. "Hey, are you sure you don't need...." He stopped mid-sentence, as his eyes fell on the newly resurrected Daven.

"How are you, Mr. Mendell?" Daven said, with a chuckle.

"What is it?" Lane crowded in the door, too. "Holy crap! What's next, walking on water? Wait! Let me get my Palm. No one's gonna believe this!" He hurried back out for his case.

"I'm not sure I believe this," Jelani said.

"Are you willing to proceed on faith?" Astan asked. "You have the fire within you to carry you along. Let us help you."

She took a deep breath, looked at her dear friends and her new partner, and thought back on her father's words. Belief was only the first step, but it was the biggest one. It was indeed time to step up to the challenge.

"So if a bird and a fish want to live together...." She looked at Astan. "I mean, now that the clan is reunited, you all will live in the woods, right? Will I be expected to give up my apartment and live in the woods? In a what, a tree? With no running water?"

"No cable modem," Crispy whispered, as Lane returned.

"That either. Electricity. Coffeemakers. Hair dryers. Hell, mail! Anything!" She hugged herself in despair. "I don't intend any disrespect, Daven. I'm sure your lifestyle is all healthy and rugged and all that, but really!"

Daven grinned. "Our people have lived in the forest for hundreds of years. Not until you were born did this change, when so many of our people took refuge with the humans. You and Astan both came of age in the human world." He leaned back in the chair. "The world is changing, and the two of you may be better prepared than any of our kin have been to deal with the question of co-existence."

"I'll help!" Crispy said, looking out the window. "I can carry messages and pick up trash and talk to the animals."

"Crisp! You're scaring the hell out of me." Lane eyed his roommate. "I think we better get you home. Soon." He looked at his watch. "Besides, I've got a WOW raid with my posse at nine.

I'll be late as it is."

"At least we have this place," Jelani said, taking a last look around the cabin. "Maybe we can call it a halfway house." She eyed the counter. "If we get a coffee pot."

With an understanding smile, Daven took her hand and kissed it. *I'm proud you're of my blood, Jelani. I swear my loyalty. I will stand by you, till the wind comes to send us onward.*

He released her and clapped Astan on the shoulder. "I think you should come with me. We need to talk about a few things, if you're going to be king."

Astan chuckled. "This better not be the one about the birds and the bees."

"The what?" Daven looked puzzled. "What about birds?"

Lane and Iris joined in then, with a hearty laugh.

"Another tender father and son moment. Okay. Let's hit the road," Lane said. "Come on, Crisp."

They left the cabin, and Jelani soon heard car doors slam.

"I'll wait for you outside, son." Daven smiled and then, although still a bit wobbly on his feet, left the cabin.

"See you later!" Iris called.

"You know she's got the hots for him," Jelani whispered to Astan.

"So if she and my father hooked up, she'd be your mother, huh?" Astan laughed. "That would be even more messed up than everything else that's happened."

"At least the rest has turned out right. Hasn't it?"

"I believe it has." He took her hands and pulled her close.

"I've rescued my mother from a tree and reunited her with my dead father. You've raised your father from the dead and saved me from evil people. You've even turned me into a believer," she said. "How many other miracles will we be able to perform together?"

"I'm not sure," Astan gave her a kiss, as they started for the door. "Let's go find out."

THE END

Acknowledgements

I owe thanks to the many people who helped make this book come to life, including:

a. Maxine, for introducing me to the beautiful mountains of the Bitterroot all those years ago, and for hosting our reminder visits.

b. My wonderful group of friends and readers, who praise me when I'm doing good work and tell me that I'm full of it when I need it, especially Sue, Kellie, Gina and Darci.

c. Elaina Lander, whose artistry is crafting beautiful bracelet giveaways for personal appearances.

d. Daughters Beth and Donna for helping me get the word out.

e. My writing critique group, who each bring their own gifts to share as we pass on our stories, one to the other-Tom, Jeff, Ed, Dave, Gene, Carm, Paul, Linda, Ginny, Christy and particularly Jean, who reads every word, wields her red pen like Zorro's sword, and makes me want to write as well as she does.

f. Eric, without whom plot holes would become plot pitfalls, who always knows "how to" do any kind of wacky thing, and who taught me everything I know about epic drops.

g. Terri Branson, who shared a vision with me and continues to push the creative process along as this story comes into your hands.

About the Author

Lyndi Alexander dreamed for many years of being a spaceship captain, but settled instead for inspired excursions into fictional places with fascinating companions from her imagination that she likes to share with others. She has been a published writer for over thirty years, including seven years as a reporter and editor at a newspaper in Homestead, Florida. Her list of publications is eclectic, from science fiction to romance to horror, from tech reporting to television reviews. Lyndi is married to an absent-minded computer geek. Together, they have a dozen computers, seven children and a full house in northwestern Pennsylvania.

Breinigsville, PA USA
01 December 2010
250469BV00001B/97/P